"Why, Diana, I do believe you're frightened,"

Lee said softly.

Diana stiffened. "That's ridiculous."

"Is it?" His hand curled around her neck, and he tugged her closer. She shivered. His mouth was only inches from hers. Firmly, before she could change her mind, she reached up and removed his hand. She backed up a few steps.

"Diana, why are you fighting this? I know you're just as attracted to me as I am to you. Why won't you admit it?"

"Whether I'm attracted to you or not is beside the point—"

"Oh?" He grinned. "And the point being—?"

She took a measured breath. "If you'd allow me to finish..."

His eyes sparkled amber in the sunlight. "By all means."

"I'm not interested in...casual sex...and I have absolutely no desire for a permanent relationship, so I think the best thing we can do is forget all about what just happened."

"I see. You've got it all figured out, do you?"

Dear Reader,

Welcome to Silhouette **Special Edition** . . . welcome to
romance. Each month Silhouette **Special Edition**
publishes six novels with you in mind—stories of
love and life, tales that you can identify with . . . as
well as dream about.

This month has some wonderful stories for you—
after all, March comes in like a lion and goes out
like a lamb! And in Lisa Jackson's new series,
MAVERICKS, we meet three men who just won't be
tamed! This month, don't miss *He's Just a Cowboy*
by Lisa Jackson.

THAT SPECIAL WOMAN!, Silhouette **Special
Edition**'s new series that salutes women, has a
wonderful book this month from Patricia Coughlin.
The Awakening is the tender story of Sara Marie
McAllister—and her awakening to love when she
meets bounty hunter John Flynn. It takes a very
special man to win That Special Woman! And
handsome Flynn is up for the challenge!

Rounding out this month are books from other
favorite writers: Elizabeth Bevarly, Susan Mallery,
Trisha Alexander and Carole Halston!

I hope that you enjoy this book, and all the stories to
come! Have a wonderful March!

Sincerely,

Tara Gavin
Senior Editor
Silhouette Books

TRISHA ALEXANDER

MOTHER OF THE GROOM

SPECIAL EDITION®

Published by Silhouette Books New York
America's Publisher of Contemporary Romance

For Kim, daughter #1, who inspired this story; Shelley, daughter #2, the owner of the real Bonnie and Clyde; and Gail Chasan, editor extraordinaire. Thanks, guys.
Special thanks to Alaina Richardson, Heather MacAllister, Elaine Kimberley and Carla Luan for their invaluable critique; and to Betty Gyenes for allowing me to share the navy night.

SILHOUETTE BOOKS
300 East 42nd St., New York, N.Y. 10017

MOTHER OF THE GROOM

ISBN: 0-373-09801-4

First Silhouette Books printing March 1993

Printed in the U.S.A.

Books by Trisha Alexander

Silhouette Special Edition

Cinderella Girl #640
When Somebody Loves You #748
When Somebody Needs You #784
Mother of the Groom #801

TRISHA ALEXANDER

was encouraged from childhood to believe she could do whatever she set out to do, and this perennial injection of confidence became the mainstay of her life. Professionally, she has held many positions, from secretary to ad salesperson. After years of considering the prospect, Trisha began writing seriously. She found that she liked everything about it: reading, research, talking about writing, the act of writing itself, writers' conferences, critiquing, revising, editing—you name it, she loves it.

Chapter One

"Whew, it's hot out there!" Diana Sorensen complained as she strode into her real estate office. "You'd think by mid-September we'd start getting some cooler weather, wouldn't you?"

Tracy Allbright, Diana's eight-months'-pregnant-and-counting receptionist, grinned. "How long have you lived in Houston, Diana?"

Diana rolled her eyes. "Too long." She set her heavy briefcase on the floor and removed the pink slips from her phone message slot on Tracy's desk. Riffling through them quickly, she noted that Leona Applegate had called. She mentally crossed her fingers. Maybe the old harridan had actually made a decision to buy the Thornwood house. "Anything exciting happen while I was out?" she asked.

"No, not really." Tracy rolled her eyes. "Unless you count the fact that Barton, Jr., kicked me about seventeen times this afternoon."

Diana gave Tracy an answering smile and bent to pick up her briefcase again.

"And the fact that Kent is waiting for you back in your office."

"He is?" Pleasure swelled Diana's heart. Kent was her twenty-four-year-old son, and she hadn't seen much of him the past couple of months. Throughout June he'd been consumed with studying for the bar exam, and once that was over in July, he'd started working long hours. And lately, all his free time seemed to revolve around that new girl he'd met over the Fourth of July weekend. A new girl Diana had met and didn't much like.

Walking out of the reception area into the large bull pen where her six full-time agents worked, she decided she wouldn't dwell on anything unpleasant for the rest of the day. Besides, Kent's infatuation with his new girlfriend was bound to pass because as far as Diana had been able to tell, the two had absolutely nothing in common.

Diana waved at the two agents who were in, then opened the door leading into her private office. Kent sat sprawled on the paisley print love seat that occupied half of one wall, his long legs spread out in front of him, a can of soda in one hand and a dog-eared paperback novel in the other hand.

Diana squinted at the title. She needed her glasses for reading. "Hmm, *Presumed Innocent.* Don't you get enough of the law at work? Do you have to read about it, too?"

Kent grinned. "Hi, gorgeous. You look hot."

"I *am* hot," Diana grumbled. "After forty-two years in this town, you'd think I'd be used to the heat."

"If you'd break down and wear something cool—"

"*You* wear suits," Diana countered. But now that she was in her office, she removed the teal linen jacket and carefully hung it on a hanger, which she hooked over the clothes tree standing in the corner.

"Just wait until January! Then it'll be jeans every day."

Diana knew Kent was referring to the fact that once he received notification that he'd passed the bar—which would, she was confident, come in November—he intended to go into business for himself. For years, ever since he'd decided he wanted to be a lawyer, he had dreamed of opening a storefront law office where the poor and underprivileged of Houston could come for low-cost legal aid. Although Diana realized that parts of Kent's dream were impractical, she was proud of her son. Unlike most young men in today's world, he wasn't out to get everything he could for himself.

She smiled at him, taking pleasure in the way he looked. Tall and muscular, Kent radiated all-American-boy good looks. His thick dark hair resisted taming, and his fresh, tanned face glowed with good health. Dark blue eyes like hers, an engaging smile and a sunny disposition completed the picture. Today he wore a dark, pin-striped suit combined with a white shirt and yellow tie.

"Is that a power tie?" she teased.

Kent laughed. "Sure. I'm really into power these days."

Diana collapsed into her swivel chair, kicked off her pumps, pulled out the bottom drawer of her desk, and propped her feet on it. "So what brings you here?" She glanced at her watch. "At only four-thirty in the afternoon?"

"I was out this way interviewing an expert we plan to use as a witness on the Mellenkamp case, so I decided to come by and talk to you. I..." Kent hesitated, and Diana had a sudden sense of foreboding. "I've been meaning to come and see you ever since last weekend."

Diana sat there waiting.

"Mom, you remember Allison Gabriel..."

Diana nodded. The new girlfriend. Her sense of foreboding grew.

"Well..." Kent grinned again, his eyes bright. "Last Saturday night I asked her to marry me."

Diana now understood exactly what was meant by the phrase *a sinking heart* because hers plummeted to her toes at Kent's proud pronouncement. But years of working with picky clients had schooled Diana in the art of masking her real feelings, so she said smoothly, "Really? And?"

Kent's grin seemed to split his face in two. "She said yes!" He leaped up, his book falling onto the floor. "Aren't you going to say something?"

"Actually, I'm speechless. You've really taken me by surprise. I had no idea you were serious about Allison. You've only known her, what, a couple of months?"

"I knew I wanted to marry her the moment I saw her," Kent declared, his expression earnest, his deep voice filled with passion. "I know it's a cliché, but—" He colored slightly. "It was love at first sight."

Oh, God. Impractical. Idealistic. And romantic, too. How had she—who was so sensible and realistic—produced this boy? Even her ex-husband—Kent's father—with all his faults, was more pragmatic than his son. But even as these thoughts formed, Diana remembered that once upon a time, when she was very, very young, she'd been just as impractical, idealistic and romantic as Kent. Those were the very reasons she now had a twenty-four-year-old son instead of a degree in computer science.

"How will this affect your plans to open your own office?"

Kent frowned. "It won't. Why should it?"

Diana shrugged. "I just wondered." She chose her next words carefully. "Don't misunderstand me, Kent. I'm happy for you if this is what you want, but it costs money to get married, and I know you're operating on a pretty tight budget. I just wondered if you and Allison had discussed your plans and how she feels about them.''

The frown smoothed out, and once more, Kent smiled happily. ''She knows what I'm planning. We haven't gone into all the details, but we'll work everything out.''

Somehow Diana wasn't as sure as Kent seemed to be that Allison Gabriel would be content to be the wife of a struggling storefront lawyer. Diana had only met the woman once, over the Labor Day weekend, when Kent had brought her to a cookout hosted by Sunny Garcia, Diana's best friend. Diana had taken one look at Allison's flawless tan, her perfectly manicured nails, her understated but expensive jewelry and her designer clothes, and known that Allison Gabriel was accustomed to the very best. Would Allison be willing to give up the luxuries she now took for granted?

Kent was still talking, and Diana wrenched her thoughts away from the dismal turn they'd taken. ''. . . and her father has invited us all to lunch tomorrow,'' he said happily. ''He's made reservations at The Rotisserie for Beef and Bird for one o'clock. You can make it, can't you?''

He sounded so eager, so proud. She knew how much he wanted her approval, and oh, God, she wanted to be happy for him. She loved him so much. ''Of course I can make it.'' She made a mental note to rearrange her schedule for the following day. Kent pulled her up and put his arms around her. They hugged hard. She *would* be happy for him, she vowed. If he wanted Allison Gabriel, and she wanted him, Diana had no right to be thinking black thoughts about the relationship. She could feel her eyes mist as she realized that from now on things would never be the same between her and Kent. He would slowly grow away from her, which was the way it should be.

"When's the wedding?" she said as they drew apart. She straightened his tie while she regained her emotional equilibrium. From the time Kent was a small boy she'd encouraged him to be independent and make his own decisions. And now he had, and he deserved her wholehearted support.

"We thought we'd get married the Saturday after Christmas. That way we'll have at least a week for our honeymoon."

"Christmas. So soon..."

"Well, it *is* soon, but I wanted to get everything settled before I start working on my own."

"Yes, I guess that makes sense."

Exuberant, Kent folded his arms around her again, giving her another hug. "I'm so happy," he whispered. "She's wonderful. You're going to love her."

And with that sentiment ringing in her ears, Diana sent up a fervent prayer that Kent was right.

At one-ten the following afternoon, Diana relinquished the keys of her three-year-old silver Buick Riviera to the valet parking attendant and walked inside The Rotisserie for Beef and Bird. Blessed coolness greeted her, and the maître d', with a smile and flourish, said, "Yes, madam?"

"I'm meeting the Gabriel party."

"Ah, yes, of course. This way, please."

Diana followed the maître d' into the sunny main dining room. He led her to a round table on the far left side where Kent was already seated with Allison Gabriel and her father. The two men stood as Diana approached. "Sorry I'm late," Diana said. "My last appointment ran overtime."

"Mother, you remember Allison?" Kent said.

"Yes, of course. Hello, Allison. It's wonderful to see you again. Kent's told me the happy news." Diana extended her hand, and after a slight hesitation, Allison reached up and placed her hand in Diana's. Diana had expected to shake hands, but obviously Allison didn't, so Diana gave her a brief squeeze and smiled down into the young woman's tawny eyes. Allison gave her an answering smile.

"And this is Allison's father, Lee Gabriel. Lee, my mother, Diana Sorensen."

Diana turned toward the tall, dark man who walked around the table and held out his hand. Her gaze lifted to meet his. Not many men topped Diana, because, in her two-inch heels, she stood five feet eleven inches tall. As her hand was grasped in a strong, cool palm and firmly shaken, her gaze was riveted to his. Lee Gabriel's eyes were the same shade as his daughter's, she thought distractedly—a warm, toasty brown dusted with gold—and ringed by thick lashes. Diana knew dozens of women who would kill for lashes like his—including her.

"It's very nice to meet you, Diana," he said in a nicely pitched, low voice.

Then he smiled.

Something down deep in Diana's stomach went *zing*, shooting straight up into her throat like a meteor shot through the heavens. Jumpin' Jehoshaphat, the man's smile was lethal! Were his teeth really that brilliantly white, or did they just look so dazzling in contrast to his darkly tanned, angular face? The smile rent deep grooves in his cheeks, enhancing his rugged appeal.

Diana didn't rattle easily. She was too toughened by life's hard knocks, too accustomed to dealing with all the problems a single mother has to face and too experienced in business to be easily impressed.

But Lee Gabriel—no, be honest, she told herself, *her reaction* to Lee Gabriel—definitely rattled her.

In her head.

In her gut.

Even down in her toes.

And the last time Diana had gotten rattled in her toes, she'd ended up pregnant and hastily married. As these thoughts tumbled through her mind, Diana only had a blurred impression of the rest of him before he finally released her hand, which still tingled from the imprint of his.

The maître d' had been standing patiently, and now, as Diana turned toward her chair, he whipped it out and smoothly seated her. Then he motioned to the waiter hovering nearby, and as Diana's water glass was filled, and she was handed a menu, she managed to get her resuscitated hormones under control.

"I've been looking forward to meeting you," Lee said. "Kent's told us a lot about you."

Diana looked at Kent who grinned happily. She knew her son was as proud of her as she was of him. Then she slowly let her gaze return to Lee's.

Yep. Lethal.

And not just his smile, which had settled into an amused tipping of the corners of his mouth, but the man himself. Covertly she studied him. He wasn't pretty-boy handsome or anything like that, she decided. No, what Lee Gabriel possessed was better than good looks. The man positively oozed sex appeal and a powerful magnetism that said he was accustomed to having people pay attention to him—women *and* men.

Diana noted his hawkish nose, his long, determined chin, the crinkles at the corners of his eyes, his thick dark hair nicely threaded with silver, the snowy cuffs showing at his wrists, the cufflinks that were probably solid gold, the tanned hands with the well-groomed fingernails and curly dark hairs on their backs. And if she wasn't mistaken, that watch on his left wrist looked suspiciously like a Rolex.

His gray suit looked as if it had cost more than most people earned in a week, maybe two. She was sure if she could see his shoes they'd be soft, supple leather—probably Italian—definitely expensive. Like his daughter, Lee Gabriel epitomized success and wealth and sophistication.

Once again Diana felt a shiver of apprehension. Allison Gabriel's world was a far different one from Kent's. Which one of them would do the changing?

"Kent tells me you own your own real estate agency," Lee said.

"Yes, I do."

"How long have you been in the business?"

"Nearly twenty years."

"I've always thought selling real estate would be fun," Allison interjected.

Diana dragged her attention away from Lee and looked at Allison. "I'm not sure I'd call it fun, but it's definitely challenging." The young woman looked particularly lovely today, Diana thought, in a tailored cocoa silk dress that hugged her petite figure. A double rope of creamy pearls filled the deep V-neckline and pearl studs adorned her small ears. Her chestnut hair shone with a healthy luster and was artfully arranged in a casual, windblown look that skimmed her shoulders.

Although Allison's eyes were the color of her father's, the rest of her obviously took after someone else, for Allison's face was small and square. Her lips were pouty, her nose dainty and she had a deep cleft in her chin. She was very beautiful, and Diana could see exactly why Kent seemed so smitten.

The waiter returned to their table. "Would you like to order wine today?" he asked Lee.

Lee looked around. "This is a celebration, right?" He turned to the waiter. "I think we'll have champagne." He gave Allison a fond look. "Let's make it Cristal, shall we?"

Allison squealed. "Oh, Daddy! Cristal!"

Diana, who had been about to say she never drank wine at lunch, kept quiet. He was right, of course. This *was* a celebration, and just because she usually got a headache if she drank wine during the day didn't mean she should throw a damper on the festivities.

Within minutes, their waiter brought them the pâté of the day, a house specialty, and the sommelier delivered the champagne nestled in a silver wine bucket. He ceremoniously uncorked it at the table and poured a bit of the champagne into one of the fluted glasses that had magically appeared. Lee raised the glass to his lips and sampled the champagne. Smiling with approval, he gave the sommelier a nod, and the man began to pour the wine into the remaining wineglasses.

"A toast," Lee said, "to our children." He raised his glass. "May they live a long and happy life together." As they all clinked glasses, Diana echoed his wish. She looked from Kent—whose eyes blazed with love as they rested on Allison's face—to Allison, whose eyes sparkled as she basked in the approval of her father and her fiancé. Allison and Kent *did* make a lovely couple, Diana thought. Perhaps she was borrowing trouble with the niggling worry that refused to disappear.

"Umm," Allison said to her father, "just as wonderful as I remembered it to be."

In spite of herself, Diana was impressed. She was the first to admit her ignorance of fine wines, but she knew enough to know Cristal was the best.

"Kent said the two of you want to be married the Saturday after Christmas," Diana said, turning to Allison.

"Yes. I love Christmas weddings, don't you?" the girl responded. "My bridesmaids will wear emerald green taffeta and carry white poinsettias. We'll be married at St. John's, of course, and I can just see the church now. Oh, it will be beautiful, with the Christmas trees and all the holly and red poinsettias and candles." She narrowed her eyes as she studied Diana. "With your blond hair and skin color, Diana, you'd look good in a color like raspberry or violet. I'll help you find a dress that will coordinate with the wedding party's."

Irritation surged through Diana. She was perfectly capable of picking out her own dress, and she almost said so. But a glance at Kent's face, so full of happiness, warned her not to make any waves today. So Diana just nodded and smiled noncommittally.

"Are we ready to order?" Lee asked as their waiter reappeared.

Everything on the menu looked too rich for Diana's tastes. Lee said, "Have you ever had the venison here?"

Diana shook her head. Just the thought of venison made her stomach feel queasy.

"Perhaps Madam would prefer the quail," said the waiter.

"No, uh... let me think about it for a minute or two," Diana said. "Take their orders, please."

Lee ordered the blackened redfish. Kent ordered the venison. And Allison ordered chateaubriand. They all looked at Diana again.

"I think I'll have the chateaubriand, too. But could I please have it plain? Without the sauce?"

The corners of Lee's mouth twitched, and his eyes held a suspicious twinkle.

Diana shrugged. "I can't help it. Rich food is wasted on me. I tend toward things like hamburgers. Tex Mex. Macaroni and cheese." Now *why* had she felt compelled to explain? Allison looked at her as if she'd suddenly sprouted two heads.

Diana could see Lee was fighting back laughter, and suddenly she laughed herself. "I know. I'm weird."

"You're *not* weird, Mother," Kent said quickly, warming Diana's heart.

Now it was her turn to give her progeny a fond smile. "You're prejudiced."

"Maybe I am." Kent returned her smile. "This is a complete change of subject, but before you came, Lee told me he's in the market for a house."

"Yes," Lee echoed. "And I don't have a real estate agent. Kent suggested you might take me on as a client."

Warning bells rang in Diana's mind. Instinctively she knew it wasn't a good idea to spend much time in Lee Gabriel's company. The effect he had on her was dangerous to her well-being. She wasn't sure she could take her hormones being in a constant state of unrest.

Besides, the relationship between real estate agent and client could become rocky, even combative. Finding the right house and getting it for the right price had a tendency to bring out the worst in people. She wasn't sure it was wise to mix a business relationship with the personal one she and Lee would share as the parents of the newly engaged couple. All these thoughts flitted rapidly through her mind as she formulated her answer.

"I'd be glad to ask one of my agents to work with you." Good. That had been an inspired idea. Her agency would still benefit from the business, but she wouldn't jeopardize the personal alliance.

"Do you have a business card with you?" Lee asked.

Diana reached for her purse and removed a card. She handed it across the table to him. As he took it, their fin-

gers brushed, and Diana's breath caught. Something smol-
dered in the depths of Lee's eyes, and Diana could feel her
heart beating. She dropped her gaze, and the moment
passed.

But for the rest of the luncheon, she was all too aware of
Lee across the table from her. She could feel his eyes on her
as she ate. She knew he was listening carefully when she and
Allison spoke to each other. Several times she caught him
studying her, and each time she did, his mouth would tip in
an almost mocking smile.

She would have given anything to know what he was
thinking. Or maybe not. Maybe it was better she didn't
know what he was thinking. Maybe the best thing that could
possibly happen to her would be never to set eyes on Lee
Gabriel again.

It was almost three o'clock before Diana got back to the
agency. After Tracy gave her a quick rundown on how many
times Barton, Jr., had kicked her in the past two hours, Diana headed for her office. Sunny Garcia, who was not only
her best friend but also her best agent, followed her inside.

"So how was the let's-get-to-know-one-another lunch?"
she asked.

Diana sighed wearily and sank into her chair. Sunny
perched on the edge of the love seat. She ran her fingers
through her short, curly red hair.

"Before I tell you about the lunch, tell me about Nikki.
How'd she take the news of Kent's engagement?" Nikki
Garcia was Sunny's twenty-three-year-old daughter.

Sunny grimaced. "Just about the way I thought she
would." Her green eyes filled with sadness. "Oh, gosh, Diana, it was awful to sit there and see the kid try to pretend
she didn't care. She was shattered. She cried all night. I
heard her."

"Oh, dear. I was afraid of this. I'm so sorry." Nikki and Kent had been inseparable from the time they were toddlers and Sunny baby-sat with Kent while Diana worked and attended real estate school. Their friendship had survived everything: their teenage years, Kent's high school crush on an airhead that Nikki despised, even the separation of college. Kent thought the world of Nikki, and Nikki had been in love with him for years. Everyone knew it: Diana, Sunny, all their friends. And Diana was sure Kent knew it, too—that he only pretended not to know how Nikki felt to keep from embarrassing her and to preserve their friendship. Unfortunately for Nikki, Kent had never shown the least bit of romantic interest in her.

"I know you are," Sunny said sadly, "but it's not your fault. Just because *we* wanted them to get together..." Her voice trailed off. She sighed. "Nikki had to face the truth sometime, Diana. Kent loves her, but he's not *in* love with her. She'll get over this. She'll have to. She has no other choice."

Diana sighed, too. Life would certainly be easier for all of them if Kent had fallen in love with Nikki. She was so much more suitable for him than Allison Gabriel, but as Diana well knew, things rarely went the way you hoped they would. She'd learned that lesson early in life.

"So tell me about lunch," Sunny said. The sadness had disappeared from her eyes, replaced with an avid curiosity.

"It went okay, I guess." Diana heard the lack of enthusiasm in her voice and knew she'd have to do better if she didn't want Kent to guess she was less than ecstatic about his impending marriage. "Oh, shoot, I don't know. Maybe I'm just being an overprotective mother. Maybe I wouldn't think any girl was good enough for Kent."

"That's garbage, and you know it. If Kent and Nikki had gotten engaged, you'd be doing cartwheels!"

Diana absently doodled on her notepad. She knew Sunny was right.

"What is it about the girl you don't like?"

"It's not that I don't like her. It's just that I don't think she's right for Kent. I can't imagine the two of them building any kind of life together."

"Why?"

"You know what he's like, Sunny. He's so...innocent. So idealistic. So completely impractical. He needs a strong woman who loves him enough to let him do what will make him happy, but someone who will also keep his feet firmly planted on the ground."

"Someone just like Nikki."

"Yes, someone just like Nikki." Diana stood and removed her suit jacket, draping it over the back of her chair. She plopped back down. "Allison is very sophisticated, very beautiful, but she also strikes me as a girl who's used to being taken care of. Just from the way she acted around her father, I know he's spoiled her and petted her. She's the kind of girl who will expect pampering and lots of attention. I simply don't see her as the kind of helpmate Kent will need."

"What's her father like?"

An image of Lee Gabriel's dazzling smile, his topaz eyes with their speculative gleam, his secretive smile, his raw, gut-level appeal, flashed through Diana's mind. She bit her lip thoughtfully.

Sunny cocked her head and narrowed her eyes. "Well?"

"Honestly?"

"Of course, honestly."

"He's an incredible hunk," she mumbled, astonished she'd voiced the thought.

"Hulk?"

"Hunk."

"I see," Sunny said, a slow grin sliding across her face. "An incredible hunk. Well, well, well, that certainly sounds promising!"

Diana laughed. "It's just an observation."

"What does this 'hunk' look like?"

"Tall, dark and dangerous."

Sunny grinned. "That sounds *really* promising. There's nothing I like better than a dangerous man."

"He's all yours, then."

"You're kidding! When do I get to meet him?"

"Actually you *are* going to meet him. He's looking for a house and asked me to help him find one. I told him I'd put one of my agents on the job. He's your client if you want him."

"I'm not stupid. You won't catch me looking a gift-horse in the mouth," Sunny quipped. "Maybe he likes short red-heads with thousands of freckles." She struck a pose. "You *did* say he was rich, didn't you?"

Diana thought of the bottle of Cristal, of the Rolex, of Allison's obviously authentic pearls. "I don't know if he's rich, but he certainly seems to be very comfortable."

"What does he do?"

"I'm not sure. He's some kind of big shot with Berringer. Kent told me Allison and her father have lived all over the world—most recently in Paris. In fact, Allison went to school at the Sorbonne."

"Yeah, I'd say they've got some bucks."

Just then Diana's intercom buzzed, and she punched the receiver button. "Yes, Tracy?"

"There's a Mr. Gabriel on Line One, Diana."

Sunny raised her eyebrows.

Diana switched her phone to the speaker box so Sunny could hear the conversation, then punched Line One. "This is Diana Sorensen."

"Hello, Diana Sorensen," he said, his low-pitched voice wrapping around her like a warm blanket. "Do you believe in love at first sight?"

Chapter Two

Diana stared at the phone. She couldn't believe she'd heard him correctly. "I beg your pardon?" she finally croaked.

He gave a low, intimate chuckle. "You heard me. Don't evade the question."

Diana couldn't look at Sunny, and she fervently wished she'd never turned on the speaker box. "No, I *do not* believe in love at first sight." They were the exact words she'd wanted to speak to Kent the day before.

"Somehow I had a feeling you were going to say that." She knew he was still smiling. She could hear it in his voice. "Well, I guess we'd better talk business then, hadn't we?"

Diana finally felt brave enough to look Sunny's way and wasn't surprised to see a delighted grin on Sunny's face. *Good grief, I'm surrounded by romantics.* "By all means," she said smoothly. "Let's talk business."

"I'm serious about wanting to buy a house."

"Good. There are a number of things we'll need to know then, but it'll be better for you to talk directly to the agent you'll be working with. I thought you'd like Sunny—"

"Wait a minute. I don't want to work with one of your agents."

"But I thought you said—"

"I want to work with you."

"Lee, I don't normally work with clients unless I've worked with them for years and they refuse to accept anyone else. I *never* take on new clients."

"Surely you'd make an exception in my case?"

Why was it that this man could make shivers snake up and down her spine just by changing the timbre of his voice? "As much as I'd like to," she lied smoothly, "my load here at the office is too heavy. I wouldn't be able to devote the time to you that you deserve." She avoided Sunny's eyes.

"Diana, I don't think you understand."

Oh, I understand all right. You're used to people jumping when you say jump. But she knew that wasn't it at all. She just wasn't ready to face the truth. "*What* don't I understand?" she said softly. Then she held her breath and cut a glance Sunny's way. From the expectant look on her friend's face, she had a feeling Sunny was holding her breath, too.

"I want you, Diana. I want you, and I intend to have you."

Diana switched off the speaker box and snatched up the receiver. She, who never blushed, felt the red creeping up her neck.

"Now," he continued as if the entire matter was settled, "what time do you leave the office?"

"The office?" she repeated, knowing she sounded like a flustered schoolgirl who'd never had a man flirt with her before.

"Yes. Since I'm anxious to begin looking at houses, and since there's no better time to start than the weekend, and since tomorrow is Friday, I thought—if you have no other plans—we could go to dinner tomorrow evening and I can give you all the details about what I want, etcetera. Then we can start looking Saturday."

Diana, who was also never speechless, couldn't think of one sensible thing to say.

"What's the matter?" he said innocently.

Diana finally found her tongue. What was the matter with her, anyway? She'd been married and divorced, she'd educated herself, she'd built her own successful business and she'd raised a wonderful son. She could handle Lee Gabriel. There was certainly nothing to be *afraid* of. So she said coolly, "Look, Lee. I'll be happy to meet you here at the office at ten o'clock Saturday morning. We can go over your housing requirements first, and after I run everything through the computer I can set up some appointments, and we'll go from there." She took a deep breath. "But I'll have to pass on dinner tomorrow night."

"So you have plans."

"Yes, I have plans." Damn. She was such a rotten liar.

"Diana..."

She closed her eyes. The way he said her name, rolling it on his tongue, made her think of warm honey. Made her think of soft pillows. Made her think of...

Her eyes popped open. Dangerous ground awaited if she continued with thoughts like these. Only fools or crazy people plunged ahead when they'd had all kinds of warning signs.

Now his voice was a husky purr. "Give me a chance, Diana. At the very least, we should be friends because our children are going to be married. Let me take you to dinner tomorrow night."

No. No way. Absolutely not.

"How about if I pick you up at seven?" he said when she didn't respond. "Come on." Then he laughed again. "I promise to behave myself."

No doubt about it. She *was* crazy. "Better make it eight. I don't close the agency until six."

Lee thought about Diana the rest of the day. He chuckled to himself every time he remembered her speechlessness when he'd asked her if she believed in love at first sight. He couldn't get over the impact she'd had on him.

When she had walked into the restaurant, he took one look and knew this woman was going to become very important to him. He liked everything about her. Her quiet dignity. Her strong sense of who she was. Her beautiful smile.

And her eyes. God, those eyes. They were the loveliest deep blue eyes he'd ever seen. They reminded him of the color of the ocean at twilight. A dark, mysterious indigo. They were eyes you could drown in. Wonderful eyes that had seen a lot of living. Thoughtful, intelligent eyes to match a thoughtful, intelligent woman. *Beaux yeux.* The French phrase meaning beautiful eyes, beautiful face, played in his mind like a long-forgotten melody.

When they shook hands, and she looked up, he hadn't wanted to let her hand go. His reaction to her was completely unexpected. Over the years he'd met many beautiful and charming women. None of them had moved him beyond a surface attraction. He was inured to beautiful women, or so he'd thought. But Diana, with her strong handshake, her lovely smile, her incredible eyes—made him feel like a kid again.

Except when I was a kid, I'd have never had the nerve to call her up and say the things I said.

He laughed out loud, causing his secretary—who picked that moment to walk into his office—to give him a strange look. "My, aren't we in a good mood today?" she said. She laid his To Be Signed document folder in his In box.

In answer Lee just smiled and waited for Britta to leave the office before letting his thoughts meander back to Diana.

He knew Diana had had the same punched-in-the-gut feeling. He could see it in the faint flush that stained her cheeks as he finally released her hand, and especially in the way she deliberately refrained from meeting his gaze after they all sat down at the table.

His first impression had only intensified as lunch progressed. Even her admission that she didn't like most of the food on the menu charmed him. He couldn't think of one other woman in his circle of friends who would ever admit to such ordinary tastes. They wouldn't want to be thought of as bourgeois.

He'd been uneasy about meeting Diana, too. Because Marianne had died when Allison was so young, he was overprotective of Allison, but he couldn't seem to help it. From what Kent had told him of his mother, Lee was afraid Diana might be one of those obnoxious, high-powered women who would roll right over Allison, or worse, condescend to her. But Diana was none of those things. It was clear that she was strong and confident and self-assured, but she hadn't lost her femininity, and she was gracious and nice to Allison.

Allison. For a moment, Lee allowed his thoughts to roam to his daughter. She was the light of his life. He would do anything for her. She was everything he'd ever wanted her to be, and more. There had been times, over the years, when Lee had worried about whether he'd ever think any man good enough for her. But Kent was a perfect choice, even

though the boy had a strong streak of idealism and roman-
ticism that could cause them difficulties down the road. But
Lee intended to work on that problem. In fact, he'd already had some ideas along those lines.

The important thing was Kent was smart. There was good
raw material there, and he adored Allison. That much was
obvious. Lee knew Kent would be good to her, and as far as
Lee was concerned, that was what counted. The rest would
come with time.

Yes, he thought with satisfaction. Kent Sorensen would
make Allison happy.

And depending on how dinner went the following day,
perhaps Kent Sorensen's mother would make Lee happy.

"So let me get this straight," Sunny said. "You aren't
interested in the man, you have no desire to get involved
with him, or any man, for that matter, and you think Kent's
and Allison's engagement is headed for big trouble. Right?"

"Right," Diana said. She still felt unsettled from Lee's
phone call even though thirty minutes had passed since
they'd hung up.

"That's why you agreed to go to dinner with tall, dark
and dangerous tomorrow night, and that's why you're going to *personally* take charge of finding him a house."

Diana gave Sunny a sheepish look.

Sunny shook her head. "Yep. That's what I thought.
You're nuts. You're also a very bad liar."

"What do you mean by that crack?"

Sunny gave her a knowing look. "We both know you're
very interested in him."

"I am not!" But even to her own ears her denial sounded
halfhearted.

"Come on, Diana, I'm your best friend. We've been as
close as two people can be for more than thirty years—"

"Thirty-six years, if you want to be exact."

"Yeah, thirty-six years. Don't you think I know how you're feeling, almost before you do?"

Diana bit her bottom lip.

Sunny stood. "You want to know what my advice is?" Without waiting for Diana's answer, she said, "Loosen up, kid. You haven't had a male interest in your life for a long time. Make the most of this." Then she giggled. "Lordy, I can't wait to meet Lee Gabriel. Any man who can get the better of Diana Sorensen has got to be one dynamite guy!" And then, still laughing, she waved and walked out of the office.

Kent looked around his apartment. To save money, he shared a two-bedroom apartment with a friend. Because he'd been too poor to date much while he was in law school, the arrangement had never cramped his style. And because he and Allison had agreed to wait until they were married before making love—well, Allison had had more to do with the decision than he did—sharing a place with Rich still didn't cramp Kent's style.

But tonight he and Allison would have privacy because Rich had tomorrow off and he'd hightailed it to Corpus to spend the weekend with his girlfriend.

And tonight Allison was coming to dinner.

Kent had taken pains with the preparation. He liked to cook, which was odd, because his mother hated to cook. She was a lousy cook, too. But even when he was little, Kent liked puttering around the kitchen.

Tonight he had baked chicken breasts and wild rice. He hoped Allison would like the meal. Her tastes were sophisticated when it came to food. He guessed that wasn't so surprising, since she and her father had lived in Paris for so many years. Maybe one of these days Kent would surprise her by taking a French cooking course.

Yeah. That'd be great. She'd like that.

Once he was satisfied that everything was ready for her, Kent took a quick shower, shaved and dressed in a pair of baggy cotton pants and a knit shirt. No socks. Moccasins. He'd just finished combing his hair when he heard the doorbell ring.

He always experienced a rush of happiness when he saw Allison. She looked gorgeous and sexy in black tights, a short black skirt, white blouse and black and white checked vest. "Hi," she said and walked in.

"Hi." He grinned at her, his heart going full speed as he gathered her into his arms and gave her a long, lingering kiss. He closed his eyes, breathing in the sweet fragrance of her hair.

Her voice was shaky when they finally drew apart, and her lipstick was smudged. She smoothed her hair back, and Kent's eyes were drawn to the graceful gesture.

"Allison," he said, reaching for her again.

She drew back. "Please, honey, I don't think we should." Her smile took the sting out of the refusal.

Kent sighed. He knew she was right. It was getting harder and harder—on both of them—to stop their lovemaking beyond a certain point.

She looked around. "Is Rich gone already?"

"Uh-huh. He took off right after work." Kent laughed. "He couldn't wait to see Stephanie. We've got the place all to ourselves." Suddenly he wished they hadn't decided to wait. He wanted her so much. He understood how Allison felt—she was old-fashioned, and he liked that about her—but it was so hard to wait. And they *were* engaged. He decided to bring the subject up again—later.

All through dinner he couldn't think about anything else but making love to her. By the time they'd finished their dinner and were sitting close together on the couch—sipping at the last of the Chardonnay, Kent's right arm resting around Allison's shoulder, the Debussy she liked so much playing softly on the stereo—he was in a fever pitch of love and longing.

He put down his glass of wine and with shaking fingers removed Allison's glass from her hand.

She gave him a questioning look, but before she could speak, Kent covered her open mouth with his. His body reacted immediately to the strong aphrodisiac of the taste of Allison as his tongue swooped inside and he took full possession of her mouth. "Allison," he muttered. "Oh, Allison." He wanted her so badly at that moment, he couldn't think. With his right arm holding her close, his left hand found her breast and he kneaded it, feeling the changes as his thumb rubbed against the hardened nub.

"You want me as much as I want you," he murmured thickly, letting his mouth drop to the enticing hollow of her neck. He could feel the pulse beating wildly, and hear her rapid breathing. She *did* want this.

He slid his hand down her torso, over her flat stomach, the feel of her fueling his desire. His hand trembled as he lifted her short skirt. When he touched the warm apex between her thighs, she shuddered and moved against him.

Desire, hot and heavy, pounded through him. The pain of it made him groan. His mouth covered hers again, and he pushed her down against the pillows of the couch, his body half covering hers as his fingers found the elastic band of her tights, and pulled them down. As soon as they cleared her hips, he delved under her panties, feeling her response to his intimate touch.

But like the shock of ice water poured over his head, she struggled against him. "No, no," she said, trying to escape his mouth. She pushed at his hand. "No, Kent! Stop!"

Kent collapsed against her. He slowly withdrew his hand. They were both breathing heavily, his heart slamming against his chest. He shut his eyes. Damn. He'd almost lost control of himself.

"Kent?"

Her voice sounded small, unsure.

"Kent? Are you mad at me?" She smoothed her hair. His heart had begun to slow down. But he still hurt. The pain of wanting her hadn't diminished at all. "I'm sorry, Kent." She sounded as if she were crying. He took a deep breath and raised himself up.

She *was* crying. "Shh," he said, using his thumb to wipe away a teardrop. Her mouth looked swollen, and her glossy hair was disheveled. She was so beautiful, so sweet. "There's nothing to be sorry about. It's just that I love you so much. I want you so much."

"I know." Her topaz eyes, smoky and golden in the muted lamplight, shone with her tears. "I want you, too, but Kent, darling, we decided to wait. Remember?" She reached up, drawing his face down to hers again. She kissed him gently. "I... I'm sorry, but I just feel strongly about this, and... I want our wedding night to be the first time for us. It'll be better if we wait... it will... I promise." Her voice was like silk, flowing over him in a soothing balm.

"I know. It's okay." He sat up, pulling her up after him. He smiled at her to show her he wasn't angry. Just disappointed. No, he wasn't disappointed. Disappointed sounded as if *she'd* disappointed him, and Allison could never disappoint him.

She sighed, then stood. "Maybe I'd better go now." She looked down at him, her beautiful eyes troubled. "Are you okay?"

"Yes, don't worry about it."

She hesitated, as if she were going to say something else, then nodded and rearranged her clothing.

Kent stood and took her hand. "Come on, I'll walk you to your car."

As they walked out into the navy night, still warm and humid from the day's heat, Kent longed for December to come. He knew he wouldn't be entirely happy until he didn't have to let Allison go back to her grandparents' house for the night.

As they reached her dark green Miata, Allison said, "You're not angry with me, are you?"

"No. Of course not."

"Do you still want to go shopping for a ring Saturday afternoon?"

Kent frowned. "Yes, of course." Had she thought he'd changed his mind? Confused by her unknown thought processes, he said, "Why wouldn't we go?"

She shrugged, the gesture as graceful as everything else about her. "I don't know. You just seemed...I don't know."

"You're silly, you know that?" he said. "Come here. Give me a kiss good-night."

Long after the taillights of her sporty little car left the parking lot, Kent stood there in the concealing darkness and waited for the ache to disappear.

"Did you have a nice evening, sweetheart?" Lee asked when Allison entered the cozy living room of her grandparents' guest house, where they'd been living since his transfer back to Houston in June.

She sat down opposite him, in the twin to his velvet wing chair. "Yes. It was fun." She picked at a thread on the chair's arm.

Lee's shrewd glance took in her slightly smudged makeup and her slightly wrinkled clothes. He was no fool. He knew the chances of two healthy young people refraining from a sexual relationship until they were married were slim to none. But that was okay, he thought, as long as they didn't flaunt it. Lee trusted Allison. He knew she was sensible and that she wouldn't do anything to endanger herself or her future. And she and Kent *were* engaged.

"Daddy?"

"What, sweetheart?"

Allison's troubled gaze met his. "Daddy, do you think Kent will give up this idea of opening a storefront law office?"

Lee considered her question before answering. "I don't know. Do you want him to?"

Allison nodded. "I don't see how we can live if he doesn't take a position in an established firm. I wouldn't mind him doing *some pro-bono* work. In fact, I think that's an admirable ambition, especially if he goes into politics someday, but I don't see how that's *all* he can do." She frowned. "Do you?"

He tented his fingers and studied her. She was very beautiful, he thought. He'd spoiled her, indulged her, but he figured she deserved indulging, not only because a beautiful woman was meant to be indulged, but because Allison had missed out on a lot in life. Losing her mother when she did, at the most vulnerable time of her life, had to have been hard on her. Lee had tried, in every way he could, to make it up to her. So he wasn't sorry he'd indulged her, and he hoped Kent would, too. "To answer your question, no, I don't think Kent can support the two of you on what he'd make as a storefront lawyer. But I figured he would eventually come to the same conclusion. Have you told him how you feel?"

"Well, sort of. I've hinted, but unfortunately, he hasn't taken the hint. I guess…I guess I was just hoping he'd come to his senses without me having to be blunt."

"Sweetheart, can we be honest with each other?"

"Of course, Daddy. We've always been honest with each other."

"Do you really love Kent?"

She never hesitated. "Yes. I love him a lot."

Lee was quiet for a moment. "Enough to marry him even if he persists in his plans? Even if you have to go out and get a job to pay the bills? Even if you have to give up a lot of the things you're used to having?"

Her topaz eyes, so like his, clouded. She chewed on her bottom lip as she considered his question. Finally she raised her eyes and answered. "I don't know. I don't know if I'm strong enough. And Daddy, we shouldn't *have* to live that way. Why, the firm that Kent's working for now has already offered him an associate's position. Of course, that firm's not good enough for Kent anyway, so I'm glad he doesn't want to stay there, but Kent graduated second in his class! He made the law review the first year! He could probably go to work for anyone he wanted to." Her face settled into anxious lines. "Do you think I'm awful?"

Lee had known the facts about Kent. He'd also suspected that Allison wouldn't be willing to sacrifice everything for love. And why should she? he asked himself. She was sensible and realistic. She knew it took a lot more than love to live on. Lack of money could eat away at the fabric of even the strongest relationship. Allison wasn't being unreasonable. And if Kent really loved her, he'd be willing to make the changes that would ensure him and Allison a

comfortable, secure future. That's what a man *should* do for
the woman he loved. "No, I don't think you're awful. But
I do think you should be patient. Kent's a smart young man.
He'll figure it out, especially when you start looking for a
place to live. Once the expenses start mounting, he'll realize something's going to have to give."

Allison nodded eagerly. "That's what I thought, too. And
I can keep dropping subtle hints. And, Daddy..."

"Yes?"

"Maybe you could help me."

Lee smiled. "If necessary, I'll talk to Kent."

Allison jumped up, crossed the short distance between
them, and leaned over to give him a hug. "I love you,
Daddy. I knew I could count on you."

"I love you, too, sweetheart, and you can always count on
me," Lee promised as he returned her hug.

Diana tried on one outfit after another. Fiddlesticks. It'd
been so long since she'd had any kind of social life, she had
nothing to wear for a dinner date.

Dinner date.

This wasn't a *date*. This was a prelude to a business relationship. This was just a get-acquainted dinner between the
mother of the groom and the father of the bride. Between a
real estate agent and a client.

*Sure. And the moon is made of green cheese, Diana.
That's why you've got the jitters. That's why it's taken you
over an hour to decide what to wear. That's why it feels as
if your stomach has turned inside out every time you think
about spending the entire evening with Lee Gabriel.*

She finally settled on a black crepe dress with a slim skirt
and cap sleeves. Dressy, but not too dressy, she thought. She
finished off her outfit with big gold hoop earrings and the
heavy gold necklace she'd given herself the first time she'd

sold a million-dollar property. Then she slipped her feet into black pumps.

After spritzing herself with perfume, she gave a finishing touch to her hair. Then she stood in front of her full-length mirror and looked at herself.

She twisted this way and that, trying to see herself from all angles.

Not bad, Sorensen, for a forty-two-year-old broad. She grinned at her reflection. She had never thought of herself as a beauty, like her sister Carol, who had been a runner-up in the Miss Texas Contest when she was eighteen, or her sister Jackie, who had done some modeling as a teenager. But Diana was satisfied with the way she looked, even though it had taken her a long time to get used to her height.

She wondered if she needed to lose a few pounds. No, she decided. She wasn't the least bit fat. She was just a tall woman who wore a size nine shoe. Diana sighed. Why was it that people were never satisfied with the way they were? She had always wanted to be small and perky, like Sunny. And Sunny had indicated, more than once, that she'd give anything to be as tall as Diana.

One thing Diana was thankful for, especially tonight, was that her hair wasn't gray. Oh, maybe there were gray hairs mingled among the gold, but her hair was so blond, no one would notice them. She patted her hair again, liking the short, sleek style she'd adopted when she turned forty.

As she stood there, her big male cat, Clyde, ogled her from his perch on the edge of her dresser.

"What's the matter, big boy?" Diana said in her Mae West imitation. "Don'tcha like what you see?"

Clyde made a sound that was a cross between a purr and a yelp. She reached over and ruffled the fur on top of his head. In turn, he nipped at her fingers.

"Testy tonight, aren't you?" Diana bent and kissed his head. "Where's your sister? Hiding behind the bed again?" Bonnie seemed to sense when Diana was expecting company, and always found a safe, hidden spot until the newcomer was gone.

Well, I'm as ready as I'll ever be, Diana thought, even though, like Bonnie, she almost felt like hiding herself. All the doubts she'd tried to submerge suddenly surfaced.

It had been such a long time since she'd felt this uncertainty. After her divorce, she'd been so unsure, so afraid she'd done something to cause Bill to turn to other women. It took a lot of years, and a lot of living, for her to realize that what had happened with Bill hadn't been due to any lack on her part. Bill was what Bill was, and she'd been too young, and too flattered by his attention, to recognize that when she'd married him.

Once she came to terms with that, she was okay. She'd been able to date other men, and she'd felt pretty confident of herself and her ability to keep them interested. She hadn't agonized over any of them.

Why was Lee Gabriel different?

Because he's the first man in years who's produced that toe-tingling feeling. Because you know he could be important to you. That's why you're so nervous.

Darn, darn, darn. She should have said no. Why was she risking her hard-fought serenity, her comfortable life-style, her peace and independence?

Oh, well. It was too late now. The die was cast. Nervous or not, ready or not, she'd accepted this date.

After taking a last look at herself in the mirror, she shut off the light and went into the living room of her town house to wait for Lee's arrival. Clyde followed her.

The grandfather clock in her foyer had just finished its eighth chime when her doorbell rang.

Taking a deep breath, Diana moistened her lips and opened the door.

Wow, she thought. Wow. Wow. Wow.

Lee looked outrageously attractive. He was dressed in tan slacks and matching shirt and some kind of nubby jacket the color of oatmeal.

When he smiled, Diana's slaphappy heart decided to play leapfrog again. What was wrong with her? You'd think she'd never been close to a man before. And above all things, she wanted to be calm and in control tonight.

"Don't you look nice?" he said with an approving smile, his gaze slowly traveling the length of her body and back up again.

"You don't look so bad yourself," she answered. *That's me, the mistress of understatement.* "Would you like to have a drink before we go?" She gestured toward the living room.

"I made reservations for eight-thirty. Why don't we just have a drink at the restaurant?"

"All right."

"I'd love to see your town house, though. Maybe when we come home?" He swept an appreciative glance around the spacious foyer. "Well, who's this?"

Clyde, aggressive as always, rubbed against Lee's pant leg.

"Clyde!" Diana grabbed at the cat. "Don't let him do that, Lee. He'll get hair all over you." Clyde's fur was long and thick, the color of champagne.

Ignoring her admonishment, Lee bent to stroke Clyde. "How's it going, tiger? Met any good-looking ladies lately?"

Clyde preened.

Lee grinned. "So have I." His gaze met hers. "Maybe we'll both get lucky."

Diana felt as if he'd just poured hot maple syrup over her. She knew that if Lee Gabriel were to wrestle her to the floor right now and try to have his way with her, she'd probably help him. She couldn't stop herself from grinning at the thought of two middle-aged people like her and Lee groping and doing a heavy-breathing routine on her Italian tile floor.

"What's so funny?" he asked as they walked out the door.

"Oh, nothing."

Parked in her driveway was a sleek, low-slung red Porsche. Diana chuckled.

"*Now* what're you laughing about?" Lee said as he opened the passenger door and helped her fold herself into the car.

"Don't you know that a red Porsche is the oldest cliché in the book for a man of your age?"

"Don't you know the reason clichés exist is that they're so true?" he countered. Then he grinned, the corners of his eyes crinkling agreeably in the hazy lavender twilight. "I love this car."

Diana nodded. It was a great car, and she had to admit, it suited Lee. "Where are we going?"

"To Las Alamedas."

"Really?" She was delighted. She'd been sure he would take her somewhere like Tony's or The Rainbow Lodge.

"I remembered what you said about the kind of food you like. I figured Las Alamedas was nice enough to be considered special, but Tex Mex enough to satisfy your picky taste buds."

That was very considerate of him, Diana thought. Especially since he probably preferred the continental cuisine of a restaurant like Tony's.

"I'll tell you something," he said as he expertly shifted gears and turned from her street onto Memorial Drive. "It's a secret."

"I'm waiting."

"I *love* Tex Mex myself."

Diana grinned. Maybe tonight would turn out okay, after all. Maybe she could actually relax and have fun with Lee. Maybe she'd been worrying too much.

"But even if I didn't—" He slanted a glance at her.

The gleam in his eyes made Diana's heart start to go bumpety-bump again. He shifted gears once more, and the car leaped forward.

"Even if I didn't, it wouldn't matter," he murmured in a silky drawl that made her shiver. "Because I decided yesterday that pleasing you is my new number one priority."

Maybe she hadn't been worrying enough.

Chapter Three

Diana loved Las Alamedas.

But Lee made her nervous.

All evening he'd been everything any woman could ask for in a date. Attentive. Charming. Fun.

So why was she still so jumpy?

Could it have something to do with the fact that when he looked at her she got the feeling he was trying to decide whether he'd rather have her as dinner or as dessert?

This man is dangerous, she repeated like a mantra, over and over again. Don't let his charm and that wonderful smile fool you into letting down your guard. If you're not careful, he'll devour you whole.

She shivered at the erotic image this thought conjured. Trying to get her mind off its risky course, she said, "Tell me about your job. All I know is that you work for Berringer. Just what is it you do?"

Lee wiped his mouth with his napkin and set down his fork. "For the past ten years I've been vice president of International Marketing, and I've been based in Europe—first in The Hague for three years, then in Paris for seven years. Berringer is a French company. Do you know much about it?"

"No."

"Our primary business is the design and manufacture of well-logging tools. For the past few years, we've made a heavy investment in the research and design of custom drill bits."

Diana nodded. "And now? What are you doing in Houston?"

"Now I've been named executive vice president with overall responsibility for both domestic and international sales. That's why Berringer sent me back to Houston."

"So you're planning to stay here."

"Yes. At least until I retire. Which isn't all that far off." He grimaced. "I'm getting closer all the time."

"You make it sound as if you're an old man."

"Is that a subtle way of asking my age?" he teased, his eyes twinkling. "It's no secret. I'm forty-seven."

The most sexy-looking forty-seven Diana had ever seen. With the exception of Paul Newman, whom she thought would look sexy at ninety.

"And how about you? You must have been a child bride," he said.

"Actually I was. I married at seventeen and was a mother at eighteen." She shrugged. "I'm getting up there, too."

"You're in the prime of your life."

There was that mocking smile again.

"Don't you know that the French believe a woman isn't even interesting until she turns forty?" he continued.

"In America youth is admired. Age is to be prevented at all costs."

"I happen to agree with the French."

Lordy, she was no good at this flirty kind of talk. She wiped her palms against her dress. She was too out of practice. Heck, she'd never been *in* practice. Look at her! She was a wreck! To change the subject, she said, "Why haven't you looked for a house yet? Kent told me you've been in Houston since June."

"Well, my in-laws have a guest house on their property—they live off lower Memorial Drive, near the Loop—and they insisted we use it." While he was talking, he'd motioned to their waiter. After ordering coffee, he said, "For two reasons, I decided to accept their offer. First of all, I hadn't lived in Houston for years, and I wasn't sure if I wanted to buy a house or build a house, and secondly, the Marlowes—Allison's grandparents—are crazy about Allison. She's their only grandchild, and with us living in Europe for so long, they didn't see nearly enough of her." He smiled. "I guess they want to make up for lost time."

So on top of a doting father, Allison had doting grandparents.

"But I'm getting itchy for a place of my own, and now that I've settled into my new job, it's time."

Over coffee and sopaipillas, they discussed the type of house he wanted and possible locations. He told Diana his price range and how he planned to finance the purchase.

"I'd still like to get started tomorrow morning," he added.

"Why don't you let me do some preliminary work in the morning, and after I get some appointments set up, I'll call you," Diana suggested.

When Lee agreed, Diana said, "Since that's settled, and since tomorrow's a working day for me, perhaps we should call it a night."

The ride back to her Memorial area town house didn't take long. Diana lived at the end of the wooded street, near the bayou, and night sounds surrounded them as he pulled into her driveway. Diana reached for the door handle automatically, then realized Lee was coming around to open her door. He took her hand to help her out, and when she stood, they were only inches apart. Her pulse quickened, and she felt a tingling anticipation. Diana slowly raised her eyes to gaze into his. For a long moment neither of them moved. The warm night, the whisper of air through the tall pines, the croak of a bullfrog, the distant hum of traffic on Memorial Drive, the buzz of cicadas, the silvery moonlight dappling her driveway, the rustle of leaves stirred by a small animal: Diana's awareness of these sensory details was heightened as her body throbbed with expectation.

She knew Lee was going to kiss her.

But she wasn't going to let him.

For she knew if she yielded to this crazy attraction, she would be inviting chaos into her life.

And Diana liked her life exactly the way it was. So when he tried to kiss her she would be very mature and quietly ask him not to.

Lee bent his head.

Diana stiffened.

And then he surprised the heck out of her. Instead of kissing her, he said, "Thank you for a wonderful evening." He casually draped his arm around her shoulder. "I'll walk you to the door."

He certainly was smooth. He probably thought he'd thrown her off by not kissing her when she expected it. Diana smothered a smile. He couldn't fool her. He would make his move at the door, but she'd be ready for him. Wouldn't he be surprised when she said, "No thanks." She was willing to bet very few women ever refused Lee Gabriel anything.

They reached her door. Diana unlocked it, then with her hand on the doorknob, turned to face him. "Goodnight, Lee," she said firmly.

"Goodnight, Diana. Talk to you tomorrow."

And then, to Diana's consternation, he gave her a little salute, then turned and strode back down the walk toward his car.

Something very like disappointment welled in her throat. She walked inside and closed the door, leaning against it for a few seconds while she tried to make sense out of her unreasonable reaction to Lee's completely reasonable behavior.

No doubt about it.

She *was* disappointed.

She didn't know whether to laugh or cry.

Saturday morning Kent stood looking out the French doors leading to the side patio of the guest house where Lee and Allison were living. The Marlowe property covered several acres, part of them wooded, and comprised not only the large Spanish-style main house and the small guest house, but a pool, a tennis court, and stables. Both Jinx and Howard Marlowe, Allison's grandparents, were avid equestrians. As a young woman Jinx had ridden competitively, and Howard had served on the committee of the Pin Oak Horse Show for a dozen years. Lately he'd been trying to convince Kent to learn to ride. Kent liked Allison's grandparents, even though he wasn't sure he'd ever feel entirely comfortable around them.

"I'm ready, Kent."

He turned at the sound of Allison's voice. As usual, she looked so beautiful she took his breath away. Today she wore a red jumpsuit with a wide gold belt around her waist and gold sandals on her feet. "You look great," he said.

His compliment brought a smile to her lips, and not for the first time, she reminded him of a sleek Siamese cat they used to have when he was a kid. The cat's name had been Jasmine, and she had preened whenever his mother fed or petted her. The rest of the time she wouldn't give either him or his mother the time of day.

He bent to kiss Allison, and everything else but how good she felt in his arms vanished from his mind. After a few seconds, Allison gently disengaged herself from the embrace. "You're going to mess up my lipstick," she warned.

"Then I'll have to go repair it."

"I'm sorry. Let's go."

They walked out into the sunny morning, and Allison, eyeing his seven-year-old Honda Civic, said, "Let's take my car today."

Kent tensed. "Why?"

She pouted. "Oh, come on, Kent. Don't be that way."

He sighed. "Honey, you're going to have to get used to the idea that I'll never be able to afford the kinds of things your father and your grandparents can afford." The jaunty green Miata had been a birthday present from Howard and Jinx. "There's not a thing wrong with my car."

"I know, but it's *such* a pretty day, and we can put the top down in my car," she wheedled, slipping her arms around his waist and tilting her head up to look at him. "Please?"

God, he couldn't resist her. But what harm was there in indulging her? All he really wanted was for her to be happy, and if riding in that car of hers made her happy, fine. "Okay. Okay. You win."

Her smile was dazzling. "I love you," she said, and pulled his head down to kiss him.

When she finally let him up for air, her eyes were shining with promise. She dug into her purse and pulled out her keys. "You drive."

Forty-five minutes later they were seated on velvet chairs and looking at diamond engagement rings at Mason's, a small local jewelers. Allison had wanted to go to Fred's or Tiffany's, but Kent had put his foot down on those suggestions. "I can't afford their prices. Sedgewick Mason is a friend of my mother's. She helped him sell a house once, and he'll give me a good deal."

Allison studied the tray of rings. She took so long, Kent felt oddly disturbed. "What's wrong?" he finally asked.

She cut a glance at Sedgewick, who discreetly looked away. "Oh, I'm sorry. I . . . I'm just having a hard time deciding."

Kent frowned. As Allison touched first one ring, then another, Kent looked—really looked—at the ring on her right hand, the ring her father had given her for her twenty-first birthday. It was a large emerald, a deep blue-green color that even Kent's untrained eye knew meant the stone was very valuable. He swallowed uncomfortably. "Honey, I know these rings are not very large, but I'll make it up to you someday. I promise."

"I understand, Kent. Really. It's okay. These rings are beautiful. Here—" She finally chose one—a small solitaire set in yellow gold. "This one is very nice."

Kent looked at Sedgewick, who kept his face impassive. Then he looked back at Allison, who he knew was trying very hard to mask her disappointment. Kent felt like a heel. He had enough money in his savings account to buy her the kind of ring she deserved. When Grandmother Sorensen had died two years ago, she'd left him twenty-three thousand dollars, and he hadn't touched a penny of it. The trouble was, the money was earmarked for his start-up costs on his storefront law office.

"Sedgewick," he said, "let's see some larger stones."

"No, Kent . . ." Allison touched his arm, her tawny eyes soft. "Really. I don't want you to spend money you don't have. It's okay."

"It's not okay." Suddenly Kent knew he couldn't hold his head up again if he didn't do this for her. Somehow the proper kind of ring symbolized everything she meant to him.

An hour later, with Allison blissfully turning her left hand from side to side to see how the sun's rays made her perfect one and a half carat diamond sparkle, they were speeding their way back to the house, and Kent's savings account had been seriously depleted.

Kent wondered what Diana would say when she saw the ring.

Diana was sure she was in the throes of a midlife crisis.

How else to explain her absurd reaction to the most innocent conduct on Lee's part? Even a casual brush of his hand caused silly flutters in her stomach. And if he actually flirted with her, her pulse rate went off the charts.

She had to get a grip on herself.

She was forty-two years old, for heaven's sake. In December, she would be forty-three.

Certainly too levelheaded and mature to let any man affect her this way.

She and Lee had been looking at houses since one o'clock that afternoon. In between looking at houses, they sat close together in the intimate confines of the Porsche. Diana hadn't wanted to use his car, but he'd insisted.

"Indulge me, okay? I hardly ever drove all the years we were in Paris. During the week I lived in a small apartment close to the office and walked to work. The weekends were the only time I ever got behind the wheel of a car, and then it was only a Peugeot.'' He stroked the gleaming chrome of the Porsche's hood. ''Nothing like this baby.''

Diana gave in.

So all day, they'd been in and out of his sexy car, and of course, because it was built low to the ground and she was a tall woman, Lee very courteously helped her in and out. So he'd touched her a lot over the course of the afternoon. And each time, Diana reacted exactly the same way.

Like a kid.

Like a foolish kid with a big-time crush.

And if all that wasn't bad enough, Lee didn't seem to like any of the houses she'd picked out for him to see. Since Diana was methodical, all the houses were located in the River Oaks or West University area. She was saving the Memorial area for Sunday.

''Too gingerbready,'' he said of the restored Victorian in West University.

Okay, she hadn't really thought he'd like the Victorian.

''Too monolithic,'' he said of the winner of several architectural awards in the River Oaks area.

It *was* a bit cold, she'd give him that.

''Too traditional.''

Well, maybe.

''Too big.''

Hadn't he said he *wanted* a big house? Hadn't he specifically said he would be doing a lot of entertaining?

''Too cramped and broken up.''

Diana bit back the remark that she didn't think he knew *what* he wanted.

''Too fussy.''

''Too stark.''

''Too rigid.''

Diana frowned, feeling the beginnings of a headache coming on. She glanced at her watch. Five o'clock. "There's one more house to look at today," she said evenly, determined not to let him see her irritation. Diana thought this last house was the best of the bunch, which was why she'd saved it for last.

As they approached the sprawling cedar ranch on the fringes of River Oaks, she watched Lee's face for his reaction.

To her intense disappointment, he frowned and shook his head.

"What's the matter with it?" She couldn't prevent her frustration and growing annoyance from showing in her tone.

He shrugged as he parked the Porsche in the wide driveway. "I don't know. I'm not crazy about the way it looks."

"Lee, are you sure you really want to buy a house?" For the first time that afternoon, the touch of his warm hand as he helped her out of the car didn't stir her senses. That's it, she thought wryly. I'll just have to stay annoyed with him. Which might not be so hard, considering the way the day was going.

He chuckled. "I'm sorry, Diana. I told you I was going to be a demanding client."

Was he laughing at her? Torn between the desire to say something sarcastic and the desire to keep him from knowing he was getting to her made Diana count to ten before she answered. "I'm used to demanding clients. Don't worry. We'll find you a house."

They walked up the driveway, and Diana found the lock box. Soon they were inside the vacant house. Late afternoon sunshine streamed through the windows, and Diana could see dust motes floating in the air.

"Let's start from the back of the house," she said as she walked through the wide center hallway that led straight into a sunroom that faced the back of the property.

Diana felt as if she'd stepped into a greenhouse. Everywhere she looked she saw green mixed in with a riot of colors from an incredible array of flowers. She smiled, enchanted with the room, then turned to see Lee's reaction.

He was standing so close to her she almost gasped. She automatically backed up a step. "This is a lovely room, isn't it?" she said, and she could hear the breathless quality of her voice.

"Lovely," he echoed, though his eyes were not on the room, but on her face.

Diana felt as if all the air had been squeezed out of her lungs as his warm, golden gaze captured hers.

Without her even knowing how it had happened, he moved closer, and his hands settled on her arms. Through the taupe gabardine of her suit jacket, Diana could feel the heat of his touch. She wanted to look away from his potent gaze, but she couldn't seem to move.

She swallowed.

When his lips touched hers, she shuddered, and then she was in his arms, and her mouth was opening under his, and her entire body felt as if it was in the middle of a hot flash.

Her last coherent thought before she gave herself over completely was, *Oh, my God, I'm in bigger trouble than I thought.*

Chapter Four

The kiss was like riding on the Ferris wheel. Teetering at the very top, high over the houses and trees and people, up among the bright, sparkly stars. Holding your breath, and then falling through the cool, clean night air—your heart beating hard, your stomach getting that hollowed-out, giddy feeling.

The kiss was like sitting in the lead car on the roller coaster as it inched its way up the first incline, excitement twisting through your belly, and then hurtling down so fast your insides shot up into your throat, and when you reached the bottom to start the next climb you couldn't speak without your voice quivering.

The kiss was like going around and around on the carousel, the calliope music swelling around you, the horses dipping and soaring while the lights swirled in endless ribbons of diamonds and rubies and gold.

Diana lost herself in the kiss. Time had no meaning. The world receded until there was only Lee.

His taste. His touch. His smell.

As he drew her further and further into the kiss, she clung to him and let the world spin around her. She had the strangest sensation that Lee was her anchor, that if she ever once let go, she'd whirl off into the stratosphere.

When he finally broke the kiss, the sense of loss was so acute it was like a sharp pain in her heart.

"I've wanted to do that from the first moment I saw you," he said, his voice husky.

Diana trembled with aftershock. Badly shaken, she couldn't meet his eyes. Her heart was still going like a triphammer, and her mind reeled in confusion.

What had happened to her? What had happened to her highly prized control that it had slipped so easily? How could it be that a simple kiss could turn her into a quivering mass of emotions? But her mind said there was nothing simple about the kiss Lee had just given her.

Confused and flustered by her feelings and behavior, she shook free of his arms and deliberately turned her back on him. Calling on all her reserves, she told herself to calm down. It was just a kiss, for heaven's sake, not the end of the world.

"Diana?" He touched her right shoulder. "Is something wrong?" His voice sounded ragged, as if he was having trouble with his own emotions.

Everything was wrong. Oh, Lord, what a mess! Why had she let him kiss her like that? Right now she'd have given anything to turn the clock back five minutes. "No, nothing's wrong," she mumbled.

"Diana, please look at me."

She didn't want to. She didn't want to see his eyes—those smoky, golden eyes that seemed to strip away all the outer layers of her defenses. But she knew if she didn't, she'd be lost. Because then he would know how shaken she was. He would know he'd gotten to her. He would know how deeply his kiss had affected her, and she wanted to prevent that at all costs. She couldn't afford to let him know how she felt. She had no intention of carrying this unwelcome attraction one step further than it had already gone.

So she turned, steeling herself to look up into his eyes with an unwavering gaze.

Lee smiled—a tender, sexy, cocky, man-smile that nearly did her in. "I knew kissing you would be fantastic." With his right forefinger, he stroked her cheek. The soft caress sent whispers of desire through her. "You're beautiful."

"Lee . . ." she said weakly.

He kept looking at her mouth. Diana's insides had turned into melted butter. Why did he keep looking at her mouth?

Now his voice was a husky murmur. "Why don't we try that again? Why don't we try it several times, in fact?" The smile that played at the corners of his mouth teased her. "Just to see if the second and third times are as good as the first . . . or maybe they'll be better. . . ."

Something molten slid through her at the promise in his voice and in his eyes. She could feel her heart knocking against her chest. She wasn't sure if she could ever breathe normally again. She fought against the weakness that threatened to overcome her. "That's not a good idea," she said. Even to her own ears her voice sounded strange.

His smile expanded. "Why, Diana," he said softly, "I do believe you're frightened."

She stiffened. "That's ridiculous."

"Is it?"

Now his hand curled around her neck, and he tugged her closer. She shivered. His mouth was only inches from hers. Fascinated, she stared at the sensuous curve of his lips, his gleaming white teeth. She swallowed. If only she could allow herself to give in to the aching need pulsing through her. But that would be madness. Madness. Why, she hardly knew this man. And she simply wasn't the kind of woman who jumped into bed with a virtual stranger. She'd learned long ago that actions carried consequences. Consequences you had to live with for a long, long time.

Firmly, before she could change her mind, she reached up and removed his hand. She backed up a few steps.

"Diana, why are you fighting this? I know you're just as attracted to me as I am to you. Why won't you admit it?"

To buy time, she smoothed down her skirt. "Look, Lee," she said when she finally raised her eyes once more, "whether I'm attracted to you or not is beside the point—"

"Oh?" There was that damned cocky grin again. "And the point being . . . ?"

She took a measured breath, then said, "If you'd allow me to finish . . ."

His eyes sparkled amber in the sunlight. "By all means, finish."

"I'm not interested in . . . casual sex . . . and I have absolutely no desire for a permanent relationship, so I think the best thing we can do is forget all about what just happened."

"I see. You've got it all figured out, do you?"

Was that a glint of anger in his eyes? Why should *he* be angry? She'd just stated the truth. Funny how men couldn't handle the truth. They talked about women being emotional, but women were much more realistic than men. Men were just like babies, especially when it came to their masculinity. They couldn't believe there was a woman alive who could resist them.

She lifted her chin. "Yes, I believe I do."

Now he no longer looked angry. He looked amused. As if he knew a secret, and she didn't. As if he were laughing at her!

Anger ignited inside her. What was so darned funny? She stared at him. "It wasn't hard to figure it out," she said tightly. "I don't think a person needs a Ph.D. to understand what happened here." *In other words, buster, I've got your number.*

"Diana..." His voice was soft. "What happened here is that I gave in to something I've wanted to do from the moment I set eyes on you. This is *not* about casual sex. Believe it or not, I'm not interested in casual sex any more than you are. I'm more attracted to you than I have been to any woman in years. In fact, I can't remember another woman who has ever affected me the way you do."

She *had* to hold on to this anger. She had to remember Lee was a sophisticated man who had probably practiced that same line on many women. Yet something about the look in his eyes told her he wasn't just giving her a line.

Now, stop that! That kind of thinking is going to land you in even more trouble! Furious with herself for weakening, she whirled and walked out of the sunroom. Whether Lee followed her or not was strictly up to him. She simply didn't intend to spend one more minute alone with him in the vacant house.

Just as she reached the front door, he caught up with her. His hand on her shoulder stopped her. He slowly turned her to face him.

"What are you so afraid of?" he challenged.

"I'm not afraid!"

He gave her that infuriating, knowing smile again. "Well, you could've fooled me," he said softly. "From where I stood, I'd have sworn you were running away."

Diana clenched her teeth. ''I've never run away from anything! I'm just bored with this conversation.'' She yanked open the door and stalked out. She wished she hadn't relented and let him drive his Porsche. She would have given anything to have her own car right now.

I'd leave him standing right here in the driveway, she told herself. She huffed over to the passenger side of his car and waited for him to open the door.

He took his sweet time about following her outside. As he walked toward her, he still had that cocky grin on his face. She felt like slapping him. But she refused to further elevate his inflated ego by responding, either verbally or by her facial expression.

Still smiling like a Cheshire cat, he strolled unhurriedly to her side of the car, leaned over and unlocked the door. He reached for her elbow. She shook off his hand and got into the car herself. She sat there and nursed her anger, telling herself he was too damned sure of himself. Who did he think he was, anyway, that he could grab her and kiss her like that, then think she would fall into his hands like a ripe peach?

Even as she berated herself, she knew Lee hadn't grabbed her. He hadn't forced her. She'd been a willing participant in that thousand-megawatt kiss. In fact, she'd loved being kissed by him. Loved it too much. Wanted the kiss to go on and on forever. Even now, just thinking about the kiss, a pulsing ache settled into her nether-regions.

She kept her chin defiantly raised as Lee started the car and backed out of the driveway. She felt absurdly close to tears, which astounded her.

She hadn't cried in years. She was tough. She'd learned early in life that tears were useless. They certainly weren't for her. Tears were for women who didn't realize it was foolish to depend on anyone other than yourself. Tears were for women who thought happily ever after came automatically with a wedding band.

She stared out the window, seeing nothing. She was so angry with herself. Why had she returned his kiss like that? You'd think she was starved for a man's attention, and nothing could be further from the truth. She didn't want a man in her life. She didn't need a man in her life. She didn't need anyone. Her life was just fine the way it was, thank you very much.

Lee didn't try to make conversation as they drove toward her town house, and she was grateful. Maybe her luck would hold and he'd make it easy on both of them by not bringing up the subject of the kiss again.

Lee slanted a glance in Diana's direction as he pulled into her driveway. What was she thinking? he wondered. He knew from the way she held her body—stiff and unyielding—that she was still upset and angry.

After he'd kissed her—after they'd kissed each other, he amended—and she wouldn't look at him, he'd thought she was just embarrassed because of the sparks they'd ignited together. After all, it wasn't every day that a first kiss was so... Even in his mind, Lee couldn't think of a word to describe the kiss.

He still couldn't get over how it had felt to kiss her. He'd always felt a little superior to men who went off the deep end for a woman. He'd always thought men who acted that way were just a bit juvenile. He'd never expected to feel like a lovesick kid again.

But damned if he didn't.

When he'd kissed her, every hormone in his body had gone haywire.

And she'd felt exactly the same way. He knew it.

He hadn't wanted to stop kissing her. He'd just come up for air, with every intention of capturing her sweet, hot mouth again. In fact, he'd wanted to explore much more than her mouth. He'd wanted to touch her as well as kiss her. He'd wanted to make love to her. Right there. If she'd have let him, he'd have had her on the floor and undressed in less than twenty seconds. His reaction to her had been elemental and gut-level.

He smiled to himself.

Me man. You woman.

He'd wanted to claim her. Stamp her his.

It was incredible.

Thinking about it, he could feel himself reacting, feel his body's response to the idea of Diana lying naked on the floor of that house, with the sunshine pouring in through the glass walls. He moaned softly as he turned off the ignition.

He had to think fast. Teasing her out of her embarrassment—if that's what it was—hadn't worked. In fact, it had backfired. What should he do now?

He looked at her.

She didn't look at him. He studied her profile, tenderness flowing through him as he saw how her chin was lifted, as if she were defying the world.

Diana. She'd been aptly named, he thought. The goddess Diana had been a huntress—strong and proud. And his Diana was strong and proud, too. She was so used to being in charge of her life and her emotions. Maybe she didn't like the loss of control they'd both experienced. Maybe that's why she was acting this way.

He reached out and touched her forearm.

Slowly she turned her head toward him. Her lovely eyes glistened in the late-afternoon sunlight. Her face was set in strained lines.

Lee was ashamed of himself for his earlier teasing. He could see that Diana really *was* frightened, but taunting her about it was not the way to change her mind about him. He had rushed her, and if he didn't want to blow his chances with her completely, he'd better back off. Diana needed her own space, and if she thought he was going to crowd her, she'd refuse to have anything more to do with him.

And Lee didn't want that.

So he said softly, "I'm sorry you're upset, Diana."

Something flickered in the depths of her eyes.

"Can we start over again?"

"What do you mean?" she said cautiously.

He could see the wariness. Diana the huntress still felt like Diana the prey.

"Let's try to be friends. Get to know each other. Spend some time together."

"We're spending time together. I'm showing you houses, remember?"

"That's business. Let's forget business for at least the rest of today. Let me take you to dinner tonight. I promise I won't try to kiss you again." He couldn't stop himself from adding, "Unless you want me to, that is."

She was shaking her head. "No, Lee. I'm tired. I went out with you last night. Tonight I just want to stay home. Alone."

He nodded. "What about tomorrow?"

"What *about* tomorrow?"

"Would you like to do something tomorrow?"

"We are doing something tomorrow. We're looking at houses."

"Forget the houses for now. I'm not even sure about what neighborhoods I like. Tell you what. Let's just spend the day tomorrow looking at Houston neighborhoods. We can ride around, let me get a better feel for the market. And . . ." He kept his voice as casual and empty of pressure as he was capable of doing. "We can have lunch together and get to know each other better." He smiled reassuringly. "Strictly friends, I promise."

She hesitated only a few seconds, then gave him a half smile and said, "All right."

Relief coursed through Lee. He squeezed her arm, then opened his door and walked around to let her out of the car. He followed her up the walk, admiring the way her long legs looked as she walked briskly in her neat pumps. She walked tall, with her head up, and that was another thing he liked about her. Diana would face everything head-on, with no apology, and very little fear. And when she *was* afraid, she pretended she wasn't. Like shaking her fist at the devil.

Lee really liked that. Diana would never cower. It was refreshing to him to find a woman so confident of herself, yet endearing to see that she was also vulnerable.

Smart and strong yet vulnerable and sexy. A perfect mix, he thought. As they reached her door, she turned. "Well..."

To put her at ease and let her know he wasn't going to try anything—that he was a man of his word—Lee held out his hand, and she took it. They shook hands briefly, which seemed incongruous to him after what they'd so recently shared, but he could see the relief in Diana's eyes. Good. She'd relaxed her guard a little.

"See you in the morning, then. I'll pick you up at ten," he said.

"All right."

"Dress casually," he added. "Might as well be comfortable."

As he strode down the walk to his car, he whistled happily.

The whistle caused a tremor of fear to slide down Diana's spine. He sounded entirely too happy. She shut the front door and leaned against it, closing her eyes, finally allowing the tension twisting her insides to dissolve. Clyde sidled up against her, meowing for attention, but she ignored him.

She shouldn't have agreed to Lee's plans for the next day. But without knowing he was doing it, he'd found her most vulnerable spot.

Sundays.

Unlike most other women she'd talked to, who seemed to hate spending Saturday nights alone, if Diana were to feel any emptiness or loneliness in her life, it would always hit her on a Sunday. Maybe that was because Sundays had always been such companionable days when she and Bill had been married, and even later, when Kent was still living at home. Since Bill was an ex-jock and a coach, Sundays had always been filled with sports. Sports and church and family outings.

And then, after the divorce, during all the years that Kent was growing up, he spent his Saturdays with his father, but Diana always made sure she saved Sundays for him. She worked hard the rest of the week, but on Sundays she and Kent were a tradition. They would pick up Diana's mother, and the three of them would go to church, then out for brunch.

On Sunday afternoons they always did whatever Kent wanted to do. They would drop Barbara at her house, because by the end of brunch Diana would have had enough of her mother's complaining, plus she felt it was important for her and Kent to spend some time alone.

If it was a rainy day, maybe they'd go to a museum or art gallery. Or maybe they'd shop, then go to the movies, then have dinner out, too. Sometimes they went to cat shows, or baseball games, or to see the Oilers play. Sometimes they went roller-skating or ice-skating at the Galleria. Once they even went out to Intercontinental Airport and for hours they watched the big jets take off. Diana smiled, remembering the starry look in Kent's nine-year-old eyes. He'd so loved the big jets. For his tenth birthday she'd bought them round-trip tickets to Dallas for a weekend, just so he could have the experience of flying in a jet. She'd never forget his wide-eyed expression when the plane hurtled down the runway, and his excited squeal when they lifted off.

In the summer they might go to the beach for the day or to Astroworld, or maybe just spend the entire day at their subdivision pool. They'd done all the things native Houstonians don't usually do, like visit the San Jacinto Monument and tour NASA and ride the Bolivar ferry. Seeing these things through Kent's eyes had made the excursions special for Diana.

She'd loved Sundays. Looked forward to them. Felt a deep contentment in the simple sharing of time with the family she loved.

So the past few years had been tough for her, because inevitably, as Kent grew older, he found other interests. He developed his own life, and although he was still attentive and still made it a point to try to spend at least one Sunday a month with her, Diana had felt a big gap in her life. And she hadn't wanted Kent to feel guilty about it, either. God knows, she sure didn't want to be like her own mother—whining and complaining about how her children neglected her. In fact, there were times Diana had had to bite her tongue to keep from saying what she was thinking whenever her mother started in on her. Diana had never neglected her mother.

And Kent had never neglected Diana.

Still . . . Sundays were tough. Even for someone like her, who really thought she had the perfect life. She really *did* have the perfect life, she mused. She could do whatever she wanted whenever she wanted. No one to answer to. No one to make demands on her time. No one to worry about.

If she felt like eating spaghetti for breakfast and cereal for dinner, she could. If she didn't feel like eating at all, she didn't have to. If she wanted to stay in her nightgown all day Sunday, there was no one to look at her as if she were a lazy slug. And if she wanted to plop onto the couch with a huge bowl of buttered popcorn and watch mindless TV shows, she could do that, too. So what was she griping about?

She pushed herself away from the door and slowly climbed up the stairway to the second level and her bedroom. Honestly, what was wrong with her? She was acting maudlin and stupid. Was that all it took? Some man to take notice of her, and she'd revert to being someone she'd stopped being years ago? Someone who wanted the security of a person to spend Sundays with?

"Diana Sorensen," she said aloud. "Stop this. You have no desire to be married again. You don't even want any kind of ongoing relationship. You know how demanding something like that is, and you haven't got room in your life for it! Can you even imagine a man putting up with the fact that you work about sixty hours a week?"

Clyde, who had followed her upstairs, butted her leg for attention, and Bonnie crept out from under the bed. Diana absentmindedly petted them both.

She continued to think about Lee as she shed her business clothes and put on her comfortable faded jeans and a T-shirt. She was right to be wary of Lee. She knew it. Even if she *did* think it would be nice to have a man to do things with, Lee Gabriel was not that man. She'd better remember that Lee Gabriel was the father of the girl her son was engaged to marry. If she and Lee were to start something, the day would come when their affair would come to its natural demise. And what then? She'd be uncomfortable around him for the rest of her life.

No. Impossible. Completely impossible. And if Lee said one word tomorrow about the two of them, she'd set him straight. Tell him everything she'd been thinking. Because any kind of romantic relationship between her and Lee would never work out.

Sunday dawned bright and clear, a perfect September day. The temperature had even cooperated. Instead of the blazing heat of the previous weeks, the mercury was only supposed to climb to the mid-seventies. Diana walked out onto her second-story deck, which Kent had laughingly said reminded him of the tree house he'd had as a boy because of the way it was tucked up under the sheltering pines and leafy ash trees prevalent in south Texas.

A squirrel, startled by her silent approach, scurried up the trunk of the nearest tree, then studied her with solemn eyes from the safety of his perch a few feet away. Diana chuckled and leaned over the railing. She took a deep breath of the fresh morning air. It really was going to be too beautiful a day to spend indoors. For a while after she'd gotten up, she'd toyed with the idea of calling Lee and canceling their appointment. She refused to call it a date.

But if she did that, she would be running away—the thing Lee had accused her of doing and she'd so vehemently denied. She'd never run away from anything. Or anyone. No, she had to set Lee straight, make him understand that they were never going to be more than friendly parents whose children were married to each other. She had to take control of the situation. After all, hadn't she always known it was the woman's job to set the tone for a man-woman relationship?

Sighing, Diana walked back inside her bedroom and shut the sliding glass door. As she dressed in jeans and a royal blue summer-weight sweater, she decided that before the day was over, she would get Lee's agreement to keep their relationship one of friendship only.

Shoot, she was probably agonizing over this for nothing. Lee was a smart man. He had probably gone home, thought about it and come to the same conclusion she'd come to. He was probably already regretting his impulsive act of the day before and had made up his mind not to repeat it.

"What are you planning to do today, Daddy?"

Lee turned at the sound of Allison's voice. She leaned against the frame of the doorway between the kitchen and the dining room. She was dressed in tennis whites and carried her racket. She looked young, fresh and beautiful. He smiled at her. "Diana is taking me around to look at Houston neighborhoods today."

An almost imperceptible frown marred her smooth forehead. "I thought you looked at houses yesterday."

"We did, but I suggested we spend today driving around the different sections of the city. I'm still not sure where I want to buy, and we're wasting her time and mine by looking at houses in too many places." He thought his explanation sounded reasonable.

"From the way Kent has bragged about his mother's expertise, I would have thought she'd do that kind of thing *first.*" The frown deepened. "I was afraid it wasn't a good idea for you to work with her. Now, even if you're unhappy with her work, you won't be able to change agents."

"Don't blame Diana, Allison. It's my fault. I didn't give her any guidelines. In fact, I told her to show me a little of everything." He waited a second, then added, "Kent's mother is doing a good job. It's going to take some time, of course, because the kind of house I want won't be found in a day, but she'll find me the right one.''

''I hope so.''

''You sound doubtful.'' He studied the cloudy look in her eyes. ''What's the matter, Allison? Don't you want me to work with her? I thought you liked Diana.''

''I do, Daddy.'' She made a visible effort to smile at him, but he thought the smile seemed forced.

''Then what's the problem?''

''There's no problem. I just know how important it is for you to have the right kind of house. I also know how exacting you can be. I don't want you to feel you owe this sale to Kent's mother because of me.'' She smiled and walked over to him. Standing on tiptoe, she kissed his cheek. He hugged her briefly and returned her kiss. She smelled good. ''Well, I'm leaving now,'' she said. ''I'm meeting Kent at the club. We're going to play tennis, then have lunch.''

''Sounds like fun. Have a nice day, sweetheart.''

''You, too, Daddy.'' She walked toward the door, hesitated, then stopped. She turned. ''How about if Kent and I pick up a few steaks? We can do them on the grill, and the three of us can eat dinner here tonight.'' Her smile was bright and innocent. ''It'll give you a chance to spend some time with Kent. Get to know him better.''

Why did her smile seem somehow wrong to him? Why did it seem to say, *look what a clever girl I am?* Why did he get the feeling she wanted to be sure he didn't spend the evening as well as the day with Diana?

He kept his tone offhand as he said, ''Thanks, honey. I appreciate your offer. But I don't know how long it's going to take us today. I may just take Diana out to dinner before I take her home. After all, she's giving up her Sunday for me.''

Annoyance flashed through Allison's amber eyes. "It's her job to spend weekends working with clients. Besides, you took her to dinner Friday night."

"So? I like her. She's very good company." Yes, his daughter was definitely annoyed. And who knows, maybe she even felt a bit possessive. She hadn't had to share him for a long time. "Come on, sweetheart, lighten up. I thought you'd be pleased that Kent's mother and I are getting along so well."

There was that frown again that said she was anything *but* pleased. "Well, of course, I'm pleased. It's just that—"

"Well, good. Since you're pleased and I'm pleased, we don't have a problem, do we?"

She looked as if she wanted to say something else, but she didn't. Instead she sighed. "No. We don't have a problem."

Chapter Five

I have a problem, Diana thought.

She knew she'd been kidding herself the minute she'd glimpsed Lee striding up her walk, looking much too sexy for her peace of mind in snug-fitting jeans, soft leather boots and an open-necked yellow shirt that emphasized his deep tan and golden-brown eyes. She took one look and knew it wasn't going to be as easy as she'd hoped to forget about what had happened between them.

Lordy, how could she hope to stay cool and professional when just looking at him made her feel hot and giddy? How could she hope to keep their relationship light and friendly when someone as potently male as Lee was around? Whether she liked it or not, there was a strong element of sexual awareness between them, and pretending it wasn't there simply wasn't going to work.

The trouble was, everything about Lee got her engine going. When she was around him, she never forgot for one minute that she was a woman and he was a man.

God knows, she was trying.

All morning she fought to keep her thoughts on houses and neighborhoods and the big fat sales commission her agency would receive from the sale of a house to Lee.

All morning her thoughts kept straying to details such as the appealing shape of Lee's hands on the steering wheel. Then inevitably, she'd imagine how those hands would feel whispering over her skin.

She got so angry with herself, she wanted to spit.

And what made it all worse was that Lee acted like a perfect gentleman. Friendly. Casual. Not even a hint of flirtation. He acted exactly the way Diana had hoped he would act. Exactly the way *she'd* intended to act.

It was enough to make a grown woman cry.

Lee was proud of himself. It had been hard, but not once during the morning had he said one thing to scare Diana off. He'd spent two hours sitting only inches away from her in the car without making a move or saying a word with sexual or personal overtones.

He'd looked at neighborhoods. He'd discussed prices, areas, types of homes and the housing market. In other words, he'd been good.

It was time for a reward.

He grinned, sneaking a look at Diana. Damn, she looked great in those jeans. She filled them out perfectly. He sure did like a woman with some meat on her bones, and Diana curved in and out in all the right places.

Today she looked gorgeous in her bright blue sweater that intensified the deep blue of her eyes. He'd never been particularly partial to blue-eyed blondes, but Diana, with eyes

he color of an Alpine sky and hair the color of sunlight,
ad certainly changed his mind.

"It's time for lunch," he announced. "My stomach is
complaining."

"Okay. Where would you like to eat?"

She turned, and his breath caught at the artless allure of
her smile. That was another thing he liked about her. She
wasn't studiedly flirtatious, constantly "on" as so many
women seemed to be. "I've already picked out a place," he
answered. "Do you mind?"

"No. Of course not."

It amazed Lee that Diana didn't ask questions. She just
settled back in her seat and waited to find out where they
were going. He wondered what she'd say when they got
there.

Her reaction was worth waiting for. Her eyes widened,
and her mouth dropped open when he pulled into the entrance to Hermann Park. Without saying anything, he got
out of the car and walked around to her side to help her out.
She still looked speechless.

"Watch it," he teased. "A bug's going to fly in if you
keep your mouth open like that!"

"We're having a picnic?" she finally said, obviously dis-
believing as she tagged after him and watched him open the
trunk and pull out the picnic basket he'd prepared earlier.
Then she laughed, the sound delightful and infectious.

"We sure are." He grinned, pleased with himself. Pleased
with her reaction. Pleased with the whole world. "I hope
you like fried chicken."

"Don't tell me *you* fried chicken?" Laughter still bub-
bled in her voice.

They walked toward one of the empty picnic tables, where
Lee, using the cloth he'd had the foresight to pack, wiped off
the benches and top of the table.

"I cannot tell a lie. I stopped and bought it on the way to your house."

She shook her head, her amusement tipping her lips. Her eyes sparkled in the sunlight, and a breeze lifted her hair. She looked fresh and lovely and much younger than her forty-two years. Lee wanted to kiss her, right there in the middle of the park, where anyone might see them.

But he didn't. He'd made a promise to himself that he would let nothing spoil this day. He wanted the day to be perfect. He wanted Diana to remember it with pleasure. He wanted her to think about it often so that she'd look forward to spending other days—and nights—with him. So he ignored his desire to kiss her, and began unpacking the picnic basket. He hoped he hadn't forgotten anything.

He had thought of everything.

Amazed, Diana watched as Lee spread a checkered cloth over the table, then laid out two earthenware plates, cutlery, and two plastic tumblers. Next came salt and pepper shakers, the box of fried chicken—the aroma of which made Diana's mouth water—a container of cole slaw, another of potato salad, rolls, pickles, olives and something that looked suspiciously like apple pie.

"Don't tell me you baked that pie?" she said.

Another of his irresistible smiles played over his mouth. "Randall's Bakery."

She nodded. She had practically supported Randall's Bakery single-handedly over the years.

"But I *did* make the iced tea."

"That's a relief. I think I can live with that."

"What do you mean?"

Diana grimaced. "Well, I'm a terrible cook. And if you'd made all this—" she gestured toward the laden table "—was going to start feeling really inadequate."

"Well..."

She narrowed her eyes. "Well, what?"

"I *am* a pretty good cook," he confessed sheepishly. "The only reason I didn't fix lunch myself is that I didn't have enough time to get it ready."

"Do you do *everything* well?" she asked, without thinking.

His warm gaze captured hers. "I don't know. Do I?"

Diana wanted to curl into a ball and disappear. *Why* had he said something so suggestive?

He laughed. "Tell you what. I'll let you be the judge of that. One of these days I'll invite you for dinner." His eyes twinkled. "Show you another of my talents."

She nodded, still embarrassed by her remark. To cover her embarrassment, she said, "Have you always been interested in cooking?"

He shrugged. "No. I got interested in cooking when we were living in France. Cooking isn't considered women's work there, you know—at least not the way it is here. Anyway, I took a couple of classes and found I really enjoyed it."

Lunch was delicious, Diana thought as she sat across from him. She felt all the tensions of the week slipping away as she soaked up the atmosphere: the soft breeze, the laughter of toddlers playing, the warmth of the sun on her shoulders, the impressive view of the Medical Center in the distance.

She couldn't imagine how anything could top this for perfect contentment. For the first time in a long time she really looked around her. She remembered the words from an old favorite song about taking time to stop and smell the roses. She really hadn't done enough of that the past few years.

She nearly sighed when Lee said, "Well, should we begin packing things up?"

"Okay." All good things must come to an end, she told herself.

But Lee had another surprise in store for her, and this one charmed her even more than the picnic lunch.

He drove from Hermann Park straight to the zoo. Pulling into a parking place with a flourish and a wicked twinkle in his eyes, he gave her a sideways glance and said, "I'm tired of looking at people-neighborhoods. I thought we'd see how the animals live."

She knew she should take him to task. She knew she should be irritated that he was so high-handed with her time. She knew she had no business having this much fun.

Instead she smiled.

What the heck, she thought. It's only one day. There's no law that says I have to be sensible every single day of my life.

Kent dropped Allison off at home with the promise that he'd be back at seven for dinner. They'd decided to grill some steaks and eat dinner at her place. Since he now had a free afternoon, he decided he would go back to his apartment, put on his bathing trunks and lie out by the pool while he caught up on some of his reading.

When Kent walked into the apartment, the first thing he checked was the answering machine. The light was blinking, so he pushed the message button.

Hi, Kent. It's me, Nikki. Mom told me about your engagement. Congratulations. Call me when you get a chance. Talk to you later....

Kent eyed the phone. He knew he should have called Nikki before this, but like a coward, he'd put it off. Although he'd never discussed it with anyone, he knew Nikki was in love with him. The knowledge made him uncomfortable, and had really put a strain on their relationship the past year, which made him feel badly, because he loved Nikki. Unfortunately, though, loving her wasn't the same as being in love with her.

Nikki was special, and he felt about her the way he imagined he would have felt about a younger sister. She was a pal, she was a friend and he'd always been able to talk to her about anything.

Until a year ago when there had been an almost imperceptible change in their relationship. He knew Nikki had tried hard not to let on how she felt about him, but he knew her so well she couldn't hide that kind of thing from him.

They'd never talked about it. He knew Nikki never would. She had too much pride.

He closed his eyes. Damn. Well, he might as well get it over with. He couldn't avoid her forever. He knew she was hurting, but there wasn't anything he could do about it. He loved being with Nikki, but he'd never wanted to kiss her. When he was with Allison, kissing her was about all he could think about.

Before he lost his nerve, he dialed Nikki's telephone number. She answered on the second ring.

"Hello?"

"Nikki? It's Kent."

"Oh, hi, Kent!" Her voice sounded cheerful. Too cheerful. "I should be really mad at you! Why didn't you call me to tell me your news? Why did I have to hear about your engagement from my mother?"

"I'm sorry, Nik. I meant to, but then Mom told me your mother knew, so I figured she'd already passed the word."

"Well... I guess I forgive you."

Pain knotted in Kent's chest as he listened to the false brightness in her tone, the faked coyness, which was so unlike Nikki. "I knew you would," he said softly.

"But don't let it happen again!" Then her voice turned serious and she added softly, "I'm happy for you, Kent. I really am. I just wanted you to know that. I wish you and . . . Allison . . . all the happiness in the world."

"Thanks, Nik. That means a lot to me. You're my best friend."

"You . . . our friendship means a lot to me, too."

He heard the ache in her voice, the pain she could no longer disguise. He also heard the determination to keep herself under control, and he admired that. Nikki was a fighter. She always had been. He'd always envied that quality in her, because he'd never been a fighter. "We'll always be friends," he said softly. "You know that, don't you?"

"Of course, I know that." She laughed. "Why are we so serious all of a sudden? This isn't a time for seriousness, this is a time for celebration. Let's party!"

He laughed, too, but more out of relief than out of amusement. Yes, she definitely was a fighter. She'd get over this. She'd meet someone else, fall in love and someday maybe they'd be able to laugh about this conversation. "That's a good idea. I'll talk to Allison. Maybe we can get a bunch of the gang together and go out on the town some night soon."

"I'd like that."

"I'd like that, too."

They talked a few more minutes, then Nikki said, "Well, I'm supposed to be somewhere at two-thirty, and if I don't get going, I'm gonna be late."

After he hung up the phone Kent sighed deeply. He was certainly glad that was over. Maybe the next time he talked to Nikki, they'd be over this awkwardness. She would have had a chance to adjust to the news, and he would be better able to smooth things over and make this transition easier for her. He had to make it easier for her. If he didn't, she would avoid him, and they would grow apart.

Kent knew he and Allison would have to make an effort to see Nikki, to let her know they valued her as a friend. So she wouldn't feel shut out. Tonight, he'd talk to Allison about Nikki, and between the two of them, they ought to be able to come up with a plan.

Going to the zoo with Lee was so much fun, Diana almost felt like a kid again. She glanced at Lee, who was striding along beside her. It was late in the afternoon, and they had just passed the monkey cage, where earlier they'd spent a pleasurable half hour watching the monkeys' antics.

"You've had a good time today, haven't you?" Lee asked. He tossed another piece of popcorn to the marauding pigeons who seemed to be everywhere.

"I *have* had a good time." She grinned. "But my feet hurt."

"Well, it's time to get you off them, then." He tossed the last few remaining pieces of popcorn into the air, and the pigeons swooped down, wings flapping and mouths squawking. "Ready to go?"

Although reluctant to see the day end and a return to the real world, Diana nodded. "I've had a really wonderful time today, Lee. I don't often get the chance to goof off like this, and it's been great. Thanks." It was probably a good thing the day *was* over. She didn't have a whole lot of her resolve left.

"I'm glad you had fun." He put his arm around her shoulders in a friendly, offhand gesture. "But it's not over yet. I have tickets for the Paul Simon concert out at the Mitchell Pavilion tonight."

Diana loved Paul Simon. She'd never seen him in person. She could feel the rest of her resolve floating off with the breeze.

Lee squeezed her shoulder. "We'll swing by your place so you can get a jacket or something, then head on out to the concert. We can stop for a sandwich or a pizza on the way. What do you say?"

"I say it looks as if you have everything all planned." *As if there was no question in your mind that I'd go.*

"I used to be a Boy Scout. I never forgot the motto. Be prepared." His smile made his eyes crinkle up at the corners. That smile was going to be her undoing, she knew it.

Diana knew she should be angry that he was so sure of himself, so certain she'd go along with his plans. It surprised her that she wasn't. It surprised her that for a change it was kind of nice to let someone else make the decisions. "I've never been to the Pavilion," she said slowly.

"I haven't, either, but my secretary tells me it's a great place when the weather's nice."

"Then what are we waiting for?" Diana said. "Let's get going."

"Kent, you're kidding yourself, you know that, don't you?" Allison said with an exasperated look. She laid aside her napkin.

"What do you mean?" Kent drained his glass of iced tea.

They had just finished dinner, and he had brought up the subject of Nikki, telling Allison about the conversation between them.

"She's head over heels in love with you, Kent. A blind person could see that. I saw it the first time I met her. So there's no way she's going to remain your friend. It would be too uncomfortable . . . for all of us."

"My friendship with Nikki is too important to me to let our engagement make a difference." He frowned. "Why *can't* we be friends?"

"Men and women can't have platonic friendships," Allison said, her tawny eyes glittering in the candlelight. "Sooner or later, the man-woman thing crops up."

"That sounds so cynical to me. Nikki and I have been friends since I was six years old. I don't want to lose that, and I don't think I have to."

"Kent, darling, what you view as cynical is simply realistic. You and Nikki were friends for so long without a problem because for most of those years, you were kids. Now you're a man and a woman, and the woman is in love with you. Can't you see how really impossible it would be to pretend everything was still the same?"

A feeling of disquiet gripped Kent. This wasn't the first time they'd had a disagreement over a fundamental principle, but this was the first time their differences had bothered him.

His face must have shown his thoughts, because Allison, voice soft, said, "You're such a romantic. It's one of the qualities I love most about you, but sometimes it can be exasperating."

"I don't know what you're talking about. What does being a romantic have to do with this?"

Allison smiled gently. "You see everything the way you think it should be. You envision an ideal world. You think that because you want something to be a certain way, it will be. Life isn't like that. Things don't always work out the way you hope they will."

Sadness flickered over her face. Her voice was husky when she spoke again. "When my mother died, I wanted to die, too. I kept thinking if only I'd done this differently, or if only I'd done that differently, she wouldn't have died. I kept looking for a reason. Finally, I realized there *was* no reason. Sometimes . . . things happen.''

Her bleak gaze finally met his, and he saw the sheen of tears in her eyes. "Kent, I wish the world were different. But it isn't. It's tough out there. I learned it when I was fourteen. Nikki's learning it now. And one of these days, you'll probably have to learn it, too."

Torn between his desire to hold her in his arms and tell her he'd never let anything hurt her again, and his wish to continue arguing the point, Kent did what was in his nature to do. He got up, walked to her side, gently pulled her to her feet and held her close.

"I love you," he whispered against her fragrant hair.

"I love you, too."

Everything about the evening was magical, Diana decided. The whisper-soft breeze, the sky that looked like purple velvet encrusted with diamonds, the soul-stirring music, the look of enchantment on the faces of the audience, the promise of autumn in the air, the scent of newly mowed grass and most important—Lee sitting beside her on the blanket she'd provided.

Every now and then, Diana's gaze would wander to Lee's face. Several times she caught him looking at her, and she'd be filled with pleasure.

The concert itself was everything she'd imagined it would be. Paul Simon blended his special magic to enthrall his listeners. The finely crafted music floated out over the audience and made Diana ache inside. Whenever she heard beautiful music or saw a beautiful painting or read a beautiful book, she always felt this way. Full of joy and awe and envy, wishing she had some special talent to share, a way to convey her innermost feelings and emotions, this ability to touch others and affect their lives.

The concert ended with "The Sounds of Silence" and for a few moments after the song was over, there was a hush, as if the enormous crowd were holding its collective breath. When Lee stirred and turned to her with a smile, Diana sighed. "It was wonderful," she said.

"Yes."

That one word was enough. Without saying anything else, they stood, gathered up their blanket and began walking slowly toward the parking lot.

The drive home was companionable and quiet. Lee inserted a Paul Simon disk into the CD player, and Diana closed her eyes and relived the concert. All too soon, Lee pulled into her driveway.

As Lee accompanied her to her doorway, Diana thought about how much she hated to see this day end. A surge of regret engulfed her: regret that the situation between them had to remain one of friendship only.

Because if Diana had discovered anything today, she had discovered that if ever she *were* to want a man in her life, that man would be Lee Gabriel.

Chapter Six

"Well, Cinderella, here we are. Home before midnight."

"Cinderella! Hardly. Cinderella was young and innocent. I'm old enough to be Cinderella's mother."

"I've always thought of Cinderella as a beautiful, mature woman who did nothing but work hard all her life and ignore her own needs to take care of everyone else's. She probably never had the time or the opportunity to have fun."

He didn't say, *like you*, but Diana knew that's what he meant. The sensitivity and perception behind his light-hearted, almost teasing words frightened her as no argument could have. How did he do it? How did he dig down and find the exact spot that was her weakest? Was that ability to read his opponent and find the most vulnerable area to work on something he'd been born with?

Diana didn't think so. She reminded herself that Lee Gabriel was a highly trained negotiator, a major player in the world of international business deals, a shrewd and effective manager who understood human nature and how to manipulate people. After all, Lee had come from middle-class beginnings, and look at him now. He'd built a personal fortune while honing his instincts and negotiating skills to a fine edge. Remember, she told herself, this is a dangerous man. Someone who identifies his objective and knows exactly which buttons to push to overcome the obstacles in his path.

Oh, Diana, be careful. He's pushing your buttons right now. She knew, as surely as she knew her own name, that despite her assurances to herself this morning, Lee had not changed his mind about her. For whatever reasons, he'd decided storming her barriers was his objective, and all his actions today had been planned with that goal in mind.

Well, she didn't need to take a back seat to anyone. She was a successful businessperson, too. She had survived in the competitive world of high-dollar real estate, and she knew just as much about human nature as he seemed to. So no matter how smooth an operator Lee Gabriel was, Diana had no reason to be afraid.

"Why, Lee Gabriel," she said, her voice just as light, just as teasing, as his had been. "I never would have thought of you as a man who believed in fairy tales."

"That's because there's a lot you still don't know about me." His voice was a silky drawl in the shadowed night.

Diana's stomach muscles tensed. *Careful, careful,* she warned herself. But she couldn't prevent the twinge of yearning that twisted through her—a yearning for what might have been. If only Lee were someone completely removed from her circle of friends and family. If only she could give in to this terrible longing, knowing that if she made a fool of herself with him, it wouldn't matter, because no one would know.

But you can't, nincompoop. How many times do you have to tell yourself before you accept it?

Smothering a sigh, she steeled herself, then raised her eyes to gaze into his. "Well, Cinderella *is* a working girl, and if you're right, and she's a mature woman, she definitely needs her beauty sleep." She held out her hand. "Good night, Lee. Thanks again for a wonderful day. Why don't you give me a call tomorrow or whenever you're ready to look at houses again?"

"Aw, Diana, come on. I was hoping you'd invite me in. Give me a cup of coffee...or something to warm me on my long journey home," he said, his voice a low rumble.

Diana felt the way she did when she held Bonnie or Clyde up close and their contented purrs vibrated through her body. "Long journey home! All of about ten minutes!"

"Distance is relative."

"To what?" *Keep it light.*

"To how far away from the maiden the man is." Although he didn't move closer, he lifted a strand of hair that had blown against her forehead and smoothed it back. Just that tiny touch made Diana feel like purring herself. But it also sent warning signals in all directions, because if just touching her hair could make her feel so...so...warm...and weak...she was in deeper trouble than she'd thought. It wouldn't take a hell of a lot for Lee to trample over the rest of her defenses and storm the fort.

Lee chuckled softly as if he had read her thoughts and knew exactly how to counteract any move she might be planning. "Come on, Diana. I promise to behave. I told you yesterday. I won't do anything unless you want me to. And I never break my word."

She could handle that.

Couldn't she?

"Just a cup of coffee and a quick tour of your home. Then I'll leave...unless...you want me to stay."

She heard sincerity. She also thought she heard a trace of wistful longing. Was Lee Gabriel *lonely?*

Oh, that's ridiculous. Lee Gabriel had everything. He was rich. He was gorgeous. He could have as many women as he wanted. Why would he be lonely?

She told herself he was a practiced wheeler-dealer who could turn sincerity or any other emotion on and off as the situation warranted.

She told herself he was probably also a consummate actor. Hadn't she had to perfect her own acting skills to succeed in sales?

She told herself if she let herself be swayed by that hint of loneliness she was a fool.

Oh, shoot. So what? What harm was there in inviting him in for just a few minutes? What could happen? She was forty-two years old! She wasn't a novice teenager who didn't know how to handle a man.

And she *wanted* to invite him in. She *wanted* to show him her home. She *wanted* to hold on to this very special day. To pretend for just a bit longer.

She unlocked the front door. "Enter at your own risk," she said. "I'm not the world's best housekeeper, and my maid isn't due for another four days." She waved toward the living room. "Go on in. Make yourself comfortable. I'll just go put the coffee on, then I'll come and give you the grand tour."

Five minutes later she joined him in the living room. He stood at the far end, by the wall of plate glass that looked out over the wooded grounds. When he turned there was a welcoming smile in his eyes. "This is a nice room. I like the high ceiling. And the windows. During the daytime it must give the illusion of being a part of the outdoors.''

Diana thought about the last room she'd been in that had given the illusion of the outdoors and what had happened there. She quickly thrust the memory out of her mind. Thinking about Lee's kiss wasn't the way to keep her emotions under control. "I know. I can't stand to feel closed in. The feeling of openness is one of the reasons I bought this town house.''

His expression didn't change, but something about the look in his eyes unnerved her. When he spoke, though, there were no overtones, no subtle nuances. "I was looking at your cat collection, too... by the way, where *is* that cat of yours?''

Clyde picked that moment to march in, bushy tail like a fat exclamation point, blue eyes bright and curious. He padded straight over to Lee and sidled up against his leg. After spending a few minutes rubbing Clyde's head, Lee said, "You really like cats, don't you?''

"Yes, I'm a cat fanatic.''

"I've always been a dog person myself. But this little guy's okay.''

Clyde, who acted as if he understood the compliment, preened, then said, *"Myup."*

"He likes you," Diana said.

"I like him, too." Lee sounded surprised.

Diana knew there were distinct differences in dog people and cat people, even though she liked both kinds of animal.

"Tell me about your cat collection," Lee said.

Together they walked over to the glass étagère that held the bulk of her collection. Lee picked up a Lalique figurine, the frosted crystal smooth and finely crafted. He turned it thoughtfully in his hand. "Lalique," he murmured. "It's lovely."

Diana remembered his long sojourn in France. "Most of the cats in my collection aren't valuable like that one. That was a birthday gift from someone special."

His gaze flicked to hers. She wondered if he thought she'd been referring to a man, when in fact, she'd been referring to Nikki Garcia, who was her godchild. But he didn't ask, and she certainly wasn't going to offer the information. Let him think whatever he wanted to think. And why did the thought that he might think a man had given her the figurine give her such a sense of sly satisfaction?

Setting down the Lalique cat, he moved to her collection of records, tapes and compact disks. He picked up a few, studying the titles. "Is Garth Brooks good?"

"You're kidding me, right?"

"No." When his gaze met hers, she could see he was perfectly serious. "I don't know anything about country music."

"I can believe that. Otherwise you'd know who Garth Brooks is." She laughed. "Garth Brooks is only the hottest, and best, of the new country music stars. His song 'The Dance' is fantastic. I played that disk so much it's a wonder I didn't wear it out."

He riffled through her Bonnie Raitt, Anne Murray, Clint Black and George Strait tapes and disks.

"What kind of music *do* you like?" Diana asked.

He shrugged. "Blues. Jazz. Classical. And, as you know, I love Paul Simon."

Diana realized it was a wild coincidence that they had both liked Paul Simon. Otherwise, they had no musical tastes in common at all. "I suppose you've never country-western danced, either."

"Nope, but I'm willing to learn."

Boy, he sure was quick. But if he thought she was going to bite, and give him another opening, he had another think coming. "Come on, I'll show you the rest of the place."

He noticed everything.

Commented on everything.

"I like your kitchen," he said as he gazed up at the ceiling where the decorator had hung dozens of baskets of all shapes and sizes. The aroma of the brewing coffee filled the room.

"I like it, too. Although for me, a kitchen is a waste of space. I usually just pop something into the microwave or stop at Randall's salad bar on the way home from work."

"Diana, Diana," he said softly. "I can see I'm going to have to take you in hand."

"Why? Just because I don't make a big deal out of meals?" She shrugged. "I lead a very busy, full life. I don't have the time to shop and cook." She was going to add, *when it's just me,* but thought better of it.

Upstairs, she showed him her study in the loft.

"Nice," he said, walking to her bookshelves. He looked at the titles. "I see you like thrillers."

"They're my favorites. Pure escape and relaxation."

"Who's Ed McBain?" he asked as he picked up one of her books.

She patiently explained who Ed McBain was. She couldn't help herself. She had to ask the question. "What kinds of books do *you* read?"

"Oh, occasionally I read a novel, but I really enjoy biographies and world history. Books about the way the world has changed. The great military leaders. I like to study the battles and the military strategy. You can learn a lot from history."

She knew it. How had she known it?

He poked his head into her guest bedroom, but didn't stop. She hesitated, then waved toward the master bedroom, which ran across the entire back of the town house. "That's the master bedroom." The double doors stood open, and the deck beyond her patio doors was illuminated by the floodlight she kept on a timer.

"I wouldn't ordinarily ask if I could enter your bedroom—" he gave her a wry smile "—but I'd like to see that deck. It must look out over the bayou."

"It does." Oh, well. There was no harm in letting him go out on the deck. She beckoned him in, turning on a lamp as she moved through the doorway.

Belatedly Diana remembered Bonnie, who was, in all likelihood, hiding under the bed. "It's okay, Bonnie. He won't hurt you," she said.

"Who're you talking to?"

Diana grinned. "Would you believe myself?"

"No. Not the Diana Sorensen I'm coming to know."

"You're right. I'm talking to my other cat, Bonnie. The fraidy-cat who's hiding under the bed, like the coward she is." She bent down to look. Sure enough. There was Bonnie, big green eyes wide, sitting exactly in the middle, as far away from each edge of the bed as she could get.

Diana chuckled. "Hi, babe. How's it goin' under there?" She straightened. "Bonnie and Clyde are litter mates."

"Bonnie and Clyde, huh? Is that a warning signal, or something?"

"Of what?"

"Is that your subtle way of telling a man he'd better watch out? That you can hold your own in any battle?"

"Who, *moi?*" Diana mugged. "Why, Mr. Gabriel, whatever would have given you that idea?"

"Call me crazy, but something tells me I'd better be very careful around you."

Diana started to laugh.

"What's so funny?"

She tried to speak and couldn't.

"Come on! That's not fair! Let me in on the joke."

"I just remembered that the last dog we had was named... Dillinger!" She dissolved into a fresh spate of giggles.

Lee laughed, too. "See what I mean? You're obviously dangerous." He looked around as if he expected to see an arsenal of guns in the room.

Diana, still chuckling, walked to the sliding doors and unlocked them. She walked out onto the deck, and Lee followed her. The fragrant night air, cool and fresh, surrounded them. A mockingbird trilled in the distance. The bayou looked dark and mysterious below.

Diana leaned against the wood railing. Lee came up behind her. He didn't touch her, but she felt him there with every fiber of her being. It was suddenly hard to breathe.

"Diana," he said softly.

She turned slowly.

They were standing in the shadows, but there was enough light for her to see the expression in his eyes.

"Diana, I really want to kiss you." He didn't move closer. "May I?"

Their gazes locked. In his she saw tenderness. She also saw desire. Her heart began to beat in slow, heavy thuds. Her breathing became shallow and erratic. Her mouth went dry.

She wanted this. She couldn't deny her feelings any longer. She'd been so smug. But it was easy to be smug when you didn't know any better. Until she met Lee she hadn't even known anything was missing from her life, but now... here... with this man...

She touched his chest, and she could feel his heart tripping under her fingers. She lifted her face, and his lips descended to meet hers.

The instant she felt his tongue swirl into her mouth, a blazing response lit her body. He pulled her close, his hands sliding over her back, and she wound her own arms around him. Their bodies aligned perfectly, and through the fabric of her sweater and jeans, she could feel every contour and plane of his. She knew he wanted her. There was no disguising his arousal.

"Lee," she said weakly, tearing her mouth away. "This is madness."

"Why?" he whispered as he tried to recapture her mouth. His hands continued their exploration, dropping lower until their heat seared the seat of her jeans. Desire, like an electrical shock, jolted through her, centering deep inside, pulsing with a life of its own. He caught her bottom lip between his teeth, nipped gently. "I want you. You want me. Why is it madness?" he said gruffly.

"Because . . . because of . . . our kids."

Her voice sounded as if she'd been running up a steep hill. Heat flooded her veins as his hands continued to mold her body like a sculptor molding clay.

"What do the kids have to do with it?" He kissed her again. A long, lingering, drugging kiss that left her knees feeling like rubber and her brain feeling like mush. Why was her body betraying her like this? The force of her need sapped her strength and ran roughshod over what little willpower and rational thought she had left. She felt as if she'd been asleep for a long time and was just now coming back to life. She wasn't sure she liked the feeling.

"You want this. I can see that you do." Deliberately, slowly, his hand moved up to cup her right breast. His thumb circled the nub until it peaked in his hand. Like a starburst, needles of pleasure exploded inside. He rubbed both peaks until Diana cried out.

"Stop that," she said weakly.

"Do you really want me to stop?" he murmured.

"Yes." But she didn't push his hands away.

He held her gaze as he cupped both breasts. His thumbs continued their lazy circles. And instead of pulling away, she leaned into him, an unconscious gesture for more. She ached with a sweet agony she wanted to go on forever.

"Should I stop?" he asked again.

She moaned. "No."

"Good, because I sure don't want to." With infinite care, he turned her in his arms so that her back was to him, then pulled her up tight against him. The hard knot of his arousal burned into her lower back. He stroked her with long, delicious, slow movements, finally lifting her sweater and unhooking her bra. At the first touch of the cool night air against her heated skin, Diana shuddered.

"Easy, easy," he whispered. He palmed her breasts, kneading them gently as they blossomed for him. Diana knew she should push his hands away, but she didn't want to. It had been so long. So long since she'd felt a man's touch like this. So long since this sweet torture had consumed her body. So long since she'd felt this wild abandon, this intense heat of desire. Her head fell back, and he lowered his lips to her neck.

But when his right hand moved unerringly down, finding that heated core, Diana gasped and jerked away. "No!" she cried. "We have to stop. This is crazy!"

My God, where was her control? Two more seconds and he'd have had her completely naked and inside the bedroom. Things were moving entirely too fast.

"This *isn't* crazy. This is the most sensible thing we've done today." He reached for her again, trying to stop her as

she fumbled to rehook her bra. Frightened of her uncharacteristic behavior and feelings, she pushed his hands away
and whirled around.

"I said no! Now, dammit, you promised me you wouldn't
do anything I didn't want you to do." She pulled down her
sweater. "And I don't want you to touch me again."

He dropped his hands wearily. "And I won't. But what
the hell is wrong with you? I know you want me as much as
I want you. You certainly weren't faking your reaction.
What happened?"

"What happened is I finally came to my senses. Sex between us would be a big mistake, Lee."

"How can you say that, Diana? I think sex between us
would be fantastic."

"You're deliberately misunderstanding me. I'm sure the
sex itself would be great. But what about afterward?" *What
about when the affair ends? What about all the rest of my
life, all the times I'll be thrown into your company because
of our kids? How am I going to deal with that?* "I . . . I told
you. I'm not interested in an affair."

"You also said you weren't interested in a permanent relationship. I wish you'd make up your mind."

She had no answer for his logic. "I don't know, Lee.
You're confusing me, twisting everything I say. The thing is,
we're just not right for each other." *Yes, that was good.
That was the right approach to take with him.* "We don't
even have anything in common except our kids and
this . . . this . . . physical desire we feel!"

"You're cheapening our feelings, Diana. I feel a lot more
than physical desire for you, and I think you do for me, too.
I think you're just afraid to admit it. And as far as having
things in common, I think we have a lot in common. I'll bet
we have all the important things in common."

"We don't. I mean, if you can't see that . . . you weren't in my house five minutes before I saw it!"

"Didn't you like the picnic?"

"Yes, but—"

"Didn't you like the zoo?"

"Yes, of course, I liked the zoo, but those kinds of things aren't enough—"

"I'll bet you like to walk in the rain, too."

"Yes, as a matter of fact, I do, but—"

"*But* is my least favorite word, did you know that?"

"Lee . . ."

"That's better. I like the way you say my name." With his fingertip, he traced the curve of her mouth. Diana closed her eyes.

"Oh, God . . ."

"How about a roaring fire on a cold winter day? Do you like that?"

"Yes," she whispered.

"How about going to the movies and eating a huge bucket of buttered popcorn? And maybe a few candy bars as well?"

She couldn't help it. She laughed softly. "Yes."

"What about staying in bed until noon on Sunday morning? Reading the papers and eating a huge breakfast and then taking a long, hot shower? Together?"

Diana shivered at the image of the two of them in the shower together.

He smiled, and her heart turned over. "I *knew* you'd like that," he said softly. "And how do you feel about Rocky Road ice cream?"

Diana sighed. "One of my biggest weaknesses."

"See? What else is there? That's all the important things."

This time when he kissed her, she didn't fight him. All the fight had gone out of her. It was simply too hard to keep denying what he could see for himself was true. They stayed locked in each other's arms for a long time, but when he whispered against her ear, saying, "Diana, give us a chance. I think we have something pretty powerful working between us. Let's see where it leads."

"I'm no good at this, Lee. I'm no good at...being part of a couple." She almost felt like crying.

"You were a kid when your marriage fell apart," he said softly. He kissed her cheek. "You're a different person now."

He was too smart for her. He was going to wear her down with his logic because she really *did* want to surrender to him.

But giving in to these feelings would be a big mistake. Who needed this? She was happy now, contented. Maybe there were no great peaks in her life, but there were no great valleys, either. She wasn't sure she could deal with the wild swings of emotion a love affair would generate.

And what about when it was over? By then they'd be the parents of a married couple, and they'd still be forced to see each other. It would be miserable for everyone concerned.

Oh, Lordy. It would be awful. She still remembered how difficult it had been after her divorce from Bill. How awkward she'd felt when she took Kent to see Bill's mother, how strained and forced the conversations had been. It had taken her a long time to regain her peace of mind and carve a good life for herself.

Now she had it. Why risk losing it?

"Look, Diana. I know you're scared. Hell, I'm a little scared myself. It's always scary when you start something new."

"Lee..."

"I can't make you any promises. I don't know what's going to happen. But I want to explore my feelings for you . . . your feelings for me. See if what there is between us is as special as I think it is."

"I don't expect you to make any promises." Oh, it was so tempting. But was the temptation worth the risk?

He touched her cheek, and she leaned into the caress. He kissed the top of her head. "What do you say?"

"I don't know. I have to think about everything."

"That's all I'm asking. Just give it a chance."

"Lee, no matter what I decide, I'm not ready to go to bed with you," she said. "I . . . it's too soon. I have to be sure."

"I won't push you. Even if you should decide you don't ever want to go to bed with me, that's okay. I'll accept your decision."

She raised her eyes to look at him. His were clear, honest. "You mean that, don't you?"

"Yes."

"I still think this is a bad idea."

"Tell me why."

She sighed deeply. "Because of Allison and Kent. It just makes everything too complicated."

"I don't understand why you say that."

"Okay, for the sake of argument, what if you and I do have a relationship? And what if it goes wrong and we break up? Can't you see the potential problems? Why, what if Kent and Allison should break up? What then?"

"Diana, you're making too much out of nothing. If you and I find we're not compatible, I think we can handle it. We're adults. And I'm sure our children could handle it. And frankly, I see no reason for Allison and Kent to have any problems at all. In fact, the only problem I can see with them is Kent's unrealistic plan to open a storefront law office, and I'm sure he'll change his mind about that."

Diana stiffened. "I don't think his plan is unrealistic. I think it's wonderful. I'm proud of him."

"I know you are. And I don't blame you. It's commendable that Kent has such a strong sense of obligation to his community and his fellowman, but face it, those two aren't going to be able to live on love. There's going to have to be some money as well."

"Kent will earn money. And what's wrong with Allison getting a job? Marriage is a partnership, not a free ride!"

"I'm sure Allison will want to help out, but she's not like you, Diana. She's been raised in Europe where women aren't nearly as independent. All she's ever wanted was to get married and have children." He frowned. "And that's what I've wanted for her, too."

"Seems to me she's getting what she wanted. Why should Kent have to give up his dream? Why can't they compromise?"

"Diana, let's not argue about the children. They'll work their problems out without our help. I want to talk about us."

"Well, I don't." The romantic mood was broken. Her body had finally calmed down, and her brain was once again working. Everything Lee had said about Kent and Allison had only confirmed what Diana already knew. He and she were poles apart in their way of thinking, just as Kent and Allison were poles apart in their way of thinking.

Sooner or later, something was going to have to give. And when it did, Diana didn't want to be the one devastated in the process. Oh, God, she thought. She'd had a narrow escape, but thank goodness, she'd come to her senses in the nick of time.

Lee didn't want to go. She could see that. But he did, and she shut the door firmly behind him, telling herself that was that.

As she walked through the downstairs turning out the lights, she was assailed by the fragrant aroma of the coffee they never did drink, and a deep sense of melancholy followed her up the stairs to her solitary bedroom.

Chapter Seven

He never did get a cup of coffee.

Lee laughed wryly. Hell. He didn't need coffee. He needed a cold shower. Lee parked the Porsche in one of the slots of his in-laws' four-car garage and walked slowly back toward the guest house. Allison's bedroom light was out and Kent's Honda wasn't parked outside, which meant one of two things: either she wasn't home yet or she'd already gone to bed.

Good, Lee thought. He didn't feel like facing his daughter's shrewd eyes tonight, especially in light of her obvious concern and disapproval about Diana earlier today. In his present state of frustration, Lee was afraid Allison might discern its cause. And he didn't want that. Not yet, anyway. Not until Diana was over her skittishness about their relationship. Lee knew his current position with Diana was tenuous at best.

So, as if he were a kid hoping his parents won't hear him coming in after curfew, Lee unlocked the front door as quietly as possible and tiptoed into his bedroom wing.

He wondered if he dared take a shower. He didn't want Allison to hear the water and come knocking on his door. Then, realizing how ridiculous it was for him to be acting this way, as if he had something to hide, he stripped off his clothes and turned on the shower.

He gasped when the cold water hit him.

Diana closed her eyes as the hot water cascaded over her body. She had a pounding headache, the result of a sleepless night. She sighed, wishing it wasn't a Monday.

She hated Mondays.

She especially hated Mondays when she'd overslept. She would miss the nine o'clock sales meeting. It would be ten o'clock before she got into the office.

She sighed again. She liked to get an early start on Mondays. Because, inevitably, if there were going to be major problems in the agency, those problems would rear their ugly heads on Mondays or Fridays. She knew this phenomenon wasn't limited to the real estate business. She'd once read an article that had stated that statistics showed that major mistakes usually occurred on a Monday or a Friday. Research had shown that workers of all ages were recuperating from their weekends on Monday and thinking about the upcoming one on Fridays.

She was definitely recuperating from her weekend.

She had a major case of Too Much Lee. Like eating rich food after a long diet of bland food. Or like a surfeit of chocolate after denying herself for months.

As she turned off the water and toweled herself dry, she decided she'd better take a couple of aspirin. She rubbed her grainy eyes and wished she could crawl back into bed, pull the covers over her head and hide from all eyes until she felt better.

Now who's the fraidy-cat? her inner voice taunted. You were making fun of Bonnie last night. Now who's the big chicken? What's the matter, Diana? Can't you handle a mere man? What's the big deal, anyway? Lee Gabriel isn't some kind of magician who can make you do things you don't want to do. He's just a plain old mortal, and all you have to do is say no.

Just say no.

Diana wondered if the advice she was giving herself would be any more effective than the former first lady's advice had been. After dressing in a candy-apple red suit—a color which always made Diana feel more powerful and in control—she gathered her briefcase and handbag and walked out to the kitchen, where she downed the aspirin. She checked the cats' bowls for food and water, made sure she'd turned off the burner under the teapot, set her security alarm and left for the office.

During the five minutes it took her to cover the miles between her town house and her agency, she repeated several times: *no matter what Lee Gabriel says or does, the answer is no.*

"Good morning!" Tracy chirped as Diana strode into her office. "My, don't you look bright and rarin' to go this morning!" She glanced up at the wall clock, which read 10:10. "I was afraid something was wrong when you weren't here at eight."

Why did Tracy have to be so relentlessly cheerful? Diana wondered. She conveniently forgot that the young woman's cheerfulness was the exact reason Diana had hired her in the first place.

"Good morning," Diana managed without frowning. "No, nothing wrong. Just a tiring weekend. How about you? Did you have a nice weekend?" She always tried to ask about her employees, remembering how she'd hated it when former bosses had never acknowledged her as a person.

"Yes, thanks," Tracy said. Her pretty face, round and smooth with impending motherhood, glowed with good health. "Barton was so sweet to me all weekend. My ankles were swollen, so he made me sit with my feet up, and he pampered me. He even cooked dinner Saturday night!"

And why shouldn't he? Diana thought. "You deserved it."

"And what did *you* do this weekend that made you so tired?" Tracy said.

Was that a knowing gleam in Tracy's eye? "Oh, the usual. Worked both days. Showed houses to Mr. Gabriel, who's turning out to be just as picky as Leona Applegate."

Tracy grinned. "Hey, they're all picky. But at least Lee Gabriel is a man instead of a crotchety old woman. Plus Sunny tells me he's gorgeous! Did you have a good time? Surely it wasn't *all* work?"

"I think things went well enough." She kept her voice noncommittal and deliberately sidestepped Tracy's other question. It certainly wouldn't do to have her employees gossiping about her and Lee.

Tracy nodded thoughtfully.

There was that expression again. What did it mean? Diana wondered.

"Is today a special occasion or something?" Tracy asked.
"No. Why?"

Tracy shrugged. "I just wondered. I mean . . . oh, never mind." There was a small, secretive smile on her face. "You'll see. . . ."

Diana frowned. What was wrong with the woman? Well, she was in no mood to fathom Tracy's inexplicable moods. Perhaps pregnancy did this to a woman, made her act a little strange. Diana pushed open the door into the bull pen, said hello to her agents, all of whom were still in and seated at their desks, then opened her office door.

The first thing she saw was roses.

Yellow roses.

A huge bouquet of yellow roses in a cut-glass vase. Dozens of them. Narrow gilt ribbons cascaded from the neck of the vase, and a creamy card was tucked up into the airy fern pillowing the blossoms.

Diana knew the roses were from Lee.

And he'd done it again.

Found something she had fantasized about. Found another vulnerable spot. Found a weakness he could exploit.

Yellow roses were her absolute favorite flower in the entire world, and a secret dream she'd had was one where some faceless Prince Charming would shower her with yellow roses, then carry her off on his white steed, enthrone her in a fairy-tale castle and adore her for the rest of her life.

And here was a wish coming true.

Funny thing about wishes, she thought, as she walked slowly over to her desk and bent to smell the flowers.

Be careful what you wish for, because you might get it.

A teacher of Diana's had once given that advice to her fourth-grade class. Diana and the other girls and boys had laughed behind their hands, certain Miss Sciutto was too old to understand about wishes. Diana and her friends hadn't understood that sometimes the fulfillment of a wish brought its own problems.

Now she did.

For Lee Gabriel, all six feet something of him, with his sexy smile and sexy eyes and sexy ways, was complicating her life to the point she wasn't sure she'd ever regain her peace of mind.

She gently removed one of the roses, a bud that still hadn't opened its petals to the world. Its delicate fragrance perfumed the air. Then slowly, she reached for the card. Her heart skittered as she read the message, scrawled in thick, strong handwriting: "These roses remind me of you. Strong, beautiful and proud. Thanks for a wonderful day. Lee."

Just say no.

Easier said than done.

There was no way she was going to be able to concentrate on work with those damned roses staring her in the face, she decided about thirty minutes later. She picked up the vase and carried it out to the reception area.

"It's silly for me to have these flowers back there where no one can see them." She placed them on the coffee table, standing back to admire them. "There. Now everyone can enjoy them." Diana avoided Tracy's speculative gaze. She knew the woman was dying to know who had sent the roses. Diana had no intention of telling her.

Or anyone.

"So who sent the poseys?" Sunny asked five minutes later. "Tall, dark and dangerous?" Her green eyes sparkled with merriment.

"What're you grinning about?" Diana said crossly.

"My, my. Did we get up on the wrong side of the bed this morning?" Sunny plopped on the couch.

"Careful. There's no such thing as job security in this shaky economy."

"So fire me," Sunny said. "Come on. Spill everything. Are the roses from Lee Gabriel?"

Diana scowled. "I don't know why I put up with your lip."

"Because you love me?"

"Try again."

"Because I know you better than anyone, and who would you talk to if you fired me?"

Diana moaned. "Sunny... what am I going to do?"

"I knew it! He *did* send them, didn't he?" A look of pure ecstasy crossed Sunny's impish features. "Oh, you're so lucky! Why doesn't some wonderful, rich, handsome man send *me* roses? What am I doing wrong?"

"I wish he *had* sent them to you!"

"Why? Diana! You're nuts!"

"Maybe."

"No 'maybe' about it. Gosh, most women would kill to be in your shoes. How many Lee Gabriels do you think there are out there? Damn few, believe me!"

"Maybe those women don't have a satisfying, consuming career like I do, or they don't earn enough money so they're looking for a man to make life easier. Maybe those women aren't happy or contented with their lives. But I am!" Diana said. She rubbed her temples. Darn. Her headache was returning.

"Why are those things and the attentions of a man like Lee mutually exclusive?" Sunny asked reasonably.

"I don't know. All I do know is that ever since I met Lee Gabriel, I haven't been able to get anything constructive done."

Sunny chuckled. "Oh, oh. That's not a good sign."

"Sunny, can I talk to you seriously for a minute?"

Sunny's grin faded to be replaced by concern. "Sure. You know you can."

"The thing is..." Diana stopped, unsure for a minute, then sighed deeply. "The thing is," she said in a firmer voice, "I not only am not getting anything constructive done, but I'm also not sleeping as well. I can't concentrate on my work. He's either phoning me or sending me something or trying to distract me in some way. And I don't like it!''

"In other words, you felt safe and comfortable in your little niche, and you don't want that safety and comfort threatened.''

"That makes me sound like the only reason I'm not happy about Lee's attentions is that I'm afraid."

"If the shoe fits, honey..."

"Maybe I am afraid," Diana said in a small voice. "I mean...I *do* want to keep seeing Lee. I *am* attracted to him. Lordy, I'm so attracted to him it makes my head spin! But what's going to happen afterward?"

"What do you mean?"

"I mean that if you look at this thing realistically, like I'm trying to do, whatever it is between me and Lee isn't something that has permanence as part of it, so what's going to happen when the thrills wear off and we call it quits?"

Sunny frowned. "Why are you so sure it won't last?"

"Think about it. Lee is a high-powered executive with a demanding job. He needs the kind of woman who would put him and his career first, be ready to drop everything if he needed her to. And I can't do that. I have a business to run, a demanding career of my own. And you know what my schedule is like. Sometimes I work sixty, seventy hours a week. I work a lot of nights and almost every weekend. How long do you think Lee would put up with that?"

"You don't *have* to work like that," Sunny said softly. "You could scale down your time at the office."

"And we have nothing in common. He's very sophisticated and cultured."

"You don't have to take a back seat to anyone, Diana."

"Oh, Sunny, I know what you're trying to do," Diana said wearily, "but believe me, it's inevitable that we'd break up. Not a question of if, but a question of when."

"So you're saying that it would be impossibly awkward for you once that split happened?"

"Yes. Can you picture it? Allison and Kent are married, maybe already have a baby, and there we all are—a cozy family getting together to celebrate Christmas, or the baby's birthday, or the kids' anniversary! Honestly, it'd be impossible!

"I see what you mean." Now it was Sunny's turn to sigh. "But, sweetie, maybe it would all work out wonderfully. You'll never know if you don't take a chance."

"Some chances are too big to take. There's too much at stake. Like my whole future relationship with Kent and Allison."

After Sunny left her office, Diana closed her eyes and laid her head down on her arms. Sunny's earlier taunt still stung, the same way it had when Lee had flung the same words at her.

They were both wrong. She wasn't afraid. Being sensible wasn't the same as being afraid.

Being sensible was . . . well, being sensible.

Being sensible was feeling pretty good every day. Knowing exactly what the day would bring.

Being sensible was early nights and busy days and quiet, calm weekends. Routine and order and peace.

Being sensible was eating microwave dinners alone and shopping for one and never having a date for the agency Christmas party.

Being sensible was the way she had lived her life for twenty years.

The question was, did she want to live the next twenty years the same way?

* * *

Diana finally quit stewing about Lee when, at eleven-thirty, she received a telephone call from her sister Carol.

"Diana?" Carol said.

"Oh, hi, Carol."

"Diana, something's just *got* to be done about Mother!"

Diana sighed wearily. "Why? What's happened?"

"What's happened is she's driving me crazy!"

Diana couldn't help but laugh. "That's nothing new. She's been driving all of us crazy for years."

"You can laugh. She doesn't call you three and four times a day, whining and complaining about everything and everyone!"

"Carol, I don't know what you expect *me* to do about it. Mother's been whining and complaining since the day she learned to talk."

Carol's voice took on an accusing tone. "Maybe so, but she wouldn't be calling me three and four times a day if she could call anyone else. Jackie's long distance, so she won't call her. And she told me you forbid her to call you at the office unless it's an emergency!"

Diana gritted her teeth. Sometimes Carol could be as big a pain in the neck as their mother. "I *have* forbidden her to call me here, Carol. I'm running a business here. I cannot field a dozen phone calls a day from Mother. I mean, I just can't."

"But you expect me to."

"I don't expect you to do anything. I've taken care of the problem from my end by explaining to her that if she keeps disturbing me when I'm trying to work that my business will suffer. Which means I'll make less money. Which means I won't be able to help *her* as much as I do." Diana rubbed her eyes. "Now, Mother understands dollars and cents if she understands nothing else." She paused. "You're going to have to figure out how to solve your problem in your own way." Of course, Diana wasn't sure Carol could ever figure it out. She'd never been able to solve *any* of her problems. And as a result, Carol was unhappy with her life. In fact, Diana thought, if Carol weren't so unhappy, she'd probably be able to cope with Barbara's calls much better than she seemed to be doing.

"That's easy for you to say! I don't have the excuse of a business to run!"

Diana counted to ten. It would accomplish nothing for her to get angry with Carol. "My business isn't an excuse. It's my livelihood and, whether you like to be reminded of this or not, I contribute more than half the money that goes to support Mother."

"Oh? Are we back to that again?" Carol said, her voice shaking with fury. "How much money *you* give to Mother, and how little Jackie and I give her? Well, I don't have the cushy life you do. Joe and I have three children. You only have one. And he's already grown. I don't own my own business. And Joe doesn't make the kind of money that you do."

Diana would have been willing to bet that Joe made every bit as much money as she did. He and Carol just didn't know how to manage it very well. It burned a hole in their pockets, as Diana's father had been fond of saying. She started to remind Carol that Joe had bought himself a fancy sports car the previous year, and that they'd had the money to put in an expensive pool two years ago. But what was the use? Carol was Carol.

Diana took a deep breath, then said, "Carol, let's not fight, okay? I never said I thought you and Jackie should be contributing more money to Mother. But I *am* saying that since I'm the one with the means to do so, it will behoove all of us to make sure I continue to have that means."

"Fine," Carol said tightly. "That's fine. But I'm still left with this problem. I can't take much more of this, Diana. I mean it."

"Why don't you get an answering machine? Keep it on, and screen your calls. If it's Mother calling, pretend you're out. Just call her back late in the day. That way you can control the amount of times you talk to her."

"Oh, *sure*. She'd have a fit if I did that. She knows I'm here most of the time."

"Well, don't be. Change your life a little bit. It'd do you good to get out and start doing some other things. Why don't you get a part-time job? Your kids are all in school. That'd be killing two birds: you wouldn't be home for Mother to pester, and you'd have some money for yourself." To Diana, it seemed the perfect solution.

"The kids need me here."

Diana rolled her eyes. That had always been Carol's excuse for not getting off her duff. If the truth were known, Carol enjoyed spending her days watching the soaps, reading and lying around the pool.

"Besides," Carol said, "what kind of job could I get? I'm not trained to do a thing."

"So get some training. Go to school."

"School! Diana, I'm forty years old."

"So? I read about a seventy-seven-year-old woman who just got her bachelor's degree from U of H. Plenty of people do it."

"I'm not the problem. Mother is the problem," Carol said stubbornly.

Oh, the hell with it. "Well, I'm fresh out of ideas. I guess you'll just have to figure this one out yourself." She glanced at her watch. "Listen, Carol, I'd love to chat, but—"

"It's not just Mother," Carol wailed. "It's everything! Everything's going wrong. I don't know what I'm going to do."

Diana wanted nothing more than to hang up. She didn't feel like listening to any more problems. Of any kind. But Carol *was* her sister, and she did love her. "What else is wrong?" she said gently.

"It's Gretchen! You ... you have no idea. I mean, yesterday that little snip informed me that she wants a prescription for birth control pills!"

"Birth control pills!" Diana exclaimed.

"Yes. She's only fifteen. Can you imagine?"

"Well, what did you say?"

"Huh! What do you think I said? I said no." Carol laughed mirthlessly. "I said *hell,* no! I told her she was not, under any circumstances, getting a prescription for birth control pills, and not only that, she'd better not even *think* about having sex at her age, because if I ever found out she did, I'd kill her!"

Privately Diana thought that was the worst approach Carol could have taken with Gretchen, who was headstrong and stubborn, but she knew Carol wouldn't take it well if Diana voiced her opinion. Carol was sensitive about her parenting skills. She'd had a lot of problems with her children, and she would view any advice Diana gave her as a criticism. "It's awfully hard to raise kids," she said softly. It was the most nonthreatening thing she could think of to say.

"Boy, that's for sure. You know, you're really lucky. You don't know how lucky. You just have Kent, and he's never given you any trouble. You don't have any idea what it's like, really, to raise three kids."

Diana thought the kind of person Kent was had nothing to do with luck, but she knew better than to voice that opinion, either. So she just made soothing noises and finally, thankfully, Carol said she had to go.

When Diana hung up the phone, she laid her head down on her arms and closed her eyes. It was a good thing she wasn't the kind of person who liked to drink at lunch, because today had definitely turned into a two-martini lunch kind of day.

At one-thirty Lee decided to call Diana. The flowers should have been delivered by then, he figured.

He was put right through.

"Hi," he said.

"Hi." He heard the wariness in her tone.

"How are you today?"

"I'm doing all right." Still guarded. Still suspicious. Still scared. He heard it all.

"Did you get the flowers?"

She sighed. "Yes. Thank you, Lee. They're beautiful."

"I dreamed about you last night," he said softly.

"Lee..." There was a catch in her voice, a shaky little sound that trembled in the air. He closed his eyes, picturing her as she'd looked last night, remembering how she'd felt in his arms. He wished he was with her right now. He wished he could hold her close and bury his face in her hair. The wish was so strong it caused an ache right around his heart.

"Did you dream about me?" he murmured.

"No." The denial had no punch.

He smiled. "Liar."

"Please, Lee. I haven't had a good morning."

"Why? Something wrong?"

"Everything is wrong."

"Do you want to talk about it?"

"No."

"Well, I'll tell you what. Why don't you let me take you to dinner tonight? Somewhere quiet and calm with good food and good wine."

"I can't."

No hesitation, just that abrupt refusal. Okay, he thought. "All right, what about houses? When are we going to look at houses again?"

"That's up to you."

Still businesslike. Still aloof. Still in her keep-your-distance mode. "Tomorrow?" he suggested.

"Don't you have to work tomorrow?"

"I have the freedom to come and go as I please. Besides, finding a house is important."

"Let me check my schedule." He heard the shuffling sound of paper, then a few seconds later, she said, "Tomorrow afternoon is clear."

They made arrangements to meet, then Lee hung up. He swiveled his chair around so he could look out the big corner window at the Houston skyline in the far distance. He'd lost ground with Diana. Somehow, between last night and today, she'd become as prickly as a pyracantha. She was holding him at a distance, and it looked as if she intended to keep him there.

Lee knew he had his work cut out for him if he were going to persuade her to change her mind.

Diana couldn't wait to get home. This Monday had been worse than any other Monday she could remember. Since she'd come to work so late this morning, and then had so many interruptions through the day, she'd stayed late to get everything done that needed doing. Now it was almost nine, and she was exhausted. All she wanted was to change into the oldest, most comfortable clothes she owned, pour herself a glass of wine, eat something filling and comforting and go to bed. Her head was pounding.

She nearly moaned when she pulled into her garage and saw Kent's car outside her unit, with Kent and Allison just getting out. But she put a bright and welcoming smile on her face, even though it nearly killed her.

"Hi," she said, walking around to meet them. "What're you two doing here?"

"Hi," Kent said, leaning over to kiss her cheek. Even Allison came close and hugged her briefly. She looked very beautiful tonight, Diana thought, in a close-fitting, short jade leather skirt and matching silk blouse. "Allison and I were on our way home after eating dinner at Carmelo's, and we decided to stop and tell you about the engagement party her grandparents are having for us."

"Well, come on in for a minute." Diana gestured toward the garage and they entered her town house that way. When they reached the living room, she inclined her head toward the bar. "Do you want something to drink?"

After they were settled with glasses of wine in hand, Diana looked expectantly toward Allison, and what she saw nearly knocked her socks off. Allison was raising her wineglass to her mouth with her left hand, and the lamp on the table next to her played off the diamond on her ring finger, sending dazzling prisms of light dancing off the stone.

Lord have mercy, Diana thought. Where had he gotten the money to buy a ring like that? The only money he had was his inheritance from his grandmother. Speechless, she couldn't keep herself from staring at the ring, which was exquisite.

Allison smiled. "It's beautiful, isn't it? We got it Saturday." She held out her hand, and Diana, mesmerized, stood and walked over to examine the ring more closely.

"Beautiful isn't the word," she said softly, slanting her glance toward Kent, whose expression was uncertain as he met her gaze. Deeply disturbed, Diana looked away. This was none of her business, she told herself. Kent was a grown man. How he chose to spend his inheritance from his grandmother was his decision. But she wondered how this was going to affect his plans to open the storefront law office, and her uneasiness intensified.

She walked back to her chair, sat, then said, "So what about this engagement party? When is it?"

"A week Saturday," Allison said eagerly, her tawny eyes alight with excitement. "It's going to be at the country club, and my grandparents have invited tons of people."

Kent smiled indulgently at Allison, and Diana tried to inject a note of genuine enthusiasm into her voice, even though she wasn't wild about big parties. "Sounds wonderful."

"I called Dad today," Kent said.

"I wondered if you'd told him about your engagement yet," Diana said. Bill and his third wife had moved from Texas to Missouri nearly six years earlier, so Kent didn't see much of them. "What did he say?"

Kent grinned. "Oh, you know Dad. He wished me luck and said he and Maggie would be here for the wedding."

Diana nodded. It would be strange to see Bill again, even though she no longer felt any animosity toward him.

"Diana, would you like to give me a list of the people you'd like to invite to the engagement party?" Allison asked. "It's kind of late notice, but..." She gave a little shrug of apology.

"Sure," Diana said, although it was the last thing she felt like doing. But she got up, found some paper and a pen and with Kent's help, began making her list. After she finished, they talked for about twenty more minutes, then Diana yawned, even though she tried to stifle it.

"You're tired," Kent said.

"It was a long day," Diana said.

"We'll get going then," Kent said.

Later that night, even though she was exhausted, Diana couldn't sleep. She lay in bed thinking about everything. Worrying about Kent and the money he'd spent that she knew he could ill afford. Worrying about Allison and whether she would be good for Kent or whether she would end by breaking his heart. Worrying about her mother and Carol and Gretchen. Not to mention worrying about her youngest sister, Jackie, and that no-good spouse of hers.

But most of all worrying about Lee and whether or not she'd be able to withstand the feelings she had for him.

Chapter Eight

"No, Lee, it isn't necessary for you to pick me up!" Diana tried not to show her annoyance, but she couldn't help it. It was the Wednesday before the engagement party.

"I insist."

"No." She had managed, quite effectively, she thought, to evade his company the past week. The only times they'd been together had been when she was showing him houses. She had turned down every invitation he'd extended, pleading work or any other excuse she could invent. She knew she wasn't fooling him, and she sure as heck wasn't discouraging him.

"Diana, you're being unreasonable," Lee said.

Oh, he was infuriating with that I'm-a-reasonable-man-and-you're-an-emotional-woman smugness in his tone. "I'm perfectly capable of driving myself to the kids' engagement party, Lee. Besides, how will it look if I come with you?"

"How will it look if you don't?"

"What do you mean?"

"I already told Kent I was going to call you and offer to bring you. Won't he wonder why you refused?"

"Kent knows me well enough to know I like doing things on my own." But Diana felt a twinge of uncertainty. Kent probably *would* wonder why she'd refused Lee's offer. And it *was* awkward to go somewhere like the country club as an unescorted woman, no matter how much she pretended it wasn't.

You want to go. Don't lie to yourself.

No, I don't.

Yes, you do.

"Oh, all right, Lee, if it makes you happy, you can pick me up! But this *isn't* a date."

Diana decided she needed a new dress. She conned Sunny into going shopping with her on Thursday night, although Sunny really didn't need much conning.

"I know just where you should look," Sunny declared. "It's a new boutique, and I love it!"

As they pulled into the parking lot of the small West University area shopping center, Diana said, "Just how expensive *is* this place?"

"Not too bad," Sunny said evasively.

Alaina's turned out to be pretty pricey, Diana thought, but she had to admit she loved the clothes. And the owner, a tall knockout of a woman with spiked hair and a beautiful smile, seemed to know exactly what would look good on Diana.

"This one," she said emphatically, holding up a royal blue lace and chiffon number with a petal skirt and plunging-to-the-waist back.

Diana was a little skeptical, but ten minutes later, she emerged from the dressing room, wearing the dress. Sunny whistled, Alaina smiled happily and two other customers nodded approvingly.

"Didn't I tell you?" Alaina said. "What do you gals think?"

One of the customers, a blonde with a Scottish accent, said, "Smashing."

The other, a redhead with long iridescent earrings, said, "I wish I filled out a dress the way you do."

Sunny said, "We'll take it."

"See?" Alaina said. "It's all settled."

"Well..." Diana thought about the price tag. Twice as much as she'd ever paid for a dress before.

Twenty minutes later, with the royal blue dress safely covered in plastic, and her checking account six hundred dollars lighter, Diana emerged from the shop. "This is madness," she said. "It's not like I can wear the darned thing for the wedding, either. Maybe I should go back, get one of the others that costs less."

"No." Sunny took her arm firmly and led her to her car. "You deserve it. And you can afford it. I don't want to hear another word."

"I still need shoes to go with it," Diana grumbled, but her protests were halfhearted. It was such a *gorgeous* dress, and she'd felt so very glamorous in it. Not like Diana Sorensen at all.

She wondered what Lee would say when he saw her in it.

Lee whistled softly. "Satan, get thee behind me," he murmured. Diana looked breathtakingly beautiful, he thought. "That's a dynamite dress," he added, recovering.

Her smile was reflected in her eyes as they met his. "Thanks."

He'd been a little uneasy about his reception because he knew he'd forced her into accepting him as an escort tonight, but she seemed relaxed.

As he helped her into the Porsche, he was struck again by how attractive she was and how much he liked her. He wished there was an easy way to get her to trust him. He still wasn't sure exactly why she was afraid to go with what they both wanted, and he knew until he understood the root of that fear he wouldn't be able to deal with it.

And deal with it he would, for he had no intention of letting Diana remain just a casual acquaintance who happened to be connected to him because of their children. No, he fully intended making that connection deep and binding, and nothing Diana did or said was going to change his mind.

"This is some party, isn't it?" Sunny said as she and Diana stood off to one side of the large room and surveyed the guests. "Boy, kiddo, that dress really looks great on you."

"Thanks." Diana thought Sunny looked pretty smashing herself tonight in a soft yellow satin cocktail dress that complemented her red-gold hair and light green eyes. She said so, and Sunny preened.

"What're you two talking about that's making my mother look so smug?" Nikki said as she joined them.

Diana smiled at the young woman. She loved Nikki, and once again she wished this engagement party was one celebrating her engagement to Kent instead of Allison's. "I was just telling your mother I thought she looked smashing. Come to think of it, you do, too."

Nikki did. Her dark hair, inherited from her father, was cut in a new, sleek style that hugged her small head and emphasized her long, graceful neck. Her green taffeta dress was the exact same shade as her eyes, and her face looked fresh and sweet with its subdued makeup and smattering of freckles. She rewarded Diana with a smile, but Diana saw the shadow that passed over her face.

This hurts her, Diana thought, looking around at the well-heeled crowd and letting her gaze settle on Kent and Allison, who were standing with Allison's grandparents. Allison looked spectacular, Diana thought, in a slinky cream satin dress that resembled a slip.

Just then Lee approached. He smiled at Sunny and Nikki, to whom he'd been introduced earlier, and said, "I've let my date wander off on her own long enough." He held out his hand to Diana, his toasty eyes twinkling. "Come on, gorgeous, there are some people I'd like you to meet."

Diana let herself be led off, her arm tingling from Lee's firm grip, her nerves taut. When he'd picked her up tonight, she really had thought everything was going to be okay. Now she wasn't so sure. He made her feel too uncomfortable. Too acutely aware of herself. Too conscious of how she felt about him.

Even now, although she wasn't looking up at him, she could feel his gaze on her. She quickly cut a glance at him. She took one look at the possessive look in his eyes, and could feel her heart going *boing*.

"Why are you looking at me like that?" he murmured into her ear. "As if I'm the big, bad wolf?"

"Aren't you?" she muttered, half amused, half scared.

His hand slid from her arm to her back, and Diana trembled as his palm touched her bare skin.

"What's it going to take to convince you, Diana?"

She shrugged. She was a big girl. She could handle this. Of course, she could.

He leaned over her, and his breath feathered her neck. "Although," he whispered seductively, "you *do* look good enough to eat."

Diana swallowed. There went her stupid heart again. Honestly, you'd think she could control herself better than this!

"Lee! *There* you are! I've been looking all over for you!"

Diana's gaze met that of a beautiful woman who looked enough like Allison to be her sister. Her older sister, Diana amended. The woman was small-boned, had the same pouty lips and cleft chin, but her hair was lighter—somewhere between brown and blonde, with streaks of gold artfully threaded through it. Her eyes were different too—a clear gray with flecks of green. She had the same kind of curvy figure, shown to advantage in a clinging black silk dress with a low-cut bodice and draped skirt. Diamonds glittered from her throat and fingers, and her heels were at least four inches high.

"Hello, Elizabeth! Allison said you'd be here." Lee bent to scoop the woman into his arms. He hugged her and kissed her cheek, and before he released her Diana saw the glitter of appraisal in the woman's eyes as she met Diana's gaze.

Diana smiled pleasantly. The woman didn't return the smile for a long moment, then she finally did. Her teeth looked toothpaste-ad perfect. Everything about her looked perfect.

"Diana, this is Elizabeth Whitman, Allison's aunt and my sister-in-law. Elizabeth, Diana Sorensen, Kent's mother and Allison's future mother-in-law."

"*Oh,*" Elizabeth Whitman said, the smile becoming genuine. "I should have known. For a minute there, I thought..." She looked coyly up at Lee. "I thought Diana might have been your most recent *friend.*" She gave Diana a conspiratorial between-us-girls look. "Lee is quite the ladies' man, as I'm sure you've figured out by now."

Someone else might not have noticed the almost imperceptible tightening of Lee's jaw, but Diana was beginning to be able to distinguish the subtle nuances of his expressions and tone of voice. "Come on, Elizabeth. You're exaggerating," he said, his tone mild.

Elizabeth peeked at Lee through her eyelashes. "He's too modest. Why, women practically mow each other down in an attempt to please him."

Diana decided she could very easily dislike Elizabeth Whitman.

The band, who had been taking a break, returned to the stage and began playing a slow song with a seductive beat.

"Come, on, Lee," Elizabeth said, "Dance with me. It's been years since we've danced together." She gave Diana a pleased-with-myself smile. "You don't mind, do you?"

"Of course I don't mind," Diana said sweetly. As if she cared who he danced with. Why, he could dance every dance with Elizabeth Whitman, for all Diana cared. Diana was proud of her nonchalance as she watched Elizabeth Whitman pour herself over Lee. They glided over the dance floor in perfect harmony—as if they were made for each other. Elizabeth's head was thrown back, and she laughed at something Lee had said to her. Diana wondered if Elizabeth resembled her sister, if she reminded Lee of his dead wife.

"Mom, would you like to dance?"

Diana turned. Kent stood there with a big grin splitting his face. Grateful to him for being so considerate, she smiled and held out her arms. She liked dancing with Kent. He was a strong, purposeful dancer with a nice, solid feel about him. She decided she'd done a pretty good job of raising him.

"Having a good time?" he asked.

"Yes, I am."

"These people are all pretty well-off." He laughed. "Maybe you'll get some clients out of this."

Diana nodded. "That would be nice."

"Mom..."

She heard the hesitation. "What? Is something wrong?"

"No, nothing's wrong. I just...well...you haven't mentioned Allison's ring."

"It's none of my business, Kent."

"I saw the way you looked at it that night."

"I was just surprised, that's all."

"You don't approve, I know you don't."

"It's not my place to approve or disapprove, Kent. I raised you to make your own decisions. You have, and I respect that."

He squeezed her tighter for a moment. "Thanks. You're the best mother in the world, you know that?"

"Oh, Kent... " Diana sighed, glancing up at him. "You've made my job easy."

He smiled down at her, and for a moment, they were in perfect harmony.

"What do you think of Allison's Aunt Elizabeth?"

"She's very beautiful."

"Yeah. Allison thinks the sun rises and sets on her. She's been wanting me to meet her for a long time."

"Where does Elizabeth live?" Diana asked casually.

"New York City."

"Oh." Her mood lightened inexplicably.

"But she's moving back to Houston."

"Oh. Why?"

"She just got divorced from some rich wheeler-dealer."

Diana scowled. So the wonderful Elizabeth of the pouty lips and sexy figure was going to be around permanently. Well, maybe now Lee would leave her alone. Elizabeth obviously had designs on him, and as far as Diana was concerned, she could have him. Now Diana would be off the hook.

"Why are you frowning, Mom?"

Diana started. "I wasn't frowning. I was thinking."

The song ended, and Kent led her back to where Allison stood talking with her grandparents and another younger couple.

Diana smiled as she met Jinx Marlowe's gray-green gaze. The older woman was tremendously attractive, Diana thought, and she had liked her from the moment she'd met her. Her slender, athletic body was shown to advantage in a long gray silk sheath, and Diana knew she probably worked at looking that good.

Howard Marlowe introduced Diana to the other couple, whose names she promptly forgot. They talked for a few minutes, then Lee and Elizabeth joined them.

Elizabeth was laughing as they walked up, teasing Lee. "I've missed you, Lee. It's going to be great fun now that we're all back in Houston again! I'm looking forward to some rousing tennis matches!"

Diana gritted her teeth. She would be pleasant to this woman if it killed her.

"Let's play tomorrow afternoon," Elizabeth continued, ignoring everyone else. "Maybe Kent and Allison could make it a foursome."

"I'm looking at houses tomorrow afternoon," Lee said.

"Oh, that's right," Elizabeth said. "Mother said you're giving up the guest house soon."

"Elizabeth thought she might move into the guest house when you and Allison move out," Jinx offered, her gravelly voice reminding Diana of old movies she'd seen with Tallulah Bankhead. Jinx smoked, Diana knew, wondering if the smoking had done that to her voice or if it were naturally husky and deep.

"Where are you looking for a house, Lee?" Elizabeth asked.

"Right around here... the Memorial and River Oaks area."

"Who're you working with? Letty Diamond?"

"No. I'm working with Diana."

Diana knew Letty Diamond. She hadn't known Lee did, too.

"Diana?" Elizabeth frowned. "This Diana?" She looked at Diana. "Do you sell real estate?"

"Yes," Diana said evenly.

"Diana's very successful. She owns her own agency," Allison interjected. "Daddy says she's doing a wonderful job."

Astonished at Allison's intervention, Diana couldn't help feeling pleased. She smiled at Allison, wondering if she'd been fair to the girl. "Thanks."

"She *is* doing a wonderful job," Lee said.

"I'd love to tag along," Elizabeth suggested. "I might be in the market for a house myself soon."

Diana clenched her jaw. Even though she wasn't looking forward to any more sessions of house hunting with Lee, she sure didn't intend to watch Elizabeth Whitman plaster herself all over him. There were limits to what a woman should have to put up with.

"Oh, you'd be bored, Elizabeth," Lee said. "When you get ready to buy, I'm sure Diana would love to work with you."

"Yes," Diana said, "I'd *love* to work with you." *I'd love to work you over.*

"Well..." Elizabeth said, her gray-green eyes speculative. She hooked her arm possessively through Lee's. "How about us attacking the buffet table? I'm famished."

Lee said, "Come on, Diana. Let's get something to eat."

"No, thanks. Not right now. I think I'd better go over and talk to my mother and sisters. I haven't spent much time with them tonight."

"We'll come, too, Mom," Kent said, taking Allison's hand.

As the three of them walked toward the table where her family was sitting, Diana seethed. She knew she should have come to this party on her own. Now if she wanted to leave, she'd look as if she wasn't having a good time.

Or something.

Like she wanted to get Lee away from Elizabeth Whitman.

Or something.

"I was just saying to Jackie that we'd hardly talked to you all night," Diana's mother said as they approached the table.

"I'm sorry, Mom. I've been trying to talk to everyone. I didn't mean to ignore you." Diana smiled at her family. Jackie winked at her, and Carol rolled her eyes. Diana thought both her sisters and her mother looked lovely tonight. Jackie and Carol were much prettier than she was, in her opinion. Both were petite blondes like Barbara. Diana, on the other hand, had inherited her father's height . . . and big feet, she thought ruefully.

Diana looked at her mother. Although Barbara Kent exasperated Diana at times, she had to admit her mother was an attractive woman who could be very charming when she chose to.

Joe Christopher, Carol's husband, stood and offered Diana his seat.

"No, that's okay," she said. "I don't mind standing."

"I want to get some fresh air anyway," he said. He walked off toward the open terrace doors.

Diana sank into the vacated seat gratefully. "Well, are you all having a good time?"

For a few minutes they talked about the party. Then Kent turned to Jackie. "Where's Uncle Chad tonight?"

"He had to go out of town," Jackie said.

Diana knew that Jackie's husband had recently quit another job. She wondered if out of town meant he'd gone to Vegas again. He seemed to have the idea that it was easier to gamble and make money than it was to work for a living.

Kent and Allison were soon engrossed in conversation with Jackie.

Barbara turned her attention to Diana. "That's a new dress, isn't it?"

"Yes."

"I'll bet you paid plenty for it."

Diana shrugged.

"I wear this dress everywhere," her mother continued, smoothing down the skirt of her mauve lace. Her tone grated on Diana's already-raw nerves.

On the other side of Diana, Carol poked her with her elbow.

"You look beautiful in it, though, Mom," Diana said. *I will not let her goad me into saying something I'll regret.*

"You *do* look beautiful, Gram," Kent said from across the table. He grinned at his grandmother. The two had always gotten along. Although Barbara found a lot of fault with Diana, she doted on her grandson.

"Thank you, dear. But I don't know *what* I'm going to wear to your wedding," Barbara said.

Diana wanted to scream. Instead, she said calmly, "I told you I'd take you shopping for a new dress, Mother."

Carol snickered. She poked Diana again.

Kent and Allison only stayed a few more minutes, then they wandered off. Diana stood. She had to get away. "I see the Steadmans over there. I'd better go say hello."

She sighed heavily as she walked away. This evening was exactly the ordeal she'd been afraid it would be. She glanced at the dance floor. It didn't take her long to spot Lee and Elizabeth. Just then, Lee turned, and for one second, their gazes met. Diana quickly looked away.

Somehow she got through the rest of the evening. Somehow she smiled and talked and acted like a gracious woman who was thrilled to death over her son's engagement. Somehow she said all the right things.

Finally the band played "Goodnight, Sweetheart," and Lee came to claim the last dance.

"I'm sorry I've neglected you tonight," he said as he drew her into his arms.

Diana held herself as stiffly as she could.

"You're not angry with me, are you?"

"Don't be ridiculous. Why should I be angry?"

In answer, he pulled her closer, and for the rest of the dance she was acutely aware of his body as it moved against hers. She wanted to stay aloof. She wanted to show him she didn't give a damn how much time he'd spent with his beautiful sister-in-law. She wanted to be cool and civilized and say something witty and clever.

"I like dancing with you," Lee murmured against her hair.

"Really? That's hard to believe."

Now *why* had she said that? Did she want him to think she was *jealous* of the time he'd spent with Elizabeth?

"What do you mean?"

"Only that I'm not a very good dancer."

"What are you talking about? You're a great dancer."

For the rest of the dance she concentrated on not letting her body overheat because of Lee's nearness. It wasn't easy.

Diana wondered what Elizabeth Whitman was thinking when, after the dance ended, Lee guided her over to say their goodbyes to the Marlowes. Elizabeth gave nothing away, though, as she said, "Diana, so nice to meet you. Perhaps we could do lunch one day?"

"Lovely," Diana answered smoothly. "Call me."

Finally they were in his car and on their way. About two-thirds of the way to her town house Lee said, "I'm glad Elizabeth is moving back to Houston."

"Yes, I could *see* that." As soon as the words were out of her mouth, she wanted to kick herself.

Lee gave her a sideways look. "I don't think you understood what I meant."

"What's there to understand?" Diana said. "You like your sister-in-law, and you're glad she's back in Houston. Seems pretty simple to me."

"I'm not glad for myself. I'm glad for Allison. It's going to be nice for her to have her aunt here. Allison misses her mother, and Elizabeth will be the next best thing."

"Of course."

"You don't sound as if you believe me."

"Why wouldn't I believe you?"

"I don't know," he said thoughtfully. "But you sound...irritated."

"That's ridiculous," Diana said hotly. "Why should I be irritated?"

"I have no idea. Unless—"

"I'm not the least bit *irritated,* as you put it."

"Diana, are you *sure* you're not angry because I spent so much time with Elizabeth tonight?"

Diana laughed. "Certainly not. I mean, after all, Elizabeth is your sister-in-law, and you haven't seen her in a long time. Why *shouldn't* you spend a lot of time with her?"

"Yes, that's what I thought."

"Well, there. We're in perfect agreement, then."

"If we're in such perfect agreement, why do I detect a note of ice in your voice?"

"You're imagining things."

"I don't think so." He put on his left turn signal, then turned onto her street. As the car glided through the soft October night, Diana thought about how glad she would be to get inside and away from his knowing remarks.

They reached her town house complex, and he pulled into the driveway of her unit. He turned off the ignition, and the quiet settled around them. He turned in his seat to face her, and the light from the nearby gas lamp bathed his face in shadows.

"Elizabeth doesn't mean anything to me, Diana," he said softly.

"You could be madly in love with her, and it wouldn't make the least difference to me," she said tightly.

He chuckled, the sound infuriating her.

"God, you've got an insufferable ego!" she said before she could stop herself. "You really think I *care*, don't you?"

"Yes, I think you care." He chuckled again, the sound tender and teasing. "Maybe I'm getting somewhere after all if I've succeeded in making you jealous." Then, before she could react, or resist, he leaned over and kissed her nose, then let his lips slide down to cover her mouth. Diana's breath caught, and her heart slammed into her chest as his hand cupped her head, holding her lips firmly against his. He deepened the kiss, and she didn't even try to resist. She just let herself go with the sensations caused by his heated mouth and his skillful possession. Her blood pounded through her veins.

When he broke the kiss, though, she allowed her fear and frustration and unhappiness to boil over.

She hated herself.

She hated this weakness in herself.

And she hated him for causing these unwelcome feelings. Breathing hard, she said, "I'm not jealous, you...you...egotistical...man!"

Furious with him, furious with herself, furious with everyone, especially that *stupid* Elizabeth Whitman, Diana yanked open the door of the Porsche, clambered out, and without saying another word, sped up the walk.

Breath coming in short spurts, fury fueling her movements, she unlocked the door and practically threw herself inside.

She was through with men.

All men.

Period.

Chapter Nine

"**I** think everything went really well tonight, don't you?" Allison said.

Kent smiled down at her. They were walking through her grandparents' garden on their way to the gazebo at the back of the property. The engagement party had been over for more than an hour, and they'd just arrived home. "Yeah, I think it was nice."

"Nice!" Allison laughed. "Is that the only word you can think of to describe it?"

Kent shrugged sheepishly. "Well, you know what I mean. It was...it was *very* nice. Everyone had a good time, I think. Even Nikki seemed to be enjoying herself. You know, I think you were wrong. I think it's going to be okay between her and us."

"Oh, Kent, please . . . she wasn't having a good time. She was miserable!"

By now they'd reached the gazebo. Allison walked ahead of him, climbing the three shallow steps leading up and into the lacy enclosure. Her dress glistened in the moonlight. Kent studied the enticing curve of her saucy rear end as it moved seductively under the clinging silk of her dress. The air whispered with the scent of the climbing roses that hugged the gazebo.

Allison turned to face him and laid her hands against his chest, smoothing the lapels of his suit. "Honestly," she said with a tolerant chuckle, "you're such a baby sometimes!"

Kent stiffened. "I don't think I care to be called a baby."

"Oh, darling, don't get angry! Not tonight." She raised herself on tiptoe and pulled his head down to meet hers. She nibbled at his bottom lip, touching it sweetly with the tip of her tongue. "Please, Kent. Don't be mad at me," she whispered, then met his lips fully. As soon as his mouth captured her warm, inviting one, Kent forgot about his irritation. Head swimming, he deepened the kiss and pulled her closer. His blood heated and his heart hammered as he slid his hands over the thin fabric gilding her body until they cupped her bottom and nestled her against him.

He closed his eyes as he felt the firmness of her warm flesh. She wasn't wearing a bra tonight, a fact he'd been aware of all night. Too aware.

Thinking about the richness of her high, full breasts, his hands moved unerringly up her torso. He could feel the storm building inside him.

"Kent..." Allison's voice was husky and breathless as she gently pushed him away.

Reluctantly he released her. He didn't look forward to the cooling-off period he'd face if he let things go any further between them. He closed his eyes for a minute. He wanted her so much, he wasn't sure he could wait nearly three more months.

Taking a deep breath, he said, "Let's sit over there."

She smiled up at him, her eyes gleaming in the dappled light. She nodded.

They sat on the circular bench, and he took her hand in his. Her diamond engagement ring winked at him as he rubbed his thumb over the back of her hand.

"I love you," he said.

"I know. I love you, too."

"It's going to get harder and harder to wait."

"I know." Her voice sounded small in the darkness.

"But I will. Because you mean more to me than anything, and I don't want to do anything to make you unhappy."

"Oh, Kent..." She squeezed his hand. "You're awfully good to me. I..."

"What?"

"It's just that sometimes you're *too* good. Too nice. You see everything through rose-colored glasses. Like Nikki, for instance..."

He sighed. "What about Nikki?"

"Well...you think she's so *nice*. You think everyone is like you. That their motives are all pure."

"She *is* nice."

"I'm not saying she isn't. But if you think the three of us are going to be friends, now or after we're married, you're kidding yourself."

Why couldn't she just drop this subject? he wondered. Obviously they were never going to agree. "Okay," he said resignedly, "maybe I was being too optimistic to think you and she would be friends. But Nikki and I...well, we'll always be friends. She's been a part of my life since I was a little kid. She's like family. But I won't force you to do things with her. I can meet her for lunch, and I'll still see her once a week for softball."

"Kent . . . that's not going to work."

There was a note of deliberate patience in her voice, a note he didn't care for, a note that sounded as if she were talking to a child instead of a grown man.

But her voice softened as she continued. "I won't be very happy if you insist on seeing Nikki after we're married. How will that look, anyway? A married man running around with an unmarried woman?"

"You can't expect me to just drop Nikki? I can't hurt her like that."

"I'm sure she expects it. I would in her shoes."

"Allison, Nikki's not like you. She wouldn't understand if I did something like that. And, on top of the fact that I don't *want* to eliminate Nikki from my life, her mother and my mother are best friends. It would be terrible for everyone if I hurt Nikki."

"But I'm telling you, none of them expect things to be the same. If you don't believe me, ask your mother. Besides, Nikki knows the score. She's not some dumb girl from the sticks, even if she *does* dress like she is."

Kent stared at her. "What's wrong with the way she dresses? I thought she looked great tonight."

Allison shrugged. "She looked better tonight than any other time I've seen her. She obviously made an effort to look her best. I mean, think about it. If you were a girl, would *you* want to look anything less than your best when you were going to the engagement party of the man you're in love with? You sure as heck don't want to look . . . dowdy!"

"Allison, we're getting nowhere. I don't want to discuss Nikki anymore, okay? Let's just drop the subject." To get her mind off Nikki, about whom he knew they would always disagree, he said, "Your father and my mother seemed to be having a good time together. You know," he added, the idea just hitting him, "it wouldn't surprise me if they got together." He grinned. "In fact, I think your father *is* interested in my mother!" The idea pleased him immensely.

He wasn't prepared for the way Allison's hand tensed in his, the rigidity he could feel in her body. Even her voice sounded tight when she answered, "That's ridiculous!"

"Why is it so ridiculous?" Kent wasn't sure he liked her tone of voice or her implication.

"Because your mother isn't my father's type at all!"

Kent bristled. "I don't know why you should say something like that. My mother's beautiful, she's smart, she's successful. Why wouldn't he be interested in her? I'd think any man your father's age would be."

"I know the type of woman that attracts my father, and it's not someone like your mother. If he were going to be interested in anyone, it would be a woman like my aunt Elizabeth, for instance."

Kent dropped her hand. Frowning, he turned to face her. He'd had a chilling thought. "You don't like my mother, do you?"

"Oh, no, Kent . . . I . . . that's not true! I didn't mean anything like that. Oh gosh, I'm sorry . . . I never thought how that must sound."

Kent still frowned. Despite her sincere-sounding apology, he hadn't liked the way she'd referred to his mother. Her inference still rankled. His mother could hold her own in any crowd, and no one, not even Allison, was ever going to say differently. At least not in *his* hearing.

She laid her hand on his forearm. "Kent, honey, really. I didn't mean anything by what I said. It's just that . . . well, Diana is so *different* from my mother . . . and . . ." Her voice dropped so low Kent could hardly hear her. "My Aunt Elizabeth is . . . she . . . she looks just like my mother."

All his displeasure evaporated. Of course. How stupid of him. She might sound self-possessed and sophisticated, even cynical at times, but down deep Allison was vulnerable, especially when it came to the subject of her father...and her mother. Kent guessed he'd been pretty insensitive. He probably never should have said what he'd said. If he hadn't been trying to get her sidetracked from the subject of Nikki, he probably wouldn't have, either.

"It's okay," he said gruffly. "I guess I'm pretty defensive when it comes to my mother."

"I know." She slid her hand into his again, and leaned her head against his shoulder. "You're proud of your mother, and you *should* be. She's accomplished remarkable things."

"I owe her a lot," he said. "She's always put me first."

"I know. And I admire that. She's a terrific woman."

Kent knew he should feel relieved that they'd straightened all this out tonight, but for some reason, even though Allison was as sweet as could be for the next thirty minutes—he still felt a faint uneasiness. Lately it seemed as if they were disagreeing about everything. To wipe this dark thought out of his mind, he put his arm around her and tilted her face up to meet his.

Then he lost himself in the honeyed recesses of her mouth and suddenly nothing else seemed important.

Lee woke early Sunday morning, even though it had been after one before he finally got to bed the previous night. The first thing he thought about was Diana's hurried exit from his car. The way she'd sounded when she'd called him egotistical. The way she'd acted about the time he'd spent with Elizabeth.

One fact kept hammering away at him. It was the only thing that had kept him from complete frustration over Diana's actions.

If Diana didn't care about him, if she wasn't interested in him, she would never have been so emotional last night.

He kept thinking about her and how he should proceed when he saw her this afternoon. He planned his strategy while he fixed his coffee. She was still on his mind while he took a shower, dressed and walked outside to get the newspaper.

He'd finally stopped thinking about Diana and was eating the scrambled eggs he'd fixed for his breakfast when Allison walked into the kitchen.

"Good morning," she said, leaning over to kiss his cheek. "Umm, that coffee smells good." She padded over to the counter, poured herself a cup of coffee, then sat across from him.

He smiled at her. Although she was in her bathrobe and didn't have makeup on, she still looked good in his eyes. Youth, he thought fondly.

"Did you have fun last night?" she said, her gaze meeting his over the rim of her cup.

"I did. It was a very nice party. I'll have to make a point of telling your grandparents what a good job they did. I didn't have a chance to tell them last night."

She was silent for a long moment, then said casually, "I'm sorry you were stuck with escorting Kent's mother. I know you probably would have liked to stay and talk to Aunt Elizabeth afterward. Didn't she look *wonderful* last night? It's so good to have her home again. Don't you think?"

Lee set his coffee cup down. "It wasn't a chore to bring Diana. I enjoyed it." He met her gaze squarely. "And yes, I'm glad your aunt is home again, because I know how much she means to you." He hesitated. This was a subject they normally avoided, for it always brought pain to Allison, something he never liked doing. "Your aunt Elizabeth reminds you of your mother, doesn't she?" he said softly.

Allison's eyes clouded. She bit her bottom lip and nodded.

Lee reached across the table and grasped his daughter's hand. He squeezed. "You still miss her, don't you?"

She nodded. "And it's...it's worse right now. I keep thinking about my wedding. How much I wish she was here to help me and share it with me." Tears glistened in her beautiful eyes. "Th—that's why I'm so glad Aunt Elizabeth is home."

Naturally. Why hadn't he realized how hard it was for her? "I'm sorry, honey."

She sighed deeply, looking away. For a long moment the only sound in the kitchen was the hum of the refrigerator. Finally she turned her gaze back to him. She no longer looked on the verge of tears. She'd gotten herself under control. "Thanks, Dad. I...maybe I don't tell you very often, but, well, it means a lot to me that you've always been there for me." She gave him a shaky smile, and his heart swelled with love. "But, still, it *will* be wonderful to have Aunt Elizabeth's help. A woman...you know."

"Yes, I know."

"Plus," she added brightly, "she's so much fun. I'm looking forward to doing things with her. And sometimes, well, maybe the three of us can do things together." Her eyes were hopeful. "It...it would be like...like having Mom with us again."

"Sweetheart..." Oh, damn. He had to be careful what he said. Her feelings were important to him, even if her obvious desire to see him hook up with Elizabeth was wishful thinking that was never going to come true. "Look," he said gently. "I loved your mother very much, and I miss her, too. I always will. But if and when I...marry someone else...it can't be because she reminds me of your mother. That wouldn't be fair. To her or to me.''

Allison bowed her head. For a long moment she said nothing.

Lee waited.

Finally she said, "You're right, of course." As she raised her head, Lee saw an expression of longing flit across her lovely features, quickly followed by a stubborn lifting of her chin. "But, Daddy, I know Aunt Elizabeth is looking forward to spending time with us. And she's *family*. There's no harm in doing things together, is there?''

An image of Diana's face as it had looked last night popped into Lee's mind. Lee knew it wouldn't be a good idea to spend much time with Elizabeth—not if he wanted to get anywhere with Diana—but he didn't want to make too much of an issue about it.

Not yet, anyway.

"We'll see," he said. "I'm going to be pretty busy, what with the new job and house hunting and everything else. But don't let my schedule stop you. I think you should spend as much time with your aunt Elizabeth as you want to." He smiled. "She loves you. The two of you will have fun together. And between her and your grandmother, you'll have lots of help in planning the wedding."

He ignored the nagging thought that it wasn't only Diana who was going to give him trouble about his feelings for her. He had an uncomfortable feeling Allison was going to oppose him every step of the way, too.

Diana's morning wasn't going well. Although she didn't feel like it, she picked up her mother at nine-thirty the way she always tried to do on Sunday mornings. Her mother grumbled all the way to the church.

"And then he said he couldn't do anything about it . . .''

Diana frowned, trying to concentrate on what her mother was saying. "Couldn't do anything about what, Mom?"

"Don't you ever listen to me, Diana? Nobody ever listens to me! I don't know why I ended up with such children. I was always a good mother to you girls, and look at the thanks I get."

Diana sighed. She glanced at her mother's rigid profile, her tight lips, the unhappy expression pinching her face. Why did her mother always seem so discontented, no matter what or how much others did for her? Why did she always seem to want more? This was a question that had nagged at Diana for years, but she still had no answers. It didn't seem to matter how many times Diana or her sisters called their mother or came to see her, Barbara Kent still accused them of neglecting her. It also didn't matter how much money Diana gave her. Her mother continued to whine about how destitute she was. All this despite the fact that she owned her Heights area home free and clear, had a car paid for and maintained by Diana, had interest income as well as her social security checks and never lacked for anything.

Even Carol, who didn't really like doing it, contributed some money to Barbara's support. Not a lot. Not as much as Diana, but still... And Jackie helped, too, although since her worthless husband never could hold a job, she couldn't really give her mother money. But she helped by cutting Barbara's hair and sharing her entertainment and soap opera magazines, which Barbara loved.

The morning was an ordeal. Diana listened with half an ear to her mother's laments, only commenting when she felt she couldn't do otherwise. Finally, in exasperation, she said, "The engagement party was a success, I thought. The Marlowes certainly didn't spare any expense."

Barbara's blue eyes gleamed. "I always knew Kent would do right by himself. I'm glad he had the sense to pick a girl who has money and a good name."

Diana knew her mother didn't think much of the choices her own daughters had made. Diana grimaced. Actually her mother was right on that score. Neither she nor her sisters *had* picked very wisely. Unfortunately she wasn't sure Kent had, either. Of course, her criteria for a wise choice was far different from her mother's.

"I was so afraid Kent would marry Nikki," Barbara added.

That did it. Before she could stop herself, Diana said, "I was *hoping* Kent would marry Nikki."

"Oh, I knew that. I'm not as dense as you think I am, Diana. I know how much you think of that girl. And she's a nice girl. I'm not saying she isn't. But she couldn't do a thing for Kent or his career. Allison can."

"You know, Mother..." Oh, Lordy, what was the use? "Well, Kent loves Allison, and he seems happy. If he's happy, I'm happy."

Finally they were on their way back to her mother's house. But she wasn't through complaining. "I know you said you'd take me shopping for a new dress, but I can't afford a new dress," her mother said, after a long tirade about the expensive dresses all the women had worn to the engagement party and how out of place she'd felt in her old mauve lace dress that she'd worn everywhere for years.

"I always intended to pay for your dress," Diana said. Why not? What was another couple of hundred dollars, anyway? She was already going to go broke over this wedding, and she was just the mother of the groom. She wondered how parents of girls afforded the astronomical costs.

Perking up immediately, her mother said, "Can we go to Penelope Stuart's?" She'd named one of Houston's most exclusive and expensive shops.

"No," Diana said. She *wouldn't* lose her temper. She wouldn't.

"I asked Jinx Marlowe where she got her dress—"

"Oh, God, Mother, you didn't!"

"—and she said from Penelope Stuart's. I've never had a dress from Penelope Stuart's."

"Mom," Diana said through gritted teeth, "I've never had a dress from Penelope Stuart's, either. I can't afford those prices."

"*You* certainly had an expensive-looking dress on last night. How much did you pay for it?"

Diana clenched her teeth harder. *Count to ten.* She kept her voice mild as she answered. "It wasn't too expensive."

"Diana Kent Sorensen, don't you lie to me. I know that dress wasn't cheap." She continued to mumble under her breath. "It's okay for *her* to spend a fortune on a dress, but her own *mother,* well, what can I expect?"

Diana counted to twenty. "I promise you I'll get you a nice dress. A very nice dress. Now can we please drop the subject?"

By the time she pulled into the driveway of her mother's home and they'd said their goodbyes, Diana was exhausted and had the beginnings of another headache. Lately it seemed as if her head was in a constant state of disrepair.

And the day wasn't over yet. She still had to face Lee and spend the afternoon house hunting. After her ignominious actions toward him the previous night, she wasn't sure she *could* face him.

She wished she could call him and cancel their house hunting plans. She wished she could assign him to someone else. She wished she could tell him to get lost.

But she didn't do any of those things.

When he arrived at the office at one o'clock, she coolly said, "Hello. You're right on time." She picked up her briefcase. "We'll take my car today." She had decided to make no mention of their conversation the night before. If she pretended nothing had happened, maybe he'd be a gentleman and take the hint.

He gave her a twisted smile, but he didn't disagree.

The afternoon was an ordeal for her. Lee behaved himself—it wasn't that. In fact, the more businesslike she was, the more businesslike he became.

By the end of the afternoon, though, the stress of trying to keep her thoughts under control was getting to her. She was just too aware of him sitting beside her in the car, walking beside her in the houses they looked at, and several times she'd caught him looking at her with an inscrutable expression on his face.

But finally the day was over.

And they still hadn't found a house Lee liked.

When they got back to her office, Lee said, "Well, where do we go from here?"

"I'll set up some more appointments for you, I guess. When do you want to look again?"

"That's not what I meant."

They were standing in the parking lot. The Sunday afternoon traffic on Memorial Drive was light, and the early October sunshine felt warm on her shoulders. She looked up at Lee. His amber eyes were reflective as he met her gaze.

Her heart skipped. "What *did* you mean?"

"I meant where do you and I go from here?"

Diana looked away. "Lee, why won't you give this topic a rest? Why can't you accept that you and I are never going anywhere? That we're not going to have a relationship?"

"Because I don't believe it."

She forced herself to meet his gaze once more. His eyes were filled with a soft understanding and certainty that sent doubt sailing through her. "You're just going to have to accept it," she said wearily. "I'm just not interested in you." She wondered if her lack of conviction showed in her voice.

"I'll never accept it."

"Well, fine, but I'm not."

"I don't believe you. You're not telling me the truth."

"What's it going to take to convince you?"

"The day you can look me straight in the eye without flinching and say you aren't attracted to me, you don't want me and you never will...then...maybe I'll believe you." His sensuous mouth quirked up at the corners, and his eyes flashed with amusement. "But only after I've kissed you thoroughly and you haven't reciprocated!"

Diana wanted to stamp her foot.

She wanted to tell him he was an arrogant ass.

She wanted to deny everything. Let him kiss her, and hold herself aloof and cold. Show him he was dead wrong.

But she didn't dare.

For she knew she could never convince him.

Heavens, she couldn't even convince herself.

The amusement faded from his eyes. "The day you're honest with me, maybe then I'll back off."

"I've been honest with you."

"I don't think so. You've thrown up a million and one excuses, but I think the real issue is your fear. I think you're afraid of getting too close to me, of needing me or anyone else."

Diana went very still. "You're wrong." How did he do it? How did he know what she was feeling?

"I don't think so."

"You don't know anything about me." But he did. He did, damn him.

"I thought I did. I thought you were strong and brave and pretty wonderful. But now I'm not sure. Maybe you're right. Maybe I really *don't* know you. Maybe you're just a garden-variety coward."

Diana swallowed. She wanted to deny his accusation, but what was the use? She *was* frightened. But she had no intention of admitting it to him. No intention of letting him know how close he'd come.

Lee's jaw hardened. Diana's glance met his again. There was no amusement in the golden-brown depths of his eyes. No soft understanding. No emotion.

"Okay, you win," he finally said. "I've tried in every way I know how to convince you to give us a chance. And frankly, I'm tired of trying. So I won't bother you again. In fact, if you want to assign another agent to help me find a house, that's okay, too." His eyes looked like cold topaz, all the warm lights hidden behind some kind of invisible wall. "That way you won't have to put up with me at all."

Diana's heart pounded. She wanted to reach out and touch him, say, *no, no, I don't want to do that at all.*

"I guess this is goodbye, then." He gave her a mocking salute. "If you change your mind, you know my number." Now his mouth slid into a cynical smile. "But don't wait too long. I've never been known for my patience."

Chapter Ten

Lee smiled grimly all the way home. He'd always been a gambler. You didn't get to his position in the business world without being a gambler.

He wondered if his gamble with Diana would pay off. He knew he'd taken a big chance. Maybe she'd be so relieved by his backing off that she really *wouldn't* make any attempt to change things between them.

If only he knew why she was so afraid. He thought he knew, but thinking, and really knowing, were two different things.

He sighed as he pulled into the Marlowes' driveway. Well, what did he have to lose by taking this gamble? He hadn't been getting anywhere the other way. Maybe purposely staying away from Diana would do the trick. Maybe, once she'd had a chance to miss him, to examine her own feelings, she'd be more receptive to him when he finally did approach her again.

But this enforced absence was going to be tough on him. He only hoped it was going to be tough on her, too.

The next couple of weeks dragged by. Somehow Diana got through them. Somehow she kept her mind focused on work and not on Lee. She took his suggestion and assigned him to Sunny, who had been working with him ever since. By the third week of October, Diana had almost recovered her equilibrium and recaptured her contentment with her life.

Almost.

She looked up as Sunny entered her office. Sunny looked particularly attractive today in a pumpkin-colored suit and dark green suede shoes. On her head was perched a sassy green felt Robin Hood hat. A perky feather curled from the brim.

Diana chuckled. "What're you? The Halloween pumpkin come to life?"

Sunny arched her eyebrows. "You're just jealous because *you* can't wear these colors."

"That's for sure. That color of orange turns my skin to mud! Seriously I love your suit. And that hat. Are they new?"

"Uh-huh. I picked the suit up at Alaina's during her end-of-the-season sale last year. Isn't it great?" Sunny smoothed down the lapels of the suit jacket, giving Diana a sly look from under her eyelashes. "I wanted to look nice for Mr. Magnificent. I was hoping he might make an indecent proposal . . . or two."

Diana used all her considerable willpower to keep from showing how Sunny's barb had pricked. "How's the house hunting going?" she said casually.

Sunny grinned. "That's what I came in to tell you, boss lady. Congratulate me! I may not have gotten any indecent

proposals from him, but Lee Gabriel gave me something
better! Only moments ago, tall, dark and dangerous signed
an offer letter on a house.''

Diana's heart quickened. ''Is he here?'' Oh, honestly, why
did she care?

Sunny's eyes narrowed knowingly. ''No, Diana, my
friend, he's not here. He *was* here. In fact, he was right out
there, not twenty feet away from your door.'' She grinned
again. ''For a whole half hour.''

Thank goodness she hadn't known. She might have
weakened, been tempted to walk out and casually stroll by.
She hadn't even laid eyes on him since his parting shot two
weeks ago. Just thinking about his final remark made the
hairs on her arms rise again. Oh, he was so darned sure of
himself! Well, she'd show him. Hell could freeze over before she'd call him.

A sudden image of her mother's face, set in angry lines,
popped into her mind. Barbara Kent had wagged her finger
at a fourteen-year-old Diana, saying, ''Diana Kent, you are
the most bullheaded, stubborn girl it's ever been my mis-
fortune to know. Why, you'd cut off your nose to spite your
face anytime!''

I am not cutting off my nose to spite my face. This situation with Lee was not at all like that. She didn't want to see
him again; she wanted him to leave her alone.

And he was.

''Which house does he want?'' she asked, forcing her
thoughts back to business.

''The Finnegan house.'' Sunny beamed.

Diana whistled softly. ''Congratulations, Sunny. That's
going to be a nice commission check for you. That's your
new listing, isn't it?''

''Yep! I'm tickled.''

''Do you think the Finnegans will accept the offer?''

"They'd be crazy not to! He's offering them only a couple of thousand less than their asking price, and I happen to know his offer is well within the range of what they'll accept. In fact, I think it's more than they hoped to get. Of course, I couldn't let Lee know that." Sunny was referring to the fact that in Texas a real estate agent represented the seller, even if she was working primarily with the buyer. Of course, in this case, Sunny was the listing agent on the house, so she was really treading a fine line.

"That's great, Sunny. Congratulations again."

"I knew that house would sell quickly." Triumph rang in Sunny's voice. "It's a dream house."

Diana hadn't seen the Finnegan house yet. As they did for all new listings, the agency had scheduled an open house for the weekend. But now the open house would be canceled, so she guessed she wouldn't see it.

Not for a long time, anyway, she mused. Not until Lee had some kind of party for Allison and Kent where she might also be included.

And then again, maybe Lee would *never* include her again.

The thought caused her heart to give a painful lurch, which she tried to ignore. You're never satisfied, she told herself after Sunny left her office. You wanted him to leave you alone. You got your wish. What's your problem?

The problem was, she missed seeing him.

She missed talking to him.

She missed . . . She shook the thought away. So she'd discovered she missed sex. So what? Big deal.

Had she made the right decision?

The thought refused to go away.

Of course I did.

But irrationally, all afternoon after her brief conversation with Sunny, Diana wondered why Lee had given up so

easily. She finally admitted that she hadn't believed him
when he'd said he was giving up. She'd really expected him
to call her again.

Or send her flowers again.

Or something.

At ten-thirty the next morning, Diana was in the reception area talking to workmen who were installing a new security system. It was costing more than Diana had wanted
to pay, but she decided it was worth it. There had been a
couple of instances of muggings in small real estate offices,
and Diana had decided that the old saw about an ounce of
prevention being worth a pound of cure was probably very
true.

The new system included a hidden button under the rim
of Tracy's desk that would send an alarm directly to the
company monitoring the system. There were also going to
be panic buttons in the bull pen and in all the individual offices.

Diana was deep in discussion when the outer door opened
and Lee walked in.

Their gazes met.

Her heart stopped.

His was inscrutable. Cool and inscrutable.

Golden brown should mean warmth, Diana thought distractedly.

He nodded, a half smile creasing his face. The smile had
no warmth, either. "Hello, Diana."

"Lee," she said, the greeting sounding more like a croak
than a word. She cleared her throat.

Lee handed some papers to Tracy, who beamed up at him.
"Hi, Mr. Gabriel. Sunny said you were dropping these off."

Now the smile warmed up. Heavenly days, Diana
thought. When he put effort into it, his smile was enough to

curl a woman's toes. But there was an ache around her heart because the smile wasn't meant for her. "I didn't expect to see you still here," he said to Tracy. "Isn't that baby of yours due?"

"Any day," Tracy said. "But I feel great, so my doctor said there's no reason I can't work right up until I go into labor."

Diana, who had finally recovered her poise, said, "We're just hoping she doesn't decide to have Barton, Jr., here."

Tracy grinned. "Nope. No chance of that."

Lee smiled again, then looked around. "I see you're having a security system installed."

"Yes."

"You having problems or something?"

"No. I've been meaning to do this for a long time."

"Well, that's good. I'm glad there's no real problem."

His gaze met hers again, and for one brief moment, something flickered in the depths of his eyes—something that made Diana's chest tighten. And then it was gone, and his impersonal mask slipped into place again.

"Well, I've got a lunch meeting at eleven-thirty, so I'd better get going. Good seeing you again, Diana. You, too, Tracy."

After he left, Diana tried to concentrate on the security system, but over and over again throughout that long day, she kept seeing Lee's face, his eyes, his expression. She kept hearing his voice with all its nuances. She kept remembering how much fun they'd had together at the zoo, at the Paul Simon concert. She relived the kisses they'd shared, and shivered with the dark, delicious memories.

Oh, Diana stop it, she told herself. *Stop it this instant! You're happy with your life. You made the right decision. You like your freedom and your independence. You like being in control of your time, your decisions, your money, your emotions. Especially your emotions. You're contented. When you need companionship, you have your family and friends and cats. When you need excitement or challenge, you have your business.*

But what about love? The question nagged at her.

Well, you have Kent. And one of these days, you'll have grandchildren.

It's not enough.

It's been enough for twenty years. Why should it suddenly stop being enough?

You know why. Now you've met Lee. Now you've tasted something else.

Just because something tastes good doesn't mean it's good for you. On and on her thoughts whirled. Finally at five o'clock, in disgust, she stuffed papers into her briefcase and put on her suit jacket.

She had to stop this. And soon.

Otherwise she was going to go nuts.

The next afternoon, Diana had finally regained her concentration and was looking over some flyers she'd received from one of the mortgage companies, when Tracy buzzed her to announce that Kent was on his way back.

"I was beginning to think you'd fallen off the face of the earth," Diana said as he walked into her office. "I haven't heard from you in weeks."

"Now, Ma," Kent said, his good nature undisturbed. "It's not like you to nag. Is something wrong?" He bent over her desk and kissed her cheek.

"No. I've just missed talking to you, that's all. How're the wedding plans coming along?"

A slight cloud passed over Kent's affable features. "Things are going well."

"You don't sound too sure."

He shrugged. "No, really, they're going fine. It's just that...well, things are costing so much. I guess I never realized a wedding was so expensive."

Diana nodded. She hadn't, either.

"Of course, Allison's father and grandparents are paying for everything, so I guess I shouldn't complain but, I don't know, it still bothers me." Kent hesitated, then added, "Her grandparents have even insisted on paying for our honeymoon trip."

"Oh, Kent!" Even though Diana knew he could ill afford the cost of a trip on top of the cost of that extravagant ring he'd given Allison, she still felt there was something wrong about the groom not paying for the wedding trip. Surely he wasn't going to let them.

He grimaced. "I know. I don't really want to, but I don't really have a choice."

"You always have a choice," Diana said quietly.

He swung his legs down from her desk, and leaned forward, elbows on knees. His expression was earnest. "Look, Mom, I know you think that's true but, well...you just don't know Allison."

Oh, but I think I do, Diana thought. And what I know disturbs me.

"See, doing things right, well, that means a lot to her. And I...I want her to be happy. She and I talked about it. I had thought we'd just take four days or so, maybe go to New Orleans, which I could have managed, but Allison wants to go to Paris."

"Paris!"

"Yeah. She wants to show me where they lived. She...she really loves the city, and she's anxious to show it off."

His eyes said, *please understand.*

Diana sighed. She hoped Allison's views about life and money didn't corrupt Kent completely. It would be so easy for him to just give in on everything, especially when not only Allison, but her grandparents and Lee seemed determined to lavish gifts on the young couple.

She wished that he'd stand up to Allison and her family. Stiffen his backbone a little bit and not let them manipulate him so easily. She knew he wanted to please Allison. She only hoped when it really counted he'd be strong.

"Her grandfather talked to me about it," Kent continued. "He explained how much they wanted to do this for us, and how much it meant to them. I . . . I couldn't refuse. It would have seemed spiteful, or something."

Yes, Diana thought, she could see how Kent felt. Actually she imagined she might have felt the same way if Howard Marlowe had put her on the spot like that. It had been very clever of Allison's grandfather to put the honeymoon trip in just those terms. No wonder Kent had conceded on this point.

"So you're going to Paris, then?" she said.

"Uh-huh. We made our reservations yesterday."

"Well, since you've decided to accept the trip, you might as well enjoy it. Paris is a wonderful city. Romantic, beautiful. It'll be a terrific place to be on your honeymoon. So don't feel guilty."

He grinned. "That's what I like about you. You're the most sensible person I know."

Diana wondered if Kent would still think so if he knew how severely her good sense had been tested where Lee was concerned.

As if he'd read her mind, Kent said, "Lee tells me he's found a house."

"Yes." She hoped her expression didn't reveal the way her heart had quickened just at the mention of Lee's name.

"He's real excited about it, too."

"Good. I'm glad."

"Allison's Aunt Elizabeth has offered to help him with the decorating."

"Oh?" *Keep your voice calm and interested. Smile.*

"Yeah. You know, I think Lee and Allison's aunt are dating."

Pain squeezed Diana's heart, a pain she tried to pretend wasn't there. "Th-that's nice," she managed.

"Allison thinks so," Kent said innocently.

Allison would.

For the remainder of Kent's visit, Diana struggled to talk normally and to keep the vision of Elizabeth Whitman and Lee out of her thoughts. By the time Kent left, she felt drained.

This is for the best, she told herself. He's found someone else, someone much more suitable than you. Now you can get on with your own life.

The following Friday, the day before Halloween, Diana's sister Jackie called from her home in Bryan. In hysterics.

"Calm down, Jackie. What's wrong?"

Diana rolled her eyes as she listened to Jackie relate the latest in a series of incidents concerning her husband, Chad.

"This is the final straw, Diana. I just can't take any more. I couldn't believe it when I got the gasoline company's bill! Do you know what he's been doing?"

"No, what?" Nothing would surprise Diana.

"He's been charging gasoline for his friends on *our* credit card. That's the way he gets cash! They pay him cash, and he charges the purchase on our bill!" Tears clogged her voice. "It's unbelievable. And after all his promises."

Diana didn't know what to say. It would sound much too cynical to say that it was a mistake to ever believe any man's promises.

"And you know, we had had such a good talk a couple of weeks ago. I thought that maybe, finally, things were going to get better. He promised me he'd really try to stick with a job, and we made out a budget and a plan to pay off all our bills. And he agreed to take an allowance and stay with it. And now this."

Diana made comforting noises, which was all she could think of doing.

"I'm leaving him," Jackie said, tears thickening her voice. "Can the kids and I come and stay with you for a while? We could go to Mom's, I guess, but I can't face it. You know how she is. She'll give me that I-told-you-so look until I'll want to puke."

Diana thought about her quiet town house. She thought about her privacy. She thought about how much she valued her calm oasis at the end of a long, tiring day. She sighed. "Yes, of course, you can come and stay with me." She wouldn't wish her mother's constant disapproving countenance on anyone.

She hoped this sacrifice wasn't going to be in vain. She hoped Jackie meant it this time. In Diana's opinion, Chad was worthless. Would always be worthless. A good-looking, good-for-nothing worthless bum. She'd always thought Jackie deserved better.

So Jackie and her kids moved in. Actually, even though Diana wasn't looking forward to the invasion by a thirty-eight-year-old woman and her ten-year-old son and twelve-year-old daughter, it wasn't as bad as she'd thought it might be.

Douglas was a nice kid—quiet and thoughtful—and he and Diana had always gotten along. She fixed a bed up in her loft so he'd have his own place. She even let him move her little TV set from the kitchen, so he could go upstairs and watch his favorite shows if he wanted to. And Clyde,

bviously adoring, latched onto Douglas, following him
verywhere. This amused Diana. All males stick together,
he thought.

Melissa, her niece, was a pretty nice kid, too. Amazingly
ice, considering the kind of turmoil she'd been raised in.
Melissa and Jackie were sharing the guest room, but nei-
her seemed to mind.

Even Bonnie got into the act. After the first day, she
rawled out from her hidey-hole under Diana's bed, and
egan to peek her little head around the corner. On the third
ay, she rubbed up against Melissa's leg and from then on,
he two were best buddies.

The day after Jackie and the kids moved in, Tracy went
nto labor, so even that worked out well, because Jackie was
crackerjack secretary, and Diana immediately put her to
ork.

"You can work for me while Tracy's off on maternity
eave. That'll give you time to look for a permanent job."

Jackie agreed. She was pathetically grateful, and Diana
new it, but she tried to downplay her role when Jackie
umbled over her thanks.

"Listen, you'd do the same for me," Diana said.

"Well, sure, but that's never gonna happen, and you
now it. You've never needed anyone."

Diana had been telling herself the same thing for years, so
hy did it feel like a hurtful criticism when Jackie said it?

Diana and Jackie fell into the habit of talking late at night
ter the kids were asleep. They talked about everything:
ckie's future, her life with Chad, their mother and Carol.
iana told Jackie about the things Carol had said the day
e'd called to complain about Barbara's phone calls.

She's jealous of you, Diana. That's why she makes those
ide remarks."

"But she's got a husband and three children, a nice home, everything she supposedly wanted. Why is she jealous?" Diana asked. She was sitting Indian fashion on her deep cushioned couch, dressed in her favorite clothes—a faded blue warm-up suit and thick socks. Overnight the weather had turned cool, and even though it was only early November, it was beginning to feel like winter.

Jackie, who was nestled into the love seat that sat at right angle to the couch, nodded thoughtfully. She'd drawn her knees up to her chin. "I know. But she'd rather have what you have, I guess. You know how it is. The grass is always greener in someone else's yard."

Diana studied her younger sister. Jackie had a lot of common sense, and she'd always had the ability to see things from someone else's point of view. That was one of the reasons it had always amazed Diana that her sister should have made such a poor choice of a husband. Diana was beginning to think all women were stupid when it came to men. Lord knows, she certainly had been. Still was, she thought wryly, since she couldn't seem to get one particular six-foot male animal out of her mind.

We let our hormones and emotions rule us instead of our brains.

Jackie pushed her heavy blond hair away from her face. She was a beauty, Diana thought. But she was no bubble head. Maybe now that she'd made the decision to give Chad his walking papers, Jackie would finally come into her own. Diana resolved to help her as much as possible.

"You know, Diana, I've always been envious of you, too," Jackie said softly.

"You? Why?"

"You always seem to have it all together. You never doubt yourself or your ability to handle anything. And I'm always riddled with doubts."

"I'm riddled with doubts, too," Diana said, then couldn't believe she'd said it.

Jackie's blue eyes widened. "Really?"

"Really." The uncharacteristic admission of weakness actually felt good.

"About what? Your business?"

"Oh, no, not the business. No, when it comes to my career, I rarely have doubts. It's my personal life that gives me fits." To her utter astonishment, Diana found herself telling Jackie all about Lee.

When she finished, Jackie said, "It sounds to me as if this guy is one in a million, Diana. Are you sure you did the right thing?"

"I told you. I'm riddled with doubts."

"Well, maybe you should think about calling him."

"I don't know. Besides, even if I wanted to, I think he's lost interest." She remembered the impersonal way he'd treated her when she'd seen him in the office the day the security people were there. She remembered what Kent had said about Lee dating Elizabeth Whitman. "I also think he's already seeing someone else."

"I don't think he sounds like the kind of man to change his mind. Sounds to me as if he might just be giving you time to realize what you're throwing away."

Diana sighed. "Maybe. Maybe not."

Two days later, she had cause to wonder if what Jackie had said was true. Diana was out showing houses to an old customer who was trading up, and she walked into the agency tired but satisfied with the day's work.

Lee was sitting there talking to Jackie.

The first thing Diana felt was happiness. The second thing she felt was a spurt of pure jealousy, because Lee seemed entirely too comfortable sitting there and too interested in Jackie. Much too interested.

Jackie looked gorgeous today, Diana thought, in a blac
dress with white piping and big black-and-white triangula
earrings.

Diana felt frumpy next to her beautiful, *younger* sister.

But when Lee looked up, his eyes flashed with pleasur
and he immediately stood. He smiled down at her, an
Diana's breath caught. His smile always managed to d
funny things to her.

"Hi," he said softly.

"Hi." For the life of her, she couldn't think of anothe
word to say.

"Allison tells me the two of you are going shopping ove
the weekend."

"Yes, she called last night to see if I wanted to see h
wedding dress. We're also going to shop for my dress for th
wedding.

"Good. I'm glad."

"Kent tells me the wedding plans are coming along ju
fine."

Lee smiled. "I guess so. I'm not very involved." His smi
got wider. "I just pay the bills."

Jackie laughed. "That's what a father is supposed to do.

"I guess Allison's aunt is helping her with the wedding,
Diana said casually.

"I guess she has been, but she's gone off to Portugal fo
two weeks. Someone she knows invited her to a big hous
party at some villa . . . or something."

He didn't seem the least bit interested in Elizabeth
whereabouts, Diana thought happily.

"I just came in to drop something off for Sunny. We'
closing on the house Friday, you know."

"I know."

Just then Sunny walked in, and in the flurry of her gree
ing to Lee, and him handing her the papers she wanted, D

ana slipped from the room. Jackie gave her a knowing look as she brushed by the desk, but Diana didn't acknowledge it. She wondered if Lee had turned around, if he realized she was leaving. She half hoped he'd call to her, but he didn't.

Just as well, she thought as she closed the door to her private office. *I made the right decision. I can't live my life on an emotional roller coaster, and I'm afraid that's exactly what would happen to me if I broke down and did call Lee.*

But there was an ache around her heart the size of a basketball. She wondered if it would ever go away.

When Diana and Jackie walked into the office on Friday morning, the phone was ringing. Jackie snatched it up before the recorder could kick in. She listened for a moment, then said, "Diana, it's Sunny. And she sounds horrible."

"I'll take it in my office."

A few minutes later, Diana listened as Sunny, whose voice sounded like sandpaper, tried to talk. "I've got laryngitis."

"I guess you *do.* You sound horrible."

Sunny had a history of laryngitis, which seemed to hit her about once a year.

"What do you want me to do for you today?" Diana asked.

"Can you cancel my appointments...or take them yourself?" Sunny croaked. "Jackie's got the list."

"All right. Anything else?"

"Lee's closing."

"Oh, that's right. He told me it was scheduled for today."

"Can you go for me?" The words were barely a whisper.

"Yes, of course. Where's it going to be?"

"Lowman Title."

Diana nodded. She knew Lowman Title well. Sid Lowman was an old friend. They'd both started out in the Houston real estate business about the same time. She'd worked with him often in the past. "Okay," she said. "No problem. What time?"

"Six."

At first Diana thought she'd heard Sunny wrong. "Six o'clock! Why so late?"

"Lee has to go out of town in the morning. I think he's going to Paris. I'm not sure. Whatever it is, it's a business trip. And he had a couple of meetings he has to take care of today before he leaves, so Sid agreed to have the closing later. I...I think Sid knows Lee. I think they're friends."

Diana felt bad about making Sunny talk so long. "It figures. Is there anything Lee Gabriel can't accomplish? Don't answer that. Save your voice...I was just grumbling, that's all."

After they'd hung up, Diana was torn between excitement and nervousness. Although she couldn't help but feel anticipation over seeing Lee, she knew that every time she did, her emotions were thrown into a tailspin. She did okay when he wasn't around. But seeing him always unsettled her, and for days she'd think about him.

Well, it couldn't be helped. She had to go to the closing. She had to go to the rehearsal dinner. And she had to go to the wedding. After those three events were over, maybe she could go back to being the Diana she was comfortable with.

When she left her office at five-thirty, it was already almost dark. The sky had a smoky lavender cast to it, and the roofs of the nearby buildings were inky black silhouettes against it. Diana had always loved this time of day. There was something about dusk that made the world seem softer place.

The closer she got to the title company's offices, the more her nerves stretched taut. Lowman Title was located in a small office building on the edge of downtown Houston near the banks of the bayou. It sat on a small rise and had its own attached parking garage.

She parked her car, walked into the building and punched the elevator button. Riding up to the sixth floor, she took deep breaths. She lectured herself. *You can handle this, kiddo. You've handled situations that were ten times worse. Twenty times worse.*

All too soon she was there. But she felt calm. She was fine. Everything was going to be all right.

She walked into the title company's offices. Cassie, the receptionist, said, "Hi, Ms. Sorensen. Go on into the conference room. You know where it is. They're waiting for you."

Diana strode rapidly down the hall and through the open conference room door. The first thing she saw was Lee. He stood with his back to her, and he was looking out the big window overlooking lower Memorial Drive. The lights of the office buildings in Houston's impressive downtown skyline filled the view.

Oh, Lordy, even the back of him is sexy. He was wearing a dark gray charcoal suit tailored to perfection. Under the beautiful material, his shoulders were an impressive width. There was something about a man in a suit, she thought, as her pulse rate speeded up.

Sid Lowman, who was seated at the end of the long conference table, shuffling some papers, looked up at Diana's entrance. His thin face broke into a broad smile. "Well, well, well! Look who's here!" He stood. "You sure are a sight for sore eyes. I didn't know you were comin'."

Lee turned slowly. His gaze met hers. A spark of—what? happiness?—flared in his eyes for one brief instant before he doused it. Then his impersonal mask slipped into place. He inclined his head and walked toward her, extending his hand. "Hello, Diana, how are you?"

"Hello, Lee. I'm fine. How about you?" She took his hand, and he shook hers briefly. Her heart skipped at the touch of his smooth, warm palm. He looked even more wonderful from a front view. With the dark gray suit he wore a dove gray dress shirt and gray-navy-and-burgundy tie in a muted paisley print. The silver threading his hair seemed more pronounced...and even more appealing. Diana swallowed.

Now he smiled. "You're looking good."

"Thank you." She was absurdly glad she'd worn her raspberry suede suit. She knew it was flattering. She slipped her hand out of his grasp and turned to Sid. "Sunny isn't coming. She's sick with laryngitis. I'm filling in for her."

"I'm sorry about Sunny," Sid said, "but I'm real happy to see you again, Diana. It's been too long. I've missed you."

Sid was such a sweetie. She smiled at him. "I've missed you, too, Sid." She turned back to Lee. "Hope you don't mind that I'm filling in for Sunny."

"Not at all. Why would I mind?" His eyes glinted with some emotion she couldn't identify. *Was* he glad to see her? She wasn't sure.

Just then a couple who looked to be in their late sixties entered the room with Cassie.

Lee moved forward. "Hello, George, Shirley." The men shook hands, then Sid introduced her to George and Shirley Finnegan, the sellers. Soon they were all seated around the table, and Sid proceeded to conduct the closing. There were no hitches, for which Diana was very glad. During the closing, she avoided Lee's gaze, although once or twice she snuck a look his way. He wasn't looking in her direction either time.

Forty-five minutes later, the closing was over. The Finnegans stood, big smiles on their faces.

"Where are you two moving?" Sid asked politely.

"Out to our ranch," George Finnegan said. "I've finally retired, and Shirl and I are lookin' forward to bein' country folks full-time."

Shirley Finnegan, a plump, gray-haired, motherly woman, beamed at her husband.

George Finnegan handed Lee some keys. "Well, son, here goes. I hope you enjoy livin' there as much as we did."

After the Finnegans were gone, Diana gathered up her copies of everything. She said goodbye to Sid and turned to say goodbye to Lee.

"I'll walk out with you," he said.

"Okay."

Sid said, "Well, Lee, enjoy your new home. I understand it's a real showplace."

"It is," Lee said. He glanced at Diana. "Don't you think so?"

"I haven't seen it," she answered.

"You haven't? I thought you saw all the houses your agency lists."

"Normally I do, but you made an offer on the house only a day or so after Sunny listed it. It was before I'd had a chance to look at it. And since then, I just really didn't see the point."

He nodded. Soon they were on their way out. She didn't look at him as they stood side by side in the elevator. Her untrustworthy heart had started beating faster, for some stupid reason. They didn't speak as the elevator slid to a stop and the doors opened noiselessly.

Diana's heels clicked on the tile floor as they walked down the hall and out into the parking garage.

"Where are you parked?"

"Over there." Diana pointed to the far corner.

"I'll just see you safely into your car."

She didn't protest. She didn't like parking garages at any time of the day, but at night, they were doubly scary.

But halfway to her car, Lee touched her arm.

Diana's heart leaped.

"Diana," he said.

She turned and slowly raised her eyes to meet his gaze.

His voice was very soft as he said, "I'm heading over to the house. Would you like to go with me and see it?"

Everything in Diana told her to say no.

Her brain.

Her common sense.

Her entire intricate system of self-preservation.

Say no.

"Yes," she said.

Chapter Eleven

He smiled, and Diana thought, what am I doing?

"Good. Let's take my car. We'll pick up your car later."

"But that'll be out of your way, won't it? Why don't I just follow you? Sunny said you're going out of town tomorrow. You must have an awful lot to do." She was crazy. That was it. She had finally slipped over the edge.

"I'm all ready to go. All packed, even. Going over to the house is the last thing on the list."

"All right." She allowed him to take her arm and lead her to the Porsche. Her backbone seemed to have disappeared along with her good intentions.

She had a weird feeling of déjà vu as they drove up Memorial Drive toward the Loop, the lights of Houston flashing by, a classical piece played by what sounded like thousands of violins flowing from the CD, and Lee sitting beside her. Every time she took a breath she smelled the faintly woodsy scent of his cologne. Every time she glanced his way and saw his killer profile, her heart went bumpety bump.

Definitely crazy.

The car passed under the Loop. Very soon he was turning left off Memorial, and the Porsche slid along the dark, winding road. Spaced intermittently were tall street lamps that cast eerie shadows over the dense foliage and towering pines.

At the very end of the street, angled kitty-corner into the cul-de-sac, loomed a sprawling, multilevel contemporary home. A row of floodlights bathed the base of a sand-colored brick wall that surrounded the structure.

Lee got out of the car and opened the gates leading into the driveway. Moments later he pulled up in front.

Diana didn't wait for Lee to walk around and help her out of the car. When he touched her, she did very foolish things.

Emerging from the car, she took a deep breath. The air felt cool and clean, and the sounds of the city seemed very remote. Although they were only minutes from Memorial Drive and the busy 610 Loop, they might have been in the middle of the country. Night sounds were all around them: the rustle of leaves disturbed by nocturnal creatures, the faint hoot of an owl, the chirp of crickets and distantly, from the direction of the bayou, the croak of a frog.

Stars winked through the intricate web of tree limbs, and a silvery parenthesis of a moon shone down upon them.

"Watch your step," Lee said, taking her arm again.

They walked through the gate in the wall and were inside a courtyard lit by two gas lamps, one on either side of the mammoth double doors. Lee unlocked the doors and beckoned her into the shadowy interior of the house.

As the doors closed behind them, Diana stopped. She wasn't a whimsical person. She had never understood most of the poetry she'd been forced to read as a student, and she wasn't given to flights of fancy. But in that moment, in that precise place, standing next to a man who made her feel things she had no business feeling, Diana experienced something she was hard pressed to explain.

It was as if the house were speaking to her. In that dark, hushed foyer, full of silence and secrets, she felt the personality of the house. It seemed to say, *I've been waiting for you.*

She swallowed, fear fluttering deep in her belly. Dear God in Heaven, she prayed.

"Don't move," Lee murmured. "Let me find the light switch."

Then the foyer shimmered with light from one of the most unusual chandeliers Diana had ever seen. When she looked around, her breath caught. The house was incredibly beautiful—just the kind of house she loved. The entryway was two stories high, with a long, sweeping staircase off to the right. Nestled inside the curve of the staircase was the chandelier, an elegant, ultramodern waterfall design.

"Isn't this great?" Lee asked, his voice ringing with pride.

"It's gorgeous," Diana agreed.

"Come on, I'll show you the rest, only be careful. I'm still not sure where the light switches are, and some of the rooms don't have overhead lighting."

Before Diana could react, Lee took her hand and led her to the left and into an enormous living room. The moment he touched her a frisson raced through her body. She tried to ignore the feeling and concentrate on her surroundings.

The light from the chandelier illuminated the massive stone fireplace and Diana could see that the entire wall at the far end was floor-to-ceiling windows. Her heels sank into plush carpeting as Lee drew her farther into the room, which she realized was actually an L shape. When they rounded the corner of the L, they were suddenly plunged into shadowy darkness again.

Lee let go of her hand and walked to the wall. She heard him groping around, then a soft click and the house was flooded with music from some kind of built-in system.

He fiddled with the system until he found the station he wanted, and once more, classical music washed over Diana, and the air of magic and mystery that had gripped her from the moment she walked into the house intensified.

Now Lee was at her side again, his hand touching the small of her back. Even through her suede jacket, Diana felt its heat, and suddenly she found it difficult to breathe.

"Diana." His voice was soft, seductive.

Diana held her breath.

"I wish you'd look at me."

Like a sleepwalker, she turned, and now both of his hands touched her upper arms, holding them lightly. There was just enough light for her to see the shape of his face, its shadows and planes and the gleam of his eyes. She could smell his unique scent, and her heart thumped heavily.

They stood that way for what seemed forever, but was in reality probably only a few seconds. The music stopped briefly, then a new piece began—a beautiful piece with a familiar melody that trembled in the air and caused Diana to tremble right along with it.

"You're not cold, are you?" Lee said, pulling her closer.

"No." Her throat was so dry, she could barely speak. "That song is beautiful. Do you know what it is?" she asked, more to break the spell that threatened to destroy her than because she really cared.

"Debussy's *'Clair de Lune,'*" he murmured, his hands sliding around to her back.

"Lee—"

"Diana—"

They both spoke at once.

"I want to kiss you." His words were gruff, full of desire, and Diana's own pent-up needs broke through the walls she'd erected to keep them imprisoned. Suddenly she no longer cared what happened tomorrow. There was only tonight. And Lee.

She lifted her arms and put them around his neck.

With a low murmur, he crushed her to him. The kiss was hungry, as if they were starving. There was no finesse about it at all, just open mouths and slick tongues and the heat of a desire too long denied. Diana's heart went wild, pounding against her chest like a crazed thing. Lee kissed her for a long time, kissed her so thoroughly she felt weak all over, and she knew, in that moment, she'd never get enough of him. He made her feel like no man, not even Kent's father, had made her feel before.

"Oh, Diana, you're wonderful," Lee whispered against her ear when he finally let her up for air. "I want you. You know that, don't you?"

She nodded, unable to speak, her silence an answer.

Very gently, he began to remove her jacket, and she let him.

She shivered when his hands began to unbutton her silk blouse. Uncertainty clawed at her.

Her breathing quickened as he found the back zipper of her skirt and she heard the rasp as he pulled it down slowly. The skirt fell in a heap at her feet.

Soon his jacket joined her clothes on the floor.

"Help me," he muttered as he fumbled with his tie. She hesitated.

"Help me," he said again. So her clumsy fingers joined his, but it was slow work, for when their hands touched, Lee stopped and kissed her again. This time his hands roamed over the wispy material of her slip, and their heat burned her skin and fueled her desire, burying her uncertainty momentarily.

Within moments he was clad only in his briefs. Diana closed her eyes as he pulled her close again, and she could feel his hard body against hers. She swallowed when his hands slipped to her bottom, holding her against him so that the heat and force of his arousal pushed against her. Shyly at first, then more boldly, she began to explore the firm contours of his body. He felt wonderful. She refused to think about what she was doing. And where she was doing it. She just absorbed the tactile sensations and let her emotions take over.

The music swirled around them, the only sound except their ragged breathing. He lifted her slip, and suddenly, Diana was terrified. It had been such a long time. What if he was disappointed in her? She stilled his hands.

"What?" he whispered.

"Lee, I'm scared."

"I know, but it's going to be okay."

"I . . . I'm not taking anything."

"That's okay, love. I'm prepared," he murmured.

"What?"

He released her long enough to bend down, find his jacket and remove something from its pocket.

"You certainly are sure of yourself." Her voice sounded odd, not like hers at all.

"No, just hoping," he said gruffly.

"Hoping, huh?"

"Yes, love, hoping."

When he called her love like that, Diana felt as if she might melt. Just melt into one big, warm puddle.

"I bought these the day after I met you," he continued softly, "and I've been carrying them around with me ever since." He kissed the tip of her nose. "I wanted to be sure that if you were ever willing, I'd be ready." And then he really kissed her. A hard, greedy kiss. A kiss that said he was ready now.

Soon they were lying on the floor, the thick carpeting cushioning them, the faint moonlight that filtered through the windows dappling them.

Diana lay on her back, and Lee, who stopped every second or so to kiss her, unfastened the front hooks of her bra, laying it open. "Lee," Diana said faintly.

When his hands touched her breasts, she shuddered. She felt the immediate response of her body, which tightened and arched toward him. Her breasts tingled as his thumbs massaged back and forth over the aching nubs and his tongue whispered over her partly open mouth.

"See?" he murmured thickly. "Nothing to be scared of."

Diana whimpered.

"What, love?"

"I . . . I *am* scared."

"But why?"

"I'm afraid I'll disappoint you."

"You won't disappoint me."

"I . . . I'm too fat."

He laughed. "You're not at all fat."

"I . . . I've never been any good at this. It . . . it's been so long."

"It's like riding a bicycle. Once you do it, you never forget how."

"Quit teasing me."

"I love teasing you."

As if to prove his point, he teased her again, only this time with his clever hands. But Diana still couldn't give herself completely over to the feelings his hands and mouth were eliciting.

"I'm afraid I won't please you," she said weakly.

His hands tightened over her breasts, then running down her waist to touch the elastic band of her panties. "Everything about you pleases me," he said.

He began to slide her panties down.

Panic caroomed into Diana's mind. "Oh, Lee, I don't know if we should keep going."

But he kept going.

"Lee—"

He sighed. "What's bothering you now?"

"I don't know if I can do this."

"Looks to me as if you're doing just fine." She could hear the smile in his husky, teasing tone.

Now his fingers crept down, taking her panties with them. Diana gasped as he found his target and began to pay it minute attention. She stopped protesting as his mouth trailed down her body. He kissed her stomach as his fingers delved deeper, finding her warmth, caressing and stroking, bringing her to a fever pitch of pulsing need.

Diana's heart pounded at the lazy promise in his husky voice. But she quit talking because her treacherous body felt as if someone had lit a match to it and the fire was burning out of control.

She forgot all her doubts. All her fears. Now she was just a mass of quivering, mindless, craving flesh. "You're driving me crazy," she moaned as he brought her up, up, up, then slowly let her down again.

"You ain't seen nothin' yet," he whispered as he continued his tender assault.

Her body was begging for release as his hands worked her, finding every spot, every hidden place.

"Please..."

"Please, what?" he said thickly.

She reached for him, but he batted her hands away. "Not yet."

"Lee . . ." She moaned.

"You like that, don't you?"

She couldn't even answer. She hated it. She loved it.

Just when she thought he was going to have mercy on her, when she finally thought her body was going to explode, he stopped.

"No," she whimpered. "Don't stop."

"First," he muttered, "let's get rid of these."

He pulled her panties down; she sat up and helped him, then they got his briefs off. Then he lowered her back to the floor and began all over again.

Her body shrieked with need as his fingers explored and softly began to move against her in a rythmic circular motion that caused her heart to go berserk.

"Oh, oh," she said. "I don't think my heart can take this."

He laughed.

"I'm not a young woman, you know."

She was climbing again. Going up and up and up. She knew that when she finally achieved her goal, she'd burst apart at the seams.

"You'd be surprised how much the human body can take . . . ." he whispered as he captured her mouth in a deep kiss. His fingers sank inside her.

"You're enjoying this . . . this . . . torture, aren't you?" she said with a half laugh, half cry, as the kiss ended.

"I can't remember when I've enjoyed anything so much."

"You're cruel," she moaned as he refused to allow her to reach the peak she was so desperately striving toward.

"You like it."

"I hate it."

"Shall I stop, then?" he asked as once more, he began to bring her back up.

"If you do, I'll kill you!"

The music that filled the room was something harsh, something that was building toward a crashing finale, and now they stopped talking. Now, as the clawing need tore through Diana, Lee didn't stop. Now he allowed her to continue to climb along with the music, and just as she reached that pinnacle and began to disintegrate, she clutched him, filling her palm with his heat.

As the waves of pleasure tore through her, she tried to guide him inside her. She wanted to feel him there, feel his strength, have him take complete possession of her.

And then he did.

And it was better than she could ever have imagined it to be. The heat. The power. The driving life force that consumed them. And now Diana felt another kind of ecstasy, something that was as much emotional as physical, and she grasped him, digging her nails into his back as he shuddered inside her.

When at last he rolled off her and gathered her close, running his hands over her body, he said, "That was perfect, wasn't it? You're perfect."

"Oh, Lee, don't try to make me feel good. I'm almost forty-three years old. I never was perfect, but at least when I was younger..."

He chuckled. "I can see I have my work cut out with you. Didn't I tell you what the French say about older women?"

"What do the French know?" She played with the curly hairs on his chest.

He kissed her ear, letting his tongue slide around for a few minutes, and tingles of pleasure slid through Diana. "The French are very wise in the ways of love, *ma chèrie.*"

My beloved. Diana closed her eyes. If only he really meant that. If only they weren't still glowing from the throes of some really terrific sex. If only she could trust her instincts instead of her brain.

He nestled her closer, stroking her hair. The music cascaded around them. Diana tried not to think.

"You're beautiful, Diana," he said.

"You're only saying that because it's dark and you can't see me," she answered.

"The next time I'll make sure there's a light on so I *can* see you."

A few minutes later he said, "I wish I didn't have to go on this trip tomorrow. I'm going to be gone for two weeks."

"I wish you didn't have to go, either," Diana said before she could stop herself.

"Diana, love, promise me something." He tipped her chin, and his gaze bore into hers.

"What?"

"Promise me you won't start doubting what we've shared tonight. I know you. I know that when you wake up tomorrow morning, you're going to start thinking this was a mistake. I know it. You're going to have regrets and doubts and all kinds of negative feelings. And I'm not going to be here to wipe them away. I should be here. Maybe I can cancel the damned trip."

"No, Lee. Don't do that." Would he *really* cancel the trip because of her? Something warm and wonderful wrapped itself around her heart.

"Will you promise me, then?" He kissed her gently, feathering her lips with sweetness.

"Yes, I promise," she whispered, hoping she could keep her word.

Later, after they'd finally got up and dressed, he held her close again. "I'll bring you something back from Paris. What would you like? Some perfume?"

"Nothing. Just you."

"You've got me. You've got me for as long as you want me."

And then he kissed her. One last, long, promise of a kiss that sent her shooting up into the stars where everything seemed possible.

Lee was too blasted smart, Diana thought, because the next morning, exactly as he'd predicted, she was racked with doubt. Every insecurity, every fault she'd ever had, loomed into her mind. All the reasons she hadn't wanted to get involved with Lee assaulted her from all sides.

She left the office at noon. She was meeting Allison at one o'clock at the Galleria. She prayed Allison wouldn't be able to tell from looking at her that Diana had spent the previous night shacked up with her father.

Shacked up.

Honestly, Diana, she lectured herself. Sex between two consenting adults isn't shameful, so there's no reason to berate yourself with harsh words.

Remember your promise to Lee.

She tried. She really tried. But still the doubts crept in, eroding her newfound happiness.

She was sure Allison knew exactly what had passed between her and Lee the night before. Hadn't that been a speculative, *condemning* look in her eyes—eyes that looked too much like Lee's for Diana's peace of mind—when Allison had greeted her?

Diana sighed. There was no way Allison could know about the previous night. She tried to empty her mind as she waited for Allison to come into the Bride's Room, where Diana was waiting to see her in her wedding dress.

"Would you like some coffee, madam? Or perhaps a glass of champagne?" an elegant saleswoman asked.

Diana shook her head.

Just then, from the left, Allison glided into the circular, mirrored room. Diana's breath caught. Allison looked heart-stoppingly beautiful. Her gown was a spun-sugar confection of delicate lace studded with hundreds of tiny pearls. Her veil, which fell three-quarters of the way down her back, was frothy tulle cascading from a lace and pearl pillbox hat. Even her shoes, which peeked from the scalloped hem of narrow skirt, were satin with lace and pearls. Her eyes were shining as she climbed to the dais in the center of the room. "Well?" she said. "What do you think?"

"I think that's the most beautiful wedding dress I've ever seen," Diana said. "It's perfect for you."

After Allison had once more changed into her street clothes, the saleswoman brought out a half-dozen dresses for Diana to look at. Their rich jewel tones shimmered in the soft lamplight. She held them up one by one.

Allison looked them over carefully.

"That one," she said, pointing to a romantic-looking tea-length silk and lace dress in a color the saleswoman called claret.

Diana knew Allison was right. But she cringed when she saw the price tag. This dress cost even more than the blue one she'd bought for the engagement party. But Diana could just see herself in the dress.

Knowing she shouldn't, she took the dress and walked into the dressing room.

She took one look at herself in the mirror, imagining the expression in Lee's eyes when he saw her in the dress, and knew her decision had been made. The dress made her look almost beautiful.

Allison echoed the sentiment when Diana walked out to show her the dress.

She smiled. "Perfect. Absolutely perfect."

Of course, the gushing sales clerk agreed, but Diana knew they were right. The dress was right.

So she bought it.

* * *

As the days slid by, Diana zigzagged between the height of happiness and the pits of despair.

Her appetite disappeared. Her work suffered. Jackie took to giving her guarded looks, but she couldn't, she simply couldn't, confide in her sister.

She spent long hours in the evening looking at herself in her bathroom mirror. Naked. Oh, Lordy, she thought. She touched the faint stretch marks left over from her pregnancy. She frowned at the tiny lines around her eyes.

That was half the time.

The other half the time, she hugged herself secretly, reliving every moment of their glorious lovemaking. Remembering every touch. Every whisper. Every incredible feeling.

She found herself blushing as she remembered her wanton behavior, the shameless way she'd begged Lee for more and yet more. Her body responded to the memories the same way it had responded to Lee's actions, and she found herself squirming uncomfortably in her chair while she tried, without success, to concentrate on her work.

Diana marked the days off on her calendar.

Nine days until Lee's return.

Eight days until his return.

Seven days.

Six.

Five.

And then it was the night before his return.

The next morning she awoke at 4:00 a.m. She was in a state of near panic. Excitement and anticipation and fear all warred together in her mind.

She couldn't wait.

She wished the day hadn't come so soon.

She wasn't ready to face him again.

What if he didn't want her anymore? What if he were feeling the regrets he'd cautioned her against? What if? What if?

She couldn't stand the tension. The entire day, she kept watching the clock, knowing his flight from Paris would be in at two o'clock.

At three o'clock, she swallowed hard. Her heart was beating so hard she was afraid she might have a heart attack.

Wouldn't that be great? she thought. They'll find me here on the floor of the office, and I'll be dead from a heart attack. Jackie will cry. Sunny will cry. And Lee. Would he cry, too?

She pictured her funeral, everyone with long, sad faces.

She felt her eyes filling with tears.

Oh, Diana, get a grip!

Three-thirty.

Why was she watching the clock? Did she honestly think Lee was going to come here, to her office? He'd go home. He'd been gone for two weeks. All he'd want was to go home.

Four o'clock.

Didn't I tell you he'd go home? Silly woman.

Four-thirty.

Her intercom buzzed.

"Yes?"

"Lee Gabriel is here to see you," Jackie said.

Diana shot up from her chair. Panic, exhilaration, excitement, fear: all clogged her throat.

The seconds ticked by.

Her door opened.

And there he was. With a huge smile on his face, joy filling his golden-brown eyes. He looked tired and rumpled from the long hours of travel. He looked wonderful.

Happiness jolted through her. She knew her own eyes were showing everything she was feeling.

He kicked the door shut behind him.

He opened his arms.

And she flew into them.

And then he kissed her, and all her doubts, all her fears, all her insecurities, vanished as if they'd never existed.

Chapter Twelve

Diana moved through the days in a fever pitch of awareness. Everything suddenly seemed more... *something*.

More exciting. More colorful. More moving. More beautiful.

Sometimes she almost felt like crying.

She laughed a lot.

She wondered if everyone was as aware of the difference in her as she was.

One day Sunny said, "You're sleeping with him, aren't you?"

Diana blushed.

"That's okay, kiddo. Don't answer that. I had no right to ask it."

At first, Lee called her constantly, and even though his attention flattered her, she asked him to stop. "I don't want my employees gossiping about me," she explained.

"You know, Diana, a person would think you were ashamed of what we're doing," Lee said tightly. "*Are* you?"

"No, of course not. But you know how I feel about this. If my agents start talking, Kent and Allison are bound to hear about it. And I don't want them to know about us."

"You've made that plain enough. I'm still not sure I understand why."

"Please, Lee..." How could she admit she was scared she'd fail again, and this time, everyone would know the failure was her fault?

No, it was far better that no one actually *know*. That way, if her fears came to pass, and things didn't work out with her and Lee, no one would know. Especially Kent and Allison.

Diana didn't want to think these black thoughts, but they had a way of creeping into her mind anyway. The only time she was able to put them completely out of her mind was when she was actually with Lee.

She spent almost all of her free time with him. She did things with him that she hadn't done for years. They went to movies. They took long walks. One cool night they built a fire in his fireplace and toasted hot dogs and marshmallows, something Diana hadn't done since Kent was a small boy.

She helped him move.

The day his furniture was delivered, they christened the house by making love on the floor of the living room—in the same place they'd made love the first time.

Diana protested. It wasn't dark out. Someone might see.

"No one's going to see," Lee said. "That privacy wall is six feet high, for heaven's sake!"

As he touched her and caressed her and brought her to a shattering peak, she clung to him. She kept thinking the sex would lose its intensity, but so far, it hadn't. If anything, it just seemed to get better as they learned each other's bodies and each other's pleasure points.

They made love all the time.

They made love in Lee's big king-size bed with candles flickering and music swelling from the stereo system.

They made love in the huge tub filled with hot water and bubbles.

They made love in the double-size shower stall, with the hot water cascading over their bodies.

They made love in the kitchen, in the dark, like kids hiding from their parents.

Once, they even made love in the hall closet, which had Diana giggling like a schoolgirl. "Why don't we go into your bedroom?" she whispered. "It'd be more comfortable." A handle of some kind was digging into her back. "It's more fun this way," Lee whispered back. "More secret. More sinful."

Diana quivered as his hands found a certain spot on her body. "I think I like sin."

Diana thought about him all the time.

She was thinking about him the day she and her mother shopped for a dress for Barbara to wear to the wedding.

"Diana, you're not paying attention again!" her mother complained. "Do you like this dress?"

Diana forced herself to concentrate. Her mother stood before her garbed in an ice blue satin dress with simple lines. The high jeweled neckline, long sleeves and close-fitting skirt were flattering to her mother. The skirt was caught up on one side by a large satin rosette, revealing her mother's legs when she walked. Her mother had nice legs, Diana thought as Barbara walked toward the triple-sided mirror in the dress shop. "Yes, I do," she finally said.

"I like it, too," her mother said.

"How much is that dress?" Diana asked the sales clerk in an aside.

The clerk named the figure, and Diana cringed. Nearly twice as much as she'd hoped to spend. Everything about this wedding had gotten out of hand.

"This is the dress I want," Barbara said. Her eyes gleamed speculatively as she met Diana's gaze in the mirror.

Diana nodded. Why fight it? The dress was perfect for her mother.

Later, as Diana was driving Barbara home, her mother said, "I hope I'm going to see you on Sunday. You've been awfully *busy* lately, haven't you?"

Diana sent her mother a sharp glance, wondering if Barbara suspected she was seeing someone. "Yes, I have been," she answered quietly. "But I'll make sure I'm free Sunday morning."

She was still thinking about her mother when she pulled into her driveway, so at first, she didn't notice the old pickup truck parked near her town house. When she did, she felt a twinge of foreboding. That truck looked suspiciously like the one belonging to Jackie's husband, Chad. Diana hoped not. Chad in Houston would only mean trouble for Jackie. It was bad enough that he called her constantly, begging her to come back to him.

But it was Chad. A repentant Chad who was playing on her sister's sympathy. A solicitous Chad who was hugging his daughter and talking to his son.

Jackie inclined her head toward the kitchen, and Diana, after giving Chad a polite greeting, followed her to the back of the house. In the kitchen, Jackie, with a worried frown, said, "Diana, don't be mad at me, okay?"

Diana sighed. "Don't tell me you've let him talk you into going back with him?"

"I'm sorry, Diana. I know you're disappointed in me."

Diana laid her purse on the table, then walked over and hugged Jackie. "I'm not disappointed in you."

"Thank you for everything," Jackie said as she hugged back. "I love you."

"I love you, too."

Later, as Diana helped Jackie pack, Jackie said, "I'm sorry to be leaving you in the lurch at the office."

Diana shrugged. "Don't worry about it. I'll hire a temp. That's what I was going to do, anyway. Your coming just made things easier for me for a while, that's all." She smiled at her sister. "Everyone's going to miss you. They all like you a lot, and you've done a wonderful job."

"I'm going to miss them, too," Jackie said in a sad little voice.

Then why are you going? You don't look very happy. Diana wished she could say the words aloud, but this wasn't her business. She loved Jackie, but she couldn't live her life for her. Jackie had to make her own decisions.

But as Jackie turned to walk downstairs, Diana laid a hand on her arm. "If things don't work out, you can come back," she said softly.

Jackie nodded.

There were tears in Diana's eyes as she bent to give Melissa a hug. Even Douglas, who like most boys his age seemed too embarrassed to show affection, hugged her. Chad, with unusual sensitivity, waited outside while his wife and children said their final goodbyes.

When the front door closed after them, Diana shut her eyes wearily. Why had Jackie gone? Why was it that all Chad had to do was give her a sad look and mouth sweet words and she caved in? What about everything she and Diana had talked about for the past weeks? What had happened to Jackie's newfound resolve? Her understanding of the hopelessness of her marriage?

You should talk. Your resolve turns to jelly when Lee is around.

As if to prove the point, the telephone rang just as the thought drummed inside Diana, and it was Lee. Happiness flooded her at the sound of his voice.

"How'd the shopping trip go?" he asked.

She told him about the dress she'd ended up buying for her mother. Then, sighing, she told him about Chad coming. And Jackie and the kids leaving.

Lee echoed her sentiments, saying, "It's her life, Diana."

"I know, but it's not going to work."

"There's nothing else you can do except be there for her."

"I know you're right"

A few minutes later, he said, "Has Jinx called you about Thanksgiving yet?"

"No."

"She's going to. She wants you and Kent to have dinner with the family."

Diana knew her sister Carol was expecting Diana to bring Barbara to Carol's house that day. She could just imagine what her mother would have to say when she found out Diana's plans had changed.

Diana sighed. She wasn't sure which would be worse—a day listening to Carol and her mother bicker or a day spent trying to keep Kent and Allison and her family from suspecting how she felt about Lee.

Kent haunted his mailbox every day. Not normally a worrier, he began to doubt himself. He'd been so sure he'd passed the bar. But what if he hadn't? What would he do then? How would he face his mother, who was so proud of

him, who was so sure he was perfect? How would he face
Allison? What would she say? He didn't think he could bear
to see her disappointment. And what would happen to his
plans to open the storefront law office? Doubts eroded his
confidence, and with each day that passed with no word, he
got tenser.

His fears proved unfounded. On the Tuesday before
Thanksgiving the envelope he'd been waiting for arrived.
With shaky fingers, Kent tore it open.

His eyes quickly scanned the page, and the only words
that mattered leaped out at him:

William Kent Sorenson . . . Passed.

"Yes!" Kent shouted as he punched the air. "Yes!" He
raced into the apartment to call first Allison, then his
mother, and share his good news.

After making the two calls, he danced around the apartment, singing, "I passed! I passed! I'm a licensed attorney
in the state of Texas!"

His euphoria lasted until precisely 8:42 p.m. that night,
when he and Allison had a serious argument. It started innocently enough, when Kent, still excited over his good
news, said, "Now I can finally get started on finding a space
and opening my office. I thought maybe the best place to
start looking is near one of the free clinics. What do you
think?"

"Kent, I . . . I think we need to talk about this," Allison
said.

Kent immediately tensed. "I thought we *were* talking
about this."

"Yes, well . . ." Allison bit her lower lip, uncertainty
clouding her beautiful eyes. She sighed. "I mean, *really*
talk."

Disquiet and something else, something very like anger,
gripped Kent. "If what you mean by *really* talk has to do

with me changing my mind, you can just forget it, Allison.''

"Kent . . .'' Her voice was soft, soothing. Frowning, she hesitated, her spoon poised in midair. They were seated in a booth at their favorite yogurt shop—Allison eating a dish of Raspberry Rhapsody, and Kent just finishing his dish of Praline Perfection. "Surely you can see how . . . how *impossible* your plan is. I . . . I thought since you hadn't mentioned the storefront office lately, maybe you'd abandoned the idea.''

Kent took a deep breath. Most of the time he avoided unpleasant subjects, but this confrontation had been a long time coming. "The truth is, I didn't bring the subject up because you never seemed very interested in hearing about it.''

"Kent! How can you say that? I'm *always* interested in you and what you're doing . . . and thinking.''

"Maybe *not interested* wasn't the right choice of words. Maybe what I should have said was, I know you're not enthusiastic about my plans, so I've avoided the topic.''

"Kent, that's not fair.''

"Was I wrong? *Are* you enthusiastic?''

Allison sighed and laid down her spoon. "It's not that I'm not enthusiastic, darling. I think your ambition to help people who have no other resources is wonderful, but I also think it's unrealistic to think you can practice this kind of law full-time.''

Kent stared at her. When he didn't answer her statement, two spots of color appeared on her cheeks, and he knew she was angry. Well, dammit, he was angry, too! Allison would just have to understand that she couldn't control his every action, his every thought. He was willing to go a long way toward making her happy. He thought he had proven that to her. But there were limits.

"Why are you looking at me that way?" she finally said, her voice tight. "You know I'm right."

"I know you *think* you're right. I don't happen to agree. And neither does Joel."

"Joel! You mean Joel Bartlett?"

Joel Bartlett had graduated from law school a year earlier and was one of Kent's closest friends. Kent and Allison had met at a barbecue given by Marcy Howard, Joel's girlfriend.

"Yes, I mean Joel Bartlett," Kent said.

Allison's expression was skeptical. "Maybe he's saying he agrees with you, but I can guarantee you, he'd never do it himself."

"Well, that's where you're wrong, because Joel has agreed to come in with me."

"I can't believe that Marcy would *ever* agree to him doing something so...foolish."

Something cold and hard knotted in Kent's chest. When he spoke, his throat felt tight. "I see. So that's how you *really* feel. You think I'm...foolish."

"That's not what I said!"

"Sounded like that's exactly what you said." He had always known, deep down, that Allison felt this way, but he'd never wanted to face it. He had always told himself that she'd come around to his way of thinking, that she loved him and would eventually share his dream. The knowledge that she wouldn't, and didn't, hurt more than he'd have believed possible.

"You're twisting everything!" Her eyes filled with tears.

Normally her distress would have bothered him, would have been enough for him to back down, say anything to make her feel better. But somehow, tonight, Kent wanted her to make *him* feel better. He sighed, knowing what he wanted wasn't going to happen. "I don't think so. I think I'm seeing everything very clearly, maybe for the first time."

"Kent . . ." A tear trembled on her lower lid, then slipped down her cheek. She brushed it away. "Please, darling, don't be angry with me. I . . . I'm only thinking of us."

"Are you sure? Are you sure you're not just thinking of yourself?"

"Kent," she gasped. "How can you say that?" Anguish and pain pooled in her eyes. "Our future together is the most important thing in my life. I thought you felt the same way."

Kent wanted nothing more than to reach across the table and comfort her. He knew he was hurting her, and he was sorry, but he couldn't give in to her on this point. On everything else, maybe, but not on this. "Look," he said softly, "let's get out of here. We can't talk here."

She nodded.

Five minutes later they were on their way to her place. Once there, Kent turned off the ignition and turned to face her. "Honey, please try to understand," he said, reaching for her hand. "This is important to me. I want you to be behind me."

Head bowed, she said, "I'm trying to understand, Kent, but I thought I was important to you, too." Her voice sounded woebegone and miserable.

"You *are* important to me." Why was he feeling guilty? He hadn't done anything wrong.

"More important than anything else?"

"Yes. You know that."

She gave him a tremulous smile. "Then I know you'll make the right decision."

Hours later, as Kent lay in bed, he kept thinking about their conversation. He had always known Allison wasn't happy about his plans, but he'd really thought she'd eventually understand. And obviously she harbored the same belief.

What should he do? He hadn't wanted to think the day would come when he'd have to make a choice between Allison and his dream, but it was beginning to look as if that's exactly what he'd have to do. Because something in Allison's eyes tonight had told him she wasn't going to back down. She wouldn't be happy unless he forgot all about his storefront law office.

The idea that he might have to work in a traditional law office made him feel cold all over.

Surely there was some other way.

There had to be.

On Thanksgiving Day, when Diana pulled into the long driveway of the Marlowes' property, her stomach was knotted with tension. She parked in the large paved area to the side of the house, then got out of her car and stood gazing around for a few minutes. It had turned out to be a beautiful day, warm and sunny with clear skies. Because of the cold snap earlier in the month, some of the leaves had turned color, and there was a scattering of leaves across the broad lawns of the estate.

Curious to see the guest house Lee had lived in for so long, she walked around to the back. Several hundred yards away, half-hidden by a thick stand of oak trees, was a charming redbrick bungalow. With a practiced eye, she took in the pool, the stables and the gazebo.

Money. The whole place shrieked of money. Old money, and lots of it.

Curiosity satisfied, she walked around to the front of the main house and rang the doorbell. Only seconds later, the front door opened, framing a smiling Jinx Marlowe.

"Diana, my dear," Jinx said. "How good to see you again."

"Hello, Mrs. Marlowe." Diana thought Jinx looked much too young to be anyone's grandmother, let alone a grown woman's. Today she was dressed in a bright red plaid pleated skirt and red silk blouse, the colors complementing her silvery hair and gray-green eyes.

"Oh, please call me Jinx. Everyone does."

Diana smiled. "All right."

"You look very lovely today," Jinx said, approval apparent as she eyed Diana's black cashmere sweater dress and pearls.

Diana wondered what Jinx would say if she knew how long Diana had agonized over what to wear, how many outfits she had tried on and discarded before settling on this one.

"The others are all in the living room."

Diana followed Jinx down the hall and to the left. She could hear laughter and conversation. Tension fisted in her gut. As they walked into the large sunshine-filled living room, the conversation stopped.

Everyone turned toward the doorway.

"Here's Diana," Jinx said, smiling as she drew Diana into the room.

All the while Diana was shaking hands with Howard Marlowe, exchanging polite greetings with Elizabeth Whitman—who looked much too beautiful in her camel colored fitted slacks and matching sweater, she was conscious of Lee only inches away. She and Allison hugged, then Kent kissed her cheek. She wondered if either of them could hear how hard her heart was beating.

Finally Diana turned toward Lee.

His eyes said, *"Don't worry."*

He smiled down at her. "Hello, Diana."

"Hi, Lee." Thank goodness her voice didn't sound as shaky as her insides felt.

He squeezed her hand reassuringly.

She knew he was telling her that everything was going to be fine, that no one suspected a thing, that she had no need to be nervous.

Still, the day was agony for her. She couldn't relax and enjoy herself. She was too conscious of Lee sitting across the table from her. Every time he spoke her eyes were drawn his way. Every time their gazes met, something warm curled into her belly, and her breath caught. She couldn't believe the others couldn't feel the electricity between them.

More than once she knew Lee was thinking about the previous evening and their lovemaking, which seemed to get better and better all the time. She could see his memories in the way his eyes gleamed as they sought hers again and again. Once, when she and Lee exchanged a glance, Diana looked away to find Elizabeth studying her with shrewd eyes.

Great. That's all I need. Elizabeth Whitman putting two and two together and saying something to Allison.

And adding to her uneasiness was the strong feeling that there was something wrong between Kent and Allison. She wondered what it could be and if everyone else was as aware of it as she was. She was particularly aware of a problem when the conversation inevitably turned to the wedding.

"Not much longer to wait," Jinx said, giving Allison a loving look. "This is going to be the wedding of the year. Certainly Allison will be the prettiest bride of the year."

Howard chuckled. "Now, Mama, I do believe we're prejudiced."

"Prejudiced, perhaps," Jinx said, "but not blind."

Allison smiled, but Diana was certain her heart wasn't in it. There *definitely* seemed to be something wrong, and Diana vowed to find out what it was.

"Allison tells me you've found a dress," Jinx said to Diana.

"Yes. She helped me pick it out."

"It's beautiful," Allison said, rousing herself from her lethargy. Then she turned to her aunt. "Aunt Elizabeth's dress is gorgeous, too. She tried it on for me last night."

"All these gals talk about, morning, noon and night, is the wedding!" Howard boomed. He sent an amused glance Lee's way. "They only need us to pay the bills, eh, Lee?"

Lee smiled indulgently. "Whatever makes them happy." Then, looking down the table toward Kent, Lee said, "To change the subject, I'd like to offer a toast to my future son-in-law." He lifted his wine glass. "Congratulations on passing the bar, Kent."

Everyone raised their glasses and echoed Lee's toast. Kent smiled. So did Allison. But Diana couldn't stop her feeling of disquiet from spreading. There was something not quite right about Kent's smile.

As a matter of fact, he looked tense and strained. Whatever it was that was bothering him, it was something important. Diana knew her son too well not to know that only something pretty earthshaking would cause him to lose his natural good cheer.

Was she the only one aware of the tension in the air? She must be, because the rest of them kept talking and laughing as if everything was peachy.

Would this day ever be over? she wondered as she tried to push her concern for Kent and her uncomfortable awareness of Lee out of her mind. She hardly tasted her food, and Thanksgiving dinner was usually one of her favorite meals. She loved turkey and corn bread dressing, and the food that

Jinx put on her table was very good, but Diana might as well have been eating dry toast. Strain stretched her nerves taut, and she couldn't wait for the day to be over.

Finally it was, and she could say her farewells.

"Thank you for inviting me, Jinx," she said. "I enjoyed it very much." She wished she were telling the truth.

As she and Kent hugged, she whispered, "Come and see me this weekend."

"Okay." She heard gratitude in his tone and knew he needed someone to talk to.

Elizabeth Whitman's eyes were cool and knowing as she said goodbye.

"I'll walk you out to your car," Lee offered.

"That's not necessary," Diana said hastily.

He came anyway. "There, that wasn't so bad, was it?" he said the moment the front door closed behind them.

Diana looked up. "Maybe not for you. I was miserable. The whole time I was in there, I kept thinking that everyone knew about us."

"No one knows anything, although I wouldn't care if they did."

"I know you don't care. But I do."

They had reached her car, and he walked around to open her door. He helped her in, and as their hands met briefly, he said, "Can I come over tonight?"

She hated this weakness in herself, this inability to say no. She had never intended to have him completely take over her life, but somehow, he had.

She sighed. "You know you can."

All the way home she thought about the heated promise in his voice as he said, "I'll see you at eight."

Only minutes before Lee was ready to walk out the door, Allison called, and she sounded so troubled, he didn't have the heart to tell her he couldn't talk to her. He looked at his watch. It was seven-thirty. Maybe he could keep the call short and still get to Diana's by eight.

"Daddy, I don't know what to do," Allison said, her voice more unhappy than he'd heard it in a long time.

"About what, sweetheart?"

He heard her sigh. "Kent."

Lee had wondered if there was something wrong between the kids. He'd had a feeling today that things weren't as rosy as they should have been. But he hadn't wanted to think about them; he'd been too wrapped up in thoughts of Diana. "What's the problem?" he said now, guilt tugging at him. He kept forgetting that Allison, even though she was almost a married woman, still needed him.

"He's determined to open his storefront law office. We had a disagreement about it the other night."

"I see." Lee had hoped Kent would have abandoned his idealistic idea by now.

"He won't listen to me! And now he's even got Joel on his side."

"That surprises me. I thought Joel was pretty sensible."

"I thought so, too, but evidently he and Kent have decided to do this thing together." She sighed again. "Daddy, I don't know what to do."

"Maybe I should try talking to him."

"Would you?"

"Yes." Lee was sure that once he explained things to Kent, the younger man would do the right thing.

"When?"

"This weekend. I'll call him tomorrow."

"You know, if Kent got a really *fabulous* offer, I'll bet he'd change his mind."

Lee smiled. She sounded more cheerful already. "Well, let me talk to him. We'll see."

"Because, you know, that firm he works for now really isn't right for him. I mean, you can't really blame him for wanting to leave them."

Lee didn't see any point in disagreeing with her, but he didn't think Kent's desire to open his storefront law office had anything to do with the merits of the firm he was currently working for. No, if Kent were to be dissuaded from his scheme, he would have to be persuaded that he would be jeopardizing Allison's well-being, and the well-being of their marriage and their children, by his stubborn insistence on sticking with his plan.

But still . . . Lee knew this was going to be touchy. He'd have to be careful not to offend Kent. Maybe the way to approach this would be to stress that as a novice lawyer, Kent would be limited in the things he could do for the people he wanted most to help. If Kent could be convinced that once he'd established himself, become a successful lawyer with some experience and contacts, he could effect more change than he ever could as a latter day Don Quixote.

Lee was still mulling over the problem when he pulled up in front of Diana's town house, only five minutes late.

As he walked up to her front door, he wondered if he should talk to Diana about this. He wanted to, but he remembered how defensive she'd been the last time they'd discussed Kent. Unfortunately whenever Lee said anything that Diana construed as a criticism of her son, she got mighty testy.

He'd better keep quiet. Diana was edgy enough as it was. Lee certainly didn't want to give her any added reason to worry. He could settle this thing with Kent quietly—man to man.

And Diana would never be the wiser.

Chapter Thirteen

"Has Allison mentioned anything to you about her and Kent quarreling?" Diana asked. She and Lee were lying in her bed, drowsy and sated after making love. It was the first time that day Diana had felt completely relaxed.

"Why do you ask?" Lee stroked her cheek, and Diana closed her eyes. At times like this it felt so wonderful to put aside her public persona, to just snuggle into Lee's arms and pretend nothing else existed. At times like this she could even imagine what they had together might last. That they might actually find a way to mesh their two lives.

"I don't know. I got the feeling today that something was wrong. Didn't you notice anything?"

"Well, actually, I *did* notice some sort of strain between them, but attributed it to nerves, which is pretty normal, what with the wedding only a month away." He squeezed her a little tighter and nuzzled his lips against her forehead. "I wouldn't worry about it. They'll be okay."

"I guess you're right...." Diana traced a lazy circle on his chest. "But I don't know...Kent looked so unhappy...I thought they might have had a fight. But if Allison didn't mention anything to you, maybe I'm wrong."

She felt him tense. The action was almost imperceptible, just a slight tightening of his body. "They're both adults. If they have problems, they'll work them out." Diana thought his answer was evasive. The thought crossed her mind that he was hiding something from her. She almost said so, but he kissed her forehead, his warm breath sending a pleasurable tingle down her spine. "By the way, I've been meaning to ask you, how's the new temporary receptionist working out?"

Diana sighed. "She isn't. She can't seem to keep anything straight. I've asked the agency to replace her." She slid her hand over Lee's torso, taking comfort from his solid strength. "I miss Jackie. I wish she hadn't gone back to Chad."

They'd been over this territory before, so Lee didn't answer. He just stroked her back. Diana sighed again. "You know, there are times when I wish I'd never opened my own agency," she admitted.

"I know."

"You do? How could you know?"

Lee chuckled. "Diana, sometimes you amaze me. Don't you know that anyone who has ever held any kind of position of authority has had self-doubts more than once? Has wondered if all the aggravation is worth it? Has wished they could just chuck everything and go off and be a beach bum?"

Diana considered this. "I'm sure that's true, but...do you ever doubt yourself, Lee?"

"Sometimes."

"Really? You always seem so sure of yourself."

He laughed. "I'm a man. I'm supposed to act as if I know everything." His laugh deepened, and he kissed her ear, whispering. "Occasionally, though, I realize I still have a few things to learn." He brushed his hand over her breasts, teasing them into attention. "You've taught me a lot, you know."

"Stop that! I'm trying to have a serious conversation with you!" She slapped his hand away playfully.

Instead of stopping, he turned her face toward his. When his lips met hers, all conversation ceased, and all thoughts of Allison and Kent, self-doubt and problems, evaporated from Diana's mind.

But later, after Lee left, Diana thought about their conversation again. She couldn't get rid of the idea that Lee had effectively sidestepped her concerns, that he really *was* hiding something from her.

Lee called Kent early Saturday morning. "I didn't wake you, did I?"

"No, sir. I've already been to the gym and back."

"I was wondering if you have any plans for the remainder of the morning?"

"Uh, no..."

"Good. How would you like to come over to my place? I'd like to talk to you about something."

"All right."

At eleven o'clock Kent arrived.

Lee clasped his shoulder and said, "Good to see you, son. Come on in."

A few minutes later they were seated in the living room. Both had fresh cups of coffee, and Lee had set out some Danish pastry. He had thought a long time about how to introduce the subject. He finally decided to be blunt. "Kent, Allison told me about the disagreement the two of you had."

Kent's blue eyes clouded.

"She wasn't telling tales or anything," Lee hastened to add. "She's unhappy, and she knows you're unhappy, and she had to talk about it to someone."

Kent nodded, strain written all over his face. "I understand. I . . . I figured she'd talk to you." He took a swallow of coffee, then set the cup on the coffee table and leaned forward. "I might as well admit it, sir. I don't know what to do."

Lee nodded. Although he knew what he was about to say was the right thing, he felt a tug of sympathy for Kent. He understood Kent's dreams. He'd had his own unrealistic dreams once himself. "You know, I understand your feelings," he began.

"I'm not sure you do," Kent said. His gaze met Lee's.

"Believe me, son, I do. But I'm Allison's father, and her welfare is more important to me than anything."

"Her welfare is important to me, too."

"Then you shouldn't have any problem making the right decision," Lee said smoothly. "You and I both know you won't be able to make enough money practicing storefront law to support the two of you."

"If I thought that, I would never consider opening the office," Kent said, jaw hardening.

Lee felt another tug, this one of admiration. The kid had backbone. He wasn't going to lie down and let Lee run over him. Allison was headstrong sometimes, so it was good to know that if necessary Kent could stand up to her. "Look, Kent," he said slowly, choosing his words with care, "by the very nature of the kind of office you want to open, fees will be almost nonexistent. Can't you compromise?"

"In what way?"

"How about, in addition to Joel, finding several other attorneys who are interested in this kind of project, and each of you committing say, one or two evenings a week, and maybe one weekend a month to it?"

"You mean work full-time for another firm? Just do the other on a part-time, volunteer basis?"

"Exactly. That way you'll have the best of both worlds."

"But—"

"Son, I know you love Allison. But love alone isn't going to pay the rent and put food on the table. Not to speak of the added things—the things that make life fun—like travel and entertainment and nice clothes." He didn't add, *the things Allison has had all of her life,* because he knew Kent wasn't stupid. "And what about later? When you have children? How will you be able to provide a secure future for them?"

Kent bowed his head, and Lee remained quiet.

Seconds ticked by, the only sound was that of the mantel clock chiming the quarter hour.

Finally Kent lifted his head. "I suppose I could think about your suggestion," he said.

"I think Allison would be very supportive of your volunteer work if you were to decide on this solution," Lee said, pressing his advantage. "I think she'd be proud of you and would do everything she could to help you out."

Kent swallowed, his expression uncertain.

Lee felt sorry for him. Growing up was hard. "I know Ben Keating real well," he said, naming the managing part-

...er in one of Houston's most prestigious law firms. "We
went to college together. I think he'd be very interested in
you." He smiled. "How would you like to work for Keating and Shaw?"

"I ... I don't know. I hadn't thought about it."

"Well, you think about it. And while you're thinking
about it, send me a copy of your résumé. I'll see that Ben
gets it."

Kent nodded.

"Uh, I wondered ... have you discussed this with your
mother?"

"No, sir. I...I thought about it, but, well...I don't want
her to worry."

Lee nodded his approval. "Good. I'm glad you haven't.
The *would* worry." Lee knew the battle wasn't over yet, but
he had a good feeling about its outcome. He thought that
once Kent had had time to mull everything over, he'd realize he really didn't have a better choice. And Lee was confident that once he had an offer in hand from Keating and
Shaw, the decision would be easy to make.

Although Diana had told Lee she wasn't going to worry
about the kids, she hadn't been able to get them off her
mind. She'd almost mentioned the subject again Saturday
evening when Lee took her to see a French mime troupe at
Jones Hall. But then something else happened, which drove
all thoughts of Kent and Allison's problems out of her mind.

It was intermission, and Lee had bought two glasses of
wine. He and Diana were standing on the mezzanine level of
the hall, sipping their wine and looking out over the chat-
tering crowd below.

"Are you enjoying the show?" Lee asked.

Diana smiled. "Yes. Much more than I thought I would."

He returned her smile. "You look very lovely tonight," he said softly. "Blue is your color."

A warm glow spread through Diana. "I don't get much chance to wear this outfit. It's hardly ever cold enough." A "blue norther" had swept across Texas that morning, and the mercury had plunged from a mild sixty-eight to a frigid thirty-seven in just two short hours. The newscasters were predicting that it would fall even further the next day.

Just then, a couple walked up to them, big smiles on their faces. "Lee!" the woman said. "What a nice surprise!"

"Hello, B.J., Paul. How are you?" Lee said.

Diana had known this moment would come—a time when someone Lee knew would see them together. She just hoped these people, whoever they were, weren't close friends. She still wasn't ready for everyone to know about the two of them.

"Diana," Lee said, turning to her, "I'd like you to meet B. J. Barrette and her husband, Paul. And this is Diana Sorensen." Diana shook hands with the couple, who were both attractive people in their forties. "How do you do?" she said politely. *B. J. Barrette. Now why does that name sound familiar?*

B. J. Barrette, who had bright, lively dark eyes, smiled at Lee. "I'd heard you were back in town. It's great to see you." She turned to Diana, giving her a careful appraisal. "Sorensen," she said. "Hmm. Are you related to Webster Sorensen?"

"No. Not that I know of," Diana said, wishing the dimming of the lights announcing the end of intermission would hurry up and happen before B.J. asked any more questions.

"I know just about everyone in Houston," B.J. continued. "So I'm sure I must know you."

Her husband laughed. "She's not exaggerating. She probably *does* know everyone in Houston."

B.J. gave him an arch look. "Well, it's my *business* to know."

"B.J. writes the 'Around Houston' column for the *Herald*," Lee explained. His gaze met Diana's for an instant, and she saw regret—and apology.

Diana wished she could disappear. 'Around Houston' was the most-read gossip column in Houston, and she suddenly had no doubt she would read her own name in it the following morning.

"What do you do?" B.J. said to Diana.

B.J.'s tenacity reminded Diana of a West Highland terrier Kent's father had given him for his fifth birthday. Once that little dog latched onto something, he'd hung on for dear life. "I'm in real estate."

"Real estate." B.J.'s eyes narrowed.

Diana could see the wheels turning. She waited for the inevitable.

"Of course," B.J. said, a triumphant smile lighting her face. "Sorensen Realty!"

"Yes," Diana said.

"Diana's son is Allison's fiancé," Lee said.

Oh, darn, darn, darn.

"Oh, of course," B.J. said again. "I should have realized! I knew I'd heard the name recently."

She gave Diana another thorough inspection, then turned her shrewd gaze on Lee and, just as Diana thought she couldn't stand the tension another minute, the lights dimmed.

"Darling," Paul Barrette said, "we'd better be getting back to our seats."

They all smiled and murmured pleasantries, and finall
the Barrettes were gone. Diana sent a fervent prayer heav
enward. Maybe B.J. would have so many interesting peopl
to write about, she would forget all about her and Lee.

Diana sighed with relief when she opened the Sunday pa
per and hurriedly found B. J. Barrette's column. Sh
scanned it quickly. Thank goodness. There was no mentio
of the previous evening.

Wait a minute. No mention at all? That was odd.

Diana looked over the column again. Slowly the realiza
tion came that the reason there was no mention of Satur
day night was that B.J. had probably already turned in he
Sunday column before their meeting at Jones Hall.

It was Monday's column Diana had to worry about.

Kent called Allison early Sunday morning. "We have t
talk," he said without preamble. They hadn't seen eac
other the previous evening. Allison had pleaded fatigue, bu
Kent suspected she was punishing him. "I'd like to com
over."

"Now?" she asked.

"Yes. I'll be there in an hour."

An hour and a half later they were seated side by side o
the love seat in the living room of the guest house. Al
though Allison's grandparents had encouraged her to mov
into the main house after Lee took possession of his nev
house, Allison still hadn't done so. Kent guessed once he
Aunt Elizabeth returned from Quebec, where she was vis
iting friends, Allison would move, since Elizabeth had in
dicated her desire to take over the guest house.

"Honey, we've got to settle this," Kent said, taking Alli
son's hand.

She bit her bottom lip and nodded. She lifted her gaze to
is, and in the depths of her big eyes he saw hope and un-
ertainty. "Daddy said he'd talked to you," she said.

"Yeah, he did. And I've been thinking about what he
aid."

"Have . . . have you made any decision?"

Kent studied her upturned face. He wished . . . he wished
were possible to make her happy and still keep his dream
tact, but he was terribly afraid he was wishing for the im-
ossible. "Not yet. But I *am* exploring all the possibilities.
ve talked to Joel, and I've contacted a couple of other guys
ho graduated with me. And Joel said he'll talk to a couple
f his buddies."

She squeezed his hand tighter. A happy light appeared in
er eyes. "Oh, Kent, that's great."

"Yeah." So why did he still feel so depressed over it? Why
ouldn't he just accept the inevitable? Why was he still
olding out a slim hope that somehow, some way, this could
e resolved in a way that everyone would be satisfied?

"Darling, you won't be sorry. I promise you."

Later, as they sat in the kitchen and ate the tuna salad
andwiches Allison had made for their lunch, Kent said,
Wednesday is my mother's birthday."

"Oh, Kent! Why didn't you tell me sooner? We need to
uy her something!"

Kent was a bit taken aback, but quickly realized Allison
as right. It *would* be nice for them to give his mother a
resent from the both of them. "Okay. We'll go shopping
omorrow night, if that's okay with you."

"Sure."

"And I thought maybe we could take her to dinner
Vednesday night."

"Of course." She smiled at him, then rose, comin
around to his side of the table. She leaned over and kisse
his cheek, her light flowery fragrance drifting over him. H
turned his head and gazed into her beautiful eyes. "Honey
you've made me so happy today," she whispered.

Kent pulled her onto his lap, and as he lost himself in th
sweetness of her mouth, he told himself that everythin
would work out. He loved her, and any sacrifice he had t
make to keep her was worth it.

Diana opened the Monday morning paper. There it was—
her worst fears confirmed. She quickly read the reference.

Spied at Jones Hall on Saturday night, looking just as
handsome and debonair as always, was Lee Gabriel
who, along with his gorgeous daughter, Allison, has
recently moved back to Our Town. Most of you will
recall that Lee, who just took over as executive v.p. at
Berringer, Houston, had been based in Paris for
many years. Saturday night he was squiring the lovely,
blond Diana Sorensen, owner of Sorensen Realty and
a familiar name in Houston real estate circles. Diana is
the mother of Kent Sorensen, whose engagement to
Allison Gabriel was recently announced. This columnist is wondering if there's something brewing between
the parents of the soon-to-be-married couple. That
would be nice for Diana but terrible for all the other
femmes around town. Guess we'll have to wait and see,
won't we, gals?

Oh, no! It was much worse than Diana had imagined
could be. It would have been bad enough if B.J. had jus
mentioned seeing Diana and Lee together, but to specula

on their relationship, to imply that there was something going on between them . . .

Diana cringed as she reread the item. She heaved a sigh. There was nothing to be done about this. Everyone read B. J.'s column. There were bound to be repercussions, so she'd better decide how she intended to play it from now on.

She was right. She was the brunt of a lot of teasing over the next couple of days. Every one of her friends and business associates managed to call her or mention the column when they saw her. She bore up under their teasing, deliberately treating the whole thing as something casual.

But she wondered what Kent and Allison were thinking. Especially Allison. She wanted to ask Lee if Allison had mentioned anything to him, but he was awfully touchy about her desire to keep their relationship a secret, so she didn't. She figured she'd find out Wednesday night when Allison and Kent took her to dinner.

"Happy Birthday!" chorused Sunny and Diana's other agents as Diana strode into the bull pen Wednesday morning.

She smiled when she saw the birthday cake and wrapped gifts. She wasn't sure how the tradition had started, but they always made a big deal out of birthdays at the agency. Actually she kind of liked it.

Later, in her office, Sunny said, "So what are you and TD&D doing tonight?"

Diana grinned. TD&D was Sunny's code name for Lee. "Kent and Allison are taking me to dinner tonight. Tall, Dark, and Dangerous doesn't even know today is my birthday."

"Why didn't you tell him? Maybe he would have given you a ring!" She laughed.

Diana threw a paper clip at Sunny's retreating bac "You'd better run," she muttered. An engagement rin Sure. But a tiny flutter of something she couldn't nan caused her to take a deep breath.

All day Sunny's teasing remark floated at the edges of h mind. *An engagement ring.* Why did the suggestion mal her feel so...so...glittery? As if someone were shaking go dust inside her?

Diana told herself to settle down. She told herself sl wasn't in love with Lee. She told herself she had no desire marry him. She said these things over and over again.

She was still saying them when, at three o'clock, the ter porary receptionist knocked on her office door. "M Sorensen? This package was just delivered for you," sl said, her breathy voice grating on Diana's nerves.

"Oh?"

The young woman handed Diana a small oblong bo about the size of a shoe box. Diana's heart started to be hard when she saw the sender's name.

Lee.

With fingers that trembled slightly, she used her lett opener to slit open the wrapping. Then she opened the i ner box and removed the shredded tissue.

What she saw nestled inside took her breath away. It w an exquisite mate to her Lalique cat, this one stretching h front paws and pointing his rear end in the air. Swallowi hard, she lifted the creamy gift card and read the scrawl message:

Happy Birthday. All my love. Lee.

How had he known?

All my love.

It didn't mean anything. People said things such as *all n love* without really considering what the words meant.

But her heart refused to believe her. Her heart expanded with a shimmering happiness. As her fingers caressed the smooth crystal, Diana thought about all the times she and Lee had been together. How her feelings for him had intensified rather than diminished since they'd first made love. How she had grown to depend upon him. How just the sight of him could make her feel like a young girl again.

She held the figurine close to her breast. She could feel her heart beating.

Face it, you ninny. You're in love with Lee.

And maybe, just maybe, he was in love with her, too.

Chapter Fourteen

Wednesday evening, when Diana arrived home, there was a message from Lee on her answering machine. Still filled with a shaky happiness over his gift, Diana pressed the familiar numbers.

"I should be angry with you," Lee said, but his voice was teasing. "Why didn't you tell me today was your birthday?"

"Birthdays aren't a big deal."

"Yes, they are."

"How *did* you find out? Did Allison tell you?"

"Yes. She mentioned that she and Kent were taking you out to dinner tonight." His voice softened. "Did you get the package I sent?"

"Yes, and...it's so beautiful, Lee. Thank you so much."

"I'm glad you like it."

"I love it." *And I love you, too.* She wanted to say the words so badly.

"Diana..." His voice dropped to a husky whisper.

Her heart thrummed in her throat.

"Are Kent and Allison picking you up tonight?"

"No. I'm meeting them at the restaurant."

"Good. Then you can come here afterward. We'll have our own private celebration."

"Oh, Lee, I shouldn't. It'll probably be late, and we both have to work tomorrow."

"I have a special night planned," he murmured seductively. "Full of all kinds of...secret...things."

Diana felt exactly the way she had the time she'd visited the Sears Tower in Chicago. She'd gone up to the observation level and looked down, and it felt as if the bottom were dropping out of her stomach. Lee's words produced the same feeling, with his hint of dark delights.

"I have another present for you, too," Lee continued softly. "One not meant for public view."

What woman could resist? As she hung up the phone, Diana hugged herself. She had never thought of herself as having a sensual nature, but lately, she'd had to revise that opinion. Lately she'd felt positively decadent. She shivered in anticipation of whatever Lee had planned for the night.

But first she had the dinner with Allison and Kent. She had mixed emotions about spending the evening with them. She hadn't been in their combined company since Thanksgiving, and she hoped whatever it was that had caused such a strain between them that day was over and done with. On top of that, she hoped they hadn't seen B. J. Barrette's column on Monday. If they had, and any mention was made of it, Diana wasn't sure how she should play it or what to say.

By the time she left for the restaurant, she was nervous and wishing the dinner was going to be just her and Kent.

The evening started out well. It was obvious to Diana that whatever had been wrong between them, Kent and Allison were okay now, and that was a relief. They seemed happy and Diana didn't sense any tension between them. And thankfully, no mention was made of the *Herald* column either. By the time they had their coffee and dessert, Diana was relaxed and chiding herself for worrying when there obviously wasn't anything to worry about.

Diana opened her birthday present from the two of them, a gorgeous gold bangle bracelet, and with misty eyes, thanked both of them. "It's so beautiful," she said, putting it on right then. "And it goes so perfectly with my necklace."

"That's what Allison said when we saw it," Kent said.

Allison smiled. "I'm glad you like it." Then, very casually, and taking Diana completely off guard, she said, "By the way, did you happen to see B. J. Barrette's column in the *Herald* Monday?"

Diana was proud of herself. She kept her voice just as casual and even managed an offhand chuckle. "Yes. Honestly! That woman must not have anything better to write about."

Allison laughed, but Diana thought there was a false note to her laughter. "Isn't that the truth! B.J. loves to print the wildest speculation—the more outrageous, the better. Usually, though, there's *some* truth in what she says."

Kent frowned. "What are you two talking about?"

"Oh, it's nothing," Diana said. "Just a silly gossip column."

"I know what column you're talking about. But what did B. J. Barrette say?"

"Evidently she saw my father and Diana at Jones Hall Saturday night, and she tried to make a big deal out of it," Allison answered. "She insinuated that they were an item." She laughed again, the sound grating on Diana's nerves. "Dad would probably like to kill her. He hates that kind of thing, but it always seems to be happening to him." She shrugged. "Oh, well. What can you do? But B.J. ought to know better!"

Kent gave Diana a bewildered look, as if to say, *What's going on here?* but Diana's gaze locked with Allison's. Her topaz eyes blazed a challenge.

"How'd you and Dad happen to go to Jones Hall, anyway?" she said, her eyes never leaving Diana's face.

"He wanted to see that French mime troup and didn't want to go alone, so he asked me," Diana said evenly. *I will not get angry. I will not say anything I will be sorry for. I will not do anything stupid.*

"It's funny he never mentioned it to *me*," Allison said. "Heavens, I would have been *happy* to go see the mimes with him. He knows that!"

Diana let the remark pass. There was no sense in getting into a tug-of-war with Allison. Diana reminded herself that Allison was possessive about her father, that losing her mother when she was a teenager had made her very vulnerable where her father was concerned.

But even as Diana told herself these things, Allison's obvious displeasure over the idea that Lee could be interested in Diana, hurt. And Diana knew Allison was suspicious. Otherwise, she wouldn't have gone to so much trouble to act as if B. J. Barrette's comments were ridiculous. No, if Allison weren't afraid there really *was* some truth in B.J.'s statements, she would have been able just to laugh and tease Diana.

For the rest of the evening, Diana was aware of Allison's speculative gaze, and she wondered just what her future daughter-in-law would think if she knew where Diana was going after she left them.

Lee had been right. Diana never *would* forget this birthday. For days afterward, she blushed every time she thought about all the things he'd done to make the night memorable.

The red lace teddy he'd given her.

The satin sheets on his bed.

The heated oil.

And, most memorable of all, the red satin bow he'd tied around...

Diana squirmed in her chair as she relived the moment Lee had opened his front door, and she'd seen him dressed in nothing but his soft velour robe.

She closed her eyes as she thought about the delicious moment when Lee, eyes smoky in the lamplight, told her to put on the teddy and model it for him. He lay back against the pillows of his bed and watched her, eyes dark with desire—as, self-conscious at first—Diana slowly walked toward him.

She shivered as she remembered how he'd smiled, then whispered, "Come here, Diana. I have a friend who's aching to see you." He patted the bed next to him.

And Diana, feeling wanton and sexy in the lacy teddy, stretched out on the bed.

"Untie my robe," Lee whispered.

Feeling as if her bones were melting, Diana did as she was told. But when she uncovered his "friend" and saw the bow, she started to laugh.

No, it wasn't likely she'd ever forget her forty-third birthday.

On December 15 Kent received an offer from Keating and Shaw. He'd known it would come. He already knew his future father-in-law well enough to know that when Lee said something was going to happen, it happened.

Kent looked at the letter, all kinds of emotions swirling around inside him. The offer was extremely generous, more than Kent would have ever dreamed possible, and with a firm such as Keating and Shaw, it was only the beginning. If Kent did well, the sky would be the limit there. He knew he should pick up the phone and call Lee and thank him. He knew he should also call Ben Keating and accept. That's what anyone with any sense would do.

He reread the letter. They wanted an answer within the next week.

Kent stared at the letter for a long time.

After her birthday, the rest of December seemed to fly by. Diana attended three showers for Allison. She did her Christmas shopping and wrote out all her Christmas cards and got them mailed. She put in her usual long hours at work. And every minute of her spare time was spent with Lee.

The wedding, scheduled for two days after Christmas, would soon be upon them.

Then a week before Christmas, Jackie called. She was leaving Chad for good. When she asked Diana if she could come back and stay with her awhile, Diana didn't hesitate.

"Yes, you know you can," she said.

"I'm filing for a divorce," Jackie said. "I told him when I came back the last time that if it happened again, that was it. No more chances."

So Jackie came to Houston the following day, and Diana, relieved, let her temporary receptionist go. Two days later Jackie was once again installed in the front office. Everyone was glad to see her back, and Diana was pleased to see how nice to her they all were.

That night, Lee had a meeting to attend, and Diana was glad because she wanted to spend the evening with Jackie and the kids. She knew that even though this decision Jackie had made was a wise one that in the long run she wouldn't regret, she also knew these first days would be tough for her and her children. Holidays were always tough, but this one would be very difficult. Diana wanted to help Jackie as much as she could.

She took them out to dinner. Afterward, once the kids were in bed for the night, she and Jackie sat over glasses of wine and talked. Diana listened as Jackie related the series of events that led up to her leaving Chad again. Finally, when Jackie was spent, Diana said, "Now it's my turn."

Jackie listened quietly as Diana told her about Lee.

"See?" Jackie said when Diana finished. "Didn't I tell you he wasn't the kind of man to lose interest?" She smiled. "I'm happy for you, Diana. He sounds wonderful."

Diana nodded.

"What's the matter?"

"Nothing." But Diana heard the doubt in her voice.

"Are you scared?" Jackie said softly.

Diana nodded again. There was a big lump in her throat, and for the life of her she couldn't imagine why.

"What're you scared of?"

Diana tried to answer but she couldn't. What was wrong with her? She felt ridiculously close to tears.

"You're scared because you're in love with him," Jackie said, reaching for Diana's hand. "That's it, isn't it?"

Slow tears trickled down Diana's face. She angrily brushed them away. "I'm being ridiculous."

"Honey, being in love is nothing to cry about." Jackie moved closer and put her arm around Diana's shoulders. "There's something else eating you. Tell me what it is."

Diana could hear her heart beating. "Even if Lee is serious about me," she finally said, "Allison will never accept me. She doesn't like me."

"So who gives a darn?" Jackie said. "Not *my* sister. Not the same sister who has never backed away from a challenge in her entire life!" Jackie chuckled. "Besides, I don't think you like her much, either!"

"Well, I'm trying to like her. She's not even trying! The minute she thinks I might be getting too close to her precious father, her claws come out."

"Well, you wouldn't be marrying Allison, honey. You'd be marrying Lee. And once that happened, Allison would have to accept it. I wouldn't waste another minute worrying about what she thinks."

"Lee hasn't said a word about marriage."

"Didn't you tell me you told him you weren't interested in marriage?"

Diana sighed. "Yes."

"Well, then? Don't you think it's up to you to let him know you've changed your mind?"

"But what if..." Diana swallowed. "What if...now that he's...gotten what he wants from me...he's not interested?" She had just given voice to her greatest fear of all.

"You mean you think that's all he wanted? Sex?"

Diana shrugged. "No. Yes. No. Oh, shoot! I don't know what I think!"

"Diana, honey, I know you. I can't imagine you being interested in any man who was that shallow. You'd have run like hell if Lee was really like that."

Diana wet her lips. "I'm not sure any woman has any judgment at all when it comes to men."

"Your judgment is just fine."

"The thing is, where he's concerned, I don't seem to have any willpower, any sense at all. I...I just get all quivery, and emotional, and all...all *needy!*" She stared at Jackie. " hate feeling needy!"

Jackie smiled. "I know. We all do. But, honey, that's the nature of the beast. We all need other people."

"Fine. Other people are fine. But why do we have to need *men!*"

Jackie started to laugh, and after a few minutes, Diana did, too. They laughed for a long time, the laughter lifting their spirits. They hugged, and Diana whispered, "I'm glad you're here."

"Me, too."

Diana was having the rehearsal dinner at the Rainbow Lodge. She'd considered having it catered and at home, but decided it would put too much pressure on her, so she quickly discarded that idea. The Rainbow Lodge was a good choice, she thought. She had booked a private room upstairs with its own balcony overlooking the wooded grounds. If it was a cool night, there would be a fire in the fireplace, and the room was decorated for Christmas.

Diana conferred with the catering manager the day before the dinner, and satisfied that everything would be to her iking, took the rest of the day off to take care of last-minute errands.

The day of the rehearsal dinner, which was the day before Christmas Eve, dawned bright and clear, but cold. Diana talked to Lee briefly that afternoon.

"After the wedding is over, we have to talk," he said.

"About what?"

"About us."

For the rest of the day, each time she thought about those two little words, her stomach tightened from nerves. What would she do if Lee proposed marriage? She knew she loved him, but did she love him enough to completely change her life? Did she really want to deal with Allison's antagonism and all the stress that being married to a powerhouse like Lee would entail? And what about their differences? Would those differences matter?

And don't forget your track record, which isn't so great.

She closed her eyes. This was such a big step she was contemplating, such an important decision. She wished she could make it the way she made other decisions, using logic and common sense. She wished she could just put aside her emotions.

But she couldn't.

And she didn't have long to think about it, either.

She was going to have to make her decision soon.

That night Diana dressed carefully. She'd bought another new dress, this one a dark blue and taupe print silk with a shirred bodice, flowing skirt and a narrow gold belt. With it she wore gold pumps and a small gold mesh evening bag. Being in love—or maybe it was all that good sex, she thought ruefully—had put a glow in her eyes and skin, and as she checked herself out in her full-length mirror, she knew she looked better than she'd ever looked in her life.

Clyde jumped up onto her dresser and eyed her "Mrrow," he growled.

Diana grinned. Maybe he thought so, too. That sure sounded like a growl of approval to her.

Diana was picking up her mother as soon as she could leave the rehearsal. She wanted to be at the restaurant a bit early, make sure everything was set up the way it was supposed to be.

The rehearsal went off without a hitch. Diana's part was over quickly. Once she'd lighted her candle and been told how and when to walk down the aisle and where to sit, she asked if she could leave.

But she was running about fifteen minutes later than she'd told her mother she thought she'd be, and Barbara griped about that for at least five minutes. For the remainder of the short trip to the restaurant, she grumbled about the black dress she'd had to wear.

"Mother," Diana finally said in exasperation, "your dress looks lovely. *You* look lovely. Now, please, would you stop complaining? I'd like to enjoy this evening."

Barbara grumbled under her breath for a few more seconds, but then she subsided, and Diana sighed with relief when they turned into the driveway of the Lodge. She relinquished her car keys to the valet parking attendant, then she and Barbara slowly climbed the wooden steps and walked across the little bridge to the main door.

Diana looked around. She'd always liked this place. The setting was fairy-tale-like with the gazebo off to the left where many weddings were held, the lights strung through the tall trees and the bayou in the distance. Small animals prowled the grounds, and Diana knew they would often get brave enough to venture onto the wooden deck that extended the full-length of the restaurant across the back. The diners always seemed to get a kick out of seeing the animals looking at them through the plate-glass windows.

They entered the restaurant and followed the hostess up the narrow, winding stairs to their private room on the second floor. The Lodge was a refurbished Victorian house that had been added to but still retained its old-world charm.

When Barbara and Diana entered the room where the dinner would be held, Diana was surprised to see Lee already there. Acutely conscious of her mother behind her, Diana said, "Lee! What are you doing here?"

"After I walked Allison up the aisle and handed her over to Kent, there wasn't any reason for me to stay. And I thought you might need some help." His eyes said, *I wish we were alone because I want to kiss you.*

Diana looked away. Her heart was beating too fast. She was very glad the only lights in the room came from the candles and the Christmas tree, otherwise she was afraid her mother would see the telltale stain of pink she knew had crept up her cheeks. "Everything is ready, as you can see," she said.

Lee turned toward Barbara. "Mrs. Kent. It's so nice to see you again." He kissed Barbara's cheek, and Barbara smiled happily. "And don't you look lovely."

"Oh, this old dress—"

Diana interrupted her. "Why don't we sit down and uncork one of these bottles of wine?" Maybe a glass of wine would relax her. Lee's eyes twinkled as if he knew exactly what she was thinking, but he didn't say anything else to rattle her. Instead, to Diana's everlasting gratitude, he devoted himself to Barbara for the next twenty minutes.

Then Allison, looking breathtakingly beautiful in a black velvet dress, and Kent—a curiously subdued Kent—looking handsome by her side, arrived.

Diana searched Kent's eyes as he walked forward. She knew him so well, and all her instincts told her something was bothering him. Oh, Lordy, she'd be glad when this wedding was over! Everyone's nerves were stretched to the limit.

Within minutes, everyone had arrived: Jackie and her children, all shiny-faced and expectant; Carol and her family; the Marlowes, including the beautiful Elizabeth Whitman, all dolled up in a clingy red crepe dress; Joel Bartlett and Marcy Howard, who were the best man and maid-of-honor; and the other four attendants and their spouses or dates. Even the minister and his wife came, and from the warm greetings given them by the Marlowes, Diana knew they must be old friends.

And finally, Kent's father and his wife.

Diana tried to remember how long it had been since she'd been in Bill's company. Not since Kent had graduated from college, and then only briefly. But tonight, even though she was nervous about many things, seeing him was not one of them.

She was able to greet him casually, and she realized that she no longer cared at all what he thought. It was a very liberating feeling.

"You're looking great, Diana," he said.

"Thanks." She turned to Maggie, his wife, an attractive brunette. Diana felt kind of sorry for Maggie, because she was certain Bill had not changed. He was probably still chasing everything in skirts. But that was Maggie's problem, not hers.

When Diana turned her attention back to the others, it didn't surprise her to find that Elizabeth Whitman had latched on to Lee and was hanging on his arm while batting her eyelashes a mile a minute. Diana turned away to hide her grin. Elizabeth no longer worried her, either.

But Kent worried her. And Lee worried her. And what would happen once this wedding was over worried her.

That was enough for one woman to worry about, she decided.

Soon they all settled into their seats, and the dinner began. Diana welcomed everyone, then the men began to make toasts. Diana was grateful that Lee wasn't seated close to her. In fact, she had to lean forward to see him, so she was spared the strain of feeling his eyes on her the entire evening.

Soon some of the women joined in the toasting, and the party livened up even more. Diana looked around with satisfaction. Everything was going well, better than she'd hoped. This curious mix of people and families had worked out just fine.

She decided to make a toast herself. She stood, raising her glass. "To Allison and Kent," she said. "May you be as happy for the rest of your lives as you are today."

Everyone clapped, and Diana, just a bit choked up by the realization that Kent was actually getting married, sat down.

Then Kent stood. "I guess it's my turn now." He smiled down at Allison, whose face was raised toward his. "To my beautiful bride. I love you."

There was a chorus of *"Ahhs,"* then more clapping. Kent sat, leaning over to kiss Allison. For a while, the kissing continued because the guests began to tap their spoons against their wineglasses, which, Carol explained to Diana, meant they wanted to see the bride and groom smooch.

The next hour passed in a blur for Diana. She was surrounded by so many people, and there was so much on her mind, and her emotions were so near the surface, that she knew she'd never remember much about this night.

But then the dinner itself was over, and the waiters cleared the tables and began to serve the dessert—chocolate mousse, Kent's favorite. Coffee came, and the laughter and good feeling in the room increased.

Diana glanced at Kent. He seemed more relaxed now than he had when he'd first arrived. She had probably imagined that something was bothering him. He had probably just been nervous because the wedding was only a few days away.

A few minutes later, Allison stood. "I'm the only one who hasn't made a toast tonight," she said. A hush fell over the room. Kent looked up at her and smiled. She returned his smile, then said, "To my future husband, who is going to set the world on fire in his new position as an associate at Keating and Shaw!"

Diana went rigid with shock as the assembled guests smiled and murmured and offered Kent their congratulations. When had Kent decided to go to work for Keating and Shaw? When had he even got an offer? She looked at her son, who looked just as unhappy about Allison's announcement as Diana felt.

"Uh, Allison," he said, touching her arm.

Eyes shining, Allison looked at him. Their gazes locked. Very slowly, her smile faded. "What?" she said.

It was obvious to everyone that something was wrong. The chatter and laughter subsided.

Kent cleared his throat. "Uh, look, honey, I...uh...I thought we'd talk about this later, but..." He took her arm. "Let's go outside for a minute."

Allison's gaze never left his face. Her tawny eyes, so full of love and happiness only moments before, dimmed as they tudied his expression. She allowed him to lead her out to he balcony.

Diana didn't know what to do. A hush had fallen over the oom.

"You *are* accepting the offer, aren't you Kent?" Alli- on's words floated clearly through the night air.

In that moment, Diana wanted to get up and race outside nd put her arms around Kent. She wanted to protect him rom everyone and everything, just the way she had when he as a baby. But she knew she couldn't. And she knew he ouldn't even want her to.

Kent's voice never wavered. "Honey, I'm sorry. I should ave told you. But I didn't want anything to spoil tonight, o I planned to tell you later. I turned down the offer this fternoon."

Diana was trying not to listen, but she couldn't help it. No ne in the room was even pretending to do anything else. hey were all caught up in the drama of the scene unfold- g on the balcony.

"You . . . turned . . . down . . . the . . . offer . . . this . . . af- rnoon." It sounded as if Allison were biting off each word. Kent, how could you? How could you do this to me?"

At that moment, Lee stood. His gaze met Diana's. She ould see the concern shadowing his face.

"Honey, it'll be okay. I promise you," Kent said.

Even though her heart ached for him, Diana was proud f Kent. He wasn't trying to weasel his way out of this. But e felt sorry for both him and Allison, because this was a rrible way and a terrible place for this to happen.

For a long moment Allison said nothing. The room was ery still. Even Diana's mother seemed speechless. Then, so ftly, Diana almost didn't catch all the words, Allison said, I'm sorry, Kent, but it's not okay."

"Please, honey..."

"Diana, what's going on?" her mother said.

Diana ignored her mother because at that moment Alli son reentered the room. Diana saw the tense set of he mouth, the way she struggled to keep her composure. Ken walked in behind her. He touched her arm.

"Allison, honey, I know you're angry..."

"I'm not angry." She bit her bottom lip, which was nov quivering uncontrollably. "I'm terribly disappointed, bu I'm not angry."

"Let's go somewhere and talk about this," Kent said "Let me explain."

Diana's chest felt tight, and even though she was as mes merized as the rest of the guests, she was aware of the shocl and dismay on Jinx Marlowe's face, and the disbelief on th faces of many others. And Lee. What was he thinking?

"I don't want to talk anymore," Allison said, not eve trying to stop the tears that now slid from her eyes. "You'v made your choice. You've decided your future. Obviousl what you want to do is more important to you than I am Nothing could be more clear, so I don't see that there' anything left to say. Except goodbye." Very slowly, sh pulled her magnificent engagement ring from her finger an held it out to Kent. "Here. I won't be needing this any more."

"Allison, you don't mean this," Kent said. "You can' mean this."

When he didn't take the ring, Allison reached forwar and dropped it into his suit pocket. Then she walked t where she'd been sitting, fumbled around until she foun her purse and without looking at anyone said, "Daddy Will you take me home, please?"

The next few minutes would always be a jumble in Diana's mind. Lee hurried to Allison's side, and Kent said, "Sir, I'm sorry. I know you went to a lot of trouble to get that offer for me, but—"

"Later," Lee said. He looked at Diana for a brief moment before putting his arm around a now-weeping Allison and leading her from the room.

Diana felt stunned by this new piece of knowledge. Lee? Lee had engineered this offer from Keating and Shaw, and had never once said a word to her?

"Mom." Kent touched her shoulder.

Diana looked up. Kent's eyes were bleak.

"Mom, I'm sorry."

Diana didn't know what to say or do. She stood, and Kent put his arms around her, holding her close for a few seconds. Then he released her, and in a calm voice said, "Dad, Gram, Mr. and Mrs. Marlowe, everybody. I'm terribly sorry. Please forgive me, but I've got to go after Allison."

They all murmured things such as "Of course" and "You go ahead" and then Kent was gone.

Diana looked around. All the faces in the room still reflected the shock she felt.

And then she felt a tug on her skirt. She looked down at her mother.

"Does this mean I have to return my dress?" Barbara said.

Chapter Fifteen

After Kent left the rehearsal dinner, Diana managed somehow to hustle everyone out of the restaurant. She drove her mother home and closed her ears to Barbara's outraged commentary on both Kent's and Allison's behavior.

When Diana arrived home, Jackie and the kids were already there.

"God, Di, I'm sorry," Jackie said. They hugged, and Diana closed her eyes. "What do you think is going to happen now? Do you think the wedding is off?"

Diana pulled away from Jackie and shook her head wearily. "I don't know." She took off her shoes and held them by the backs. Her head was pounding. She sighed heavily. "Listen, do you mind if I go up to bed? I'm exhausted."

"No. Of course not."

"And Jackie? Turn the phone off when you go to bed will you? I'm going to unplug the one in my room. And if Lee calls before then..."

"Yes?"

"Tell him I'm not here."

As she climbed the stairs to the second floor, she could feel Jackie watching her.

Finally she reached the privacy of her room. She shut the door behind her, and without turning on any lights, groped for the phone and yanked the cord out; then she threw herself across her bed. She lay there for a long time, trying not to think about what happened, but unable to stop that godawful scene from replaying in her mind.

Over and over again she saw Kent's stricken face, Allison's misery, and Lee...

She swallowed against the tears clogging her throat.

Lee.

Lee had betrayed her. He had gone behind her back and arranged for a position for Kent. She had trusted him, and he had been sneaky and sly. That night when she'd asked him if he thought something was wrong between Allison and Kent, she'd thought he was hiding something from her. This had probably been it. He had probably lied even then.

What else has he been lying to you about?

The thought refused to go away.

She'd thought he was different. But now he'd lied to her, just as Bill had lied to her.

It hurt. Oh, God, how it hurt.

Maybe all along Lee had been pretending to care about her. Maybe all he'd ever been interested in was getting her into bed. Maybe everything had been a lie.

A long time later, Diana got up and got undressed. Still not turning on any lights, she crawled into bed. She refused to cry, although she wanted to weep and weep until there were no tears left.

It was over.

It was over between Allison and Kent.

And it was over between her and Lee.

The next day Diana dragged herself out of bed. She felt numb. When she walked into the bathroom and looked at herself in the mirror, she looked haggard.

She forced herself to go through her normal morning ritual. She showered and washed her hair. She had half a grapefruit and a glass of milk for breakfast. She brushed her teeth and put on her makeup. She blow-dried her hair and pulled a camel-colored coat dress from her closet.

At eight o'clock she left for the office. Jackie would come closer to nine, when the agency actually opened its doors. Diana returned the greetings of the two agents who were already there, and escaped into her office as quickly as she could.

Today was Christmas Eve. A day that should be a celebration of life and joy and hope. A day that would instead be full of misery and unhappiness and the death of dreams.

She sat at her desk and stared at the papers she'd left there the previous day. She tried not to think.

At nine o'clock, Jackie buzzed her on the intercom. "Diana, Lee is on the phone."

Diana thought about refusing to talk to him, but she knew Lee: he'd only call again.

Feeling cold all over, she picked up the phone. "Yes?" she said.

"Diana?"

"Yes."

"Diana, love, I'm so sorry about last night."

"Yes, well, you should be."

"What do you mean by that?"

"Just what I said. You should be."

"I think you'd better explain yourself." He sounded angry. Very angry.

"I think you're the one who has the explaining to do. It seems to me that if you hadn't interfered, if you hadn't engineered that offer to Kent, none of this would have happened."

"Diana, I know you're upset. Hell, we're *all* upset. But this isn't my fault! This problem has been brewing for a long time. I tried to help out, tried to make Kent see reason, but it didn't work."

"You lied to me." Diana shivered. She hadn't felt so cold in a long time.

"I didn't lie to you."

"You did. You never told me about what you were doing. As far as I'm concerned, you lied to me."

"Diana, please be reasonable."

"You know, Lee, I'm sick and tired of you telling me to be reasonable every time I disagree with you. Actually I think I *am* being reasonable. All I ever expected from you was honesty. I think that's very reasonable."

"I've always been honest with you."

"Oh, really?"

"I was only trying to keep you from worrying unnecessarily. I saw no reason to involve you in this."

"What else have you lied to me about?"

"What's that supposed to mean?" Now his voice no longer sounded angry. It sounded hard. And cold.

"You're a smart man. You figure it out." And Diana hung up the phone. She stared at the instrument for a few seconds, then she buzzed Jackie. "Jackie, I don't want to talk to Lee Gabriel again. If he calls, tell him I'm out with a client.''

"Diana—"

"Just do as I say, please."

At ten o'clock, Kent knocked on her door.

Diana's heart constricted at the sight of him. He looked even worse than she felt. He looked as if he hadn't slept at all the night before. At least she'd managed three or four hours. But Kent looked beat. He was dressed in boots, jeans and a turtleneck sweater.

She stood, and he walked over to her and gathered her in his arms. They held each other for a few minutes, and Diana could feel his heart beating against hers. Tears filled her eyes, tears she quickly tried to blink away. She ached for him and wished she could say something to make things better.

Finally he released her, and holding her hand, he led her to the love seat. They sat next to each other.

"Mom..."

Diana met Kent's gaze. His blue eyes were filled with a sadness so profound that seeing it was like a knife wound through her heart.

"I'm afraid it's all over with me and Allison," he said.

"I'm sorry," she whispered.

"I...I tried to talk to her last night. I went to the house, but...Mrs. Marlowe said Allison didn't want to see me." He bowed his head. "She moved out of the guest house over the weekend. If she'd been there, maybe she would have talked to me." He raised his head. The pain on his face twisted the knife deeper. "Do you think I was wrong?"

Diana shook her head. "No, but...I do think you should have told Allison before the dinner."

"I…I tried." Then he sighed deeply. "No, that's not true. didn't really try. I started to say something, but I knew he'd get upset, and I guess I just hoped some miracle would appen. I should have told her."

Diana knew he felt terrible enough, so she didn't say nything else.

"I wish…" His voice trailed off, and he looked away. "I vish I could have done what Lee suggested."

"What did he suggest?"

"That I get some of my friends to go in with me on the torefront thing. That I work full-time at Keating and Shaw nd just devote a couple nights a week and maybe one day n the weekend to the storefront."

Diana hated to admit it, but Lee's suggestion made sense. till, he'd had no right to interfere—or lie to her. And othing would change that. "Was that suggestion so un- easonable?" she asked softly.

"Maybe not to someone else." His voice sounded grim.

Diana studied his profile. The clean, clear lines. The sweet urve of his mouth. The firm chin. She swallowed hard. If nly she could do something, say something. She squeezed is hand.

He took a deep breath. "I thought I'd try talking to Al- son one last time. I'm going to go over to the Marlowes' ouse now."

They stood. "Good luck," Diana said softly as they ugged again. "Call me and let me know what happens."

At ten-thirty, Jackie buzzed her. "Diana, Lee called gain. I just thought you might want to know."

"I don't."

Jackie sighed. "Why don't you give the man a chance?"

"He had his chance."

Jackie sighed again, but she didn't argue. "The phone
have been going crazy. Everyone's been calling, wanting to
know if the wedding's on or off."

"What have you been telling them?"

"That we know as much as they do!"

At eleven-thirty, Kent called. "Allison's gone," he said
without preamble.

"Gone," Diana echoed.

"Yes," he said tonelessly. "Her grandmother said she
took off for Paris this morning. I guess Lee arranged it."

Lee again. Diana wondered if this coldness would ever go
away.

"Have you talked to him, Mom?"

"Why would I talk to him?"

"Come on. We both know you two have been seeing each
other. I didn't say anything because obviously you didn't
want us to know, but I knew."

"Yes, I talked to him."

Perhaps because of her tone of voice, Kent said, "Don't
be mad at him, Mom. What happened was inevitable, I
think. It's not Lee's fault. I . . . I would have done the same
thing in his shoes."

After they hung up, Diana put her head down on her
desk. She wished she could just crawl into a dark place
somewhere where she wouldn't have to see anyone, or talk
to anyone, or pretend that her life was normal.

Why had Lee lied to her?

Why had he made her think he loved her?

Why had she let him get under her skin?

*This was bound to happen. Why are you so upset? Didn't
you tell yourself from the very beginning that there was no
future for the two of you?*

Her intercom buzzed. "Diana, Lee Gabriel's here to see ou."

Diana's heart leaped into her throat. "Damn you, ackie," she said in a tight voice. "I told you to tell him I as out with a client."

"I did. He didn't believe me. He said to tell you if you on't come out of that office this minute he's coming in and e won't leave until you see reason."

Diana looked around wildly. There was no lock on her ffice door. Maybe she could wedge a chair under the knob. hen she realized just how ridiculous she was acting. She as an adult. She would face him like an adult. Taking a eep breath to fortify herself, she stood and smoothed down e skirt of her dress. Then, lifting her chin, she walked to e door.

She opened it.

Only three of Diana's agents were in. Most had taken the ay off; the others would only be there until noon.

Just then Lee appeared in the far doorway, the one that d into the reception area, and their gazes met.

Diana's heart was beating so hard she was sure everyone the room could hear it.

Lee charged across the bull pen, his eyes blazing, and veryone in the room stared at him. Diana backed up a few teps. When he reached her, he stopped. She opened her iouth to say something, but before she could, he grasped er arms and yanked her into his embrace. Then he lowered is head and kissed her.

The entire world spun.

The kiss was hard, angry, demanding and possessive. He issed her so long, and so thoroughly, that when he finally eleased her, Diana would have fallen if he hadn't held on

to her arms. "Now what *is* this craziness all about?" he de-
manded.

"Lee—"

There was a discreet cough, and Diana, who had completely forgotten the existence of her employees, realize
they were all gaping at her and Lee. "L—let's go into m
office," she said.

"Fine. Let's."

Diana stumbled when she turned, but made it into he
office without falling, and he followed her. He slammed th
door behind him.

She turned to face him, struggling to regain control of he
emotions. Very slowly, she raised her eyes.

She shivered. He was so angry. She could see the fury i
his golden-brown eyes. His jaw was set in stern lines, and h
mouth was tight-lipped and uncompromising.

"I repeat, Diana, just what in hell is all this garbag
about?"

"Y—you know what it's about."

"No, I do not."

"Look, Lee, can't we just part as friends? Do we have t
have a scene? Did you have to come to my office? God! M
employees are out there, probably listening to every word."
She tried to keep her voice low, but she was so disconcerte
and felt at such a disadvantage that she wasn't very suc
cessful.

"I don't give a good rat's ass who's listening! I want som
answers, and I want those answers to make sense!"

Now Diana was getting angry herself. Her senses had fi
nally stopped swimming from that devastating kiss. Wha
right did Lee have to be so angry? *She* was the injured part
here, not him. "Okay, you asked for it. You lied to me
You've *been* lying to me. And I don't want to have any

ing to do with you anymore. There! Are you satisfied
ow?''

"I never lied to you, Diana. Allison asked me to talk to
ent, and I did. After we talked, he and I discussed whether
should tell you about our conversation, and he said, no,
didn't want to worry you. And that's the truth.''

Diana stared at him. His words had the ring of truth.

"Do you believe me?''

She wanted to. "I . . . I don't know.''

"Have I ever lied to you before?'' Lee continued relent-
ssly.

"Not that I know of.''

"Then why were you so quick to assume I was lying to
ou about this?''

Suddenly Diana could feel all her anger evaporating. She
ook her head. "I don't know.''

His voice softened. "So you believe me now?''

"Yes.''

He moved closer.

She swallowed. She could see his intent in his eyes. "No,''
e said. "No, Lee. Please. I believe you about this, but it's
er between us.''

"It's not over.''

Now he was only inches away. She slowly raised her eyes,
eeting his gaze. What she saw there knocked the breath
t of her. A smoldering desire. And an unyielding deter-
ination.

He touched her shoulders, and she shuddered. With his
ght forefinger, he traced the curve of her cheek and jaw,
d the shudder raced through her again. She wanted to
sh him away. But she couldn't move to save her life.

"Diana," he whispered, rubbing his thumb over her lips. "I love you. Don't you know that? I love you. I will always love you."

"Lee—"

"I want to marry you."

She wanted to believe him. "But, Lee—"

"Remember when I told you that 'but' is my least favorite word?" He smiled for the first time, and all the anger and determination faded from his eyes, to be replaced by something soft and warm and wonderful. Something Diana wanted desperately to believe in. Something that curled into her belly and filled her heart with hope.

"I—" she started.

"You talk too much," he muttered. "Shut up and kiss me."

She looked into his eyes for a long moment, then she lifted her arms and his mouth took hers again. This kiss said everything. It said how much they loved each other. And how much they wanted each other. And how sorry they were that everything had happened the way it did. It also said that they believed in the future.

He kissed her for a long time, and when he finally released her mouth, he held her close to him, and she could feel his strong heart beating against hers.

"I don't want to wait," he said as he stroked her hair. "Let's get married as soon as possible."

"But Lee, what about Allison? And Kent?"

Lee put his hands on either side of her face and kissed her nose. "What about them?"

"Isn't this all going to be terribly awkward for everyone?"

"They'll survive. They're adults."

"But—"

Lee sighed. "I can see I have my work cut out for me. There you go with that word again." He pulled her close again, cradling her head against his chest. "Listen, love, Allison and Kent made their choice. Now I'm making mine, and you're making yours. Sure, it might be awkward the first time we're all together, but we'll work it out."

Diana thought about what he'd said. He was right. She knew he was right. Suddenly she felt lighter and freer than she had in years, and a great happiness filled her. She knew it was risky, but anything worth having was risky. She raised her face to Lee's. "I love you," she said.

"Finally! I didn't think I'd ever hear you say it!"

She laughed. It felt wonderful to say it. She tested the words again. "I love you. Oh, I love you."

He kissed her again and again, but then there was a faint tapping on the door.

"Oh, my God," Diana said. "I forgot all about my agents." She smoothed her hair and straightened her clothes. Then she opened the door.

A twinkling-eyed Jackie stood there. "Uh, Diana, I'm sorry to bother you." Jackie looked over Diana's shoulder and grinned at Lee. "But, uh, you *did* say everyone could leave at noon?"

"Yes, of course. Would…uh, would you tell them I said Merry Christmas? I don't really want to go out there right now."

Jackie's grin expanded. "Good idea." She winked and gave a little wave. "See ya later! I'll lock the door on my way out."

Diana could just imagine how she looked. She was sure she had no lipstick at all left on her mouth, and it was probably obvious to Jackie exactly what she and Lee had been doing in here.

Lee was sitting on the edge of her desk, smiling, when she closed the door and turned to face him again. "Tell you what," he said. "I've got the church. I've got the country club. Everything's already paid for, and the invitations have been mailed. Why don't you and I have a wedding?"

"You mean..."

He grinned. "Can't you just see it? Everyone will show up thinking they're going to see our kids get married. And instead they'll see us?"

"But—"

"I hate that word!"

Diana giggled. She couldn't help it. Something about his proposition appealed to her. "What about licenses and all?"

"I know a few judges. Even though it's Christmas Eve, think I can arrange it."

"You're good at arranging things, aren't you?"

"Hey, no sass from you, woman." He crooked a finger and beckoned her closer.

She went.

A long time later, when he let her up for air, he said, "S what do you say?"

"I say...yes. Yes, yes, yes!"

Much later, Diana started to laugh.

"What's so funny?" Lee said.

"Oh, I was just thinking. My mother sure will be happy."

"Well, good."

Diana laughed harder. "Now she won't have to return her dress!"

Epilogue

From the pages of the *Houston Herald:*

Around Houston
by B. J. Barrette

Locals were shocked Friday evening when they arrived at St. John's Church expecting to attend the wedding of Allison Gabriel and Kent Sorensen and instead found themselves witnessing the wedding of Lee Gabriel and Diana Sorensen, the parents of the younger couple. Rumor has it that Kent and Allison broke their engagement in a stormy scene at The Rainbow Lodge during their rehearsal dinner. Rumor also has it that the lovely Diana, who as most of you already know, owns Sorensen Realty, and the dynamic Lee, the recently appointed executive v.p. of Berringer, International, have been carrying on a torrid affair for months. Of course, if you'll recall, this columnist broke the news of their involvement first. Diana looked beautiful, if untraditional, in a tea-length, claret silk and lace dress. She carried white poinsettias and wore a magnificent diamond necklace, a gift from her bridegroom. Her only attendant was Sunny Garcia, her long-time friend and business associate. Standing up for Lee was Diana's son, Kent. Once the guests got over their shock at the substitution of the major participants, a good time was had by all. This reporter has it on good authority that the champagne flowed freely, and the buffet at the lavish country club reception included delicacies from all over the world. The guests danced until the wee hours to the music of Harry Thompson and his band. The new Mr. and Mrs. Lee Gabriel left the reception early for parts unknown. We'll be sure to let you know when the newlyweds get back to town.

* * * * *

SPRING FANCY

Three bachelors, footloose
and fancy-free...until now!

Spring into romance with three
fabulous fancies by three of
Silhouette's hottest authors:

ANNETTE BROADRICK
LASS SMALL
KASEY MICHAELS

When spring fancy strikes, no man is immune!

Look for this exciting new short-story collection
in March at your favorite retail outlet.

Only from

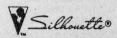

Silhouette®

where passion lives.

Take 4 bestselling love stories FREE

Plus get a FREE surprise gift!

It takes a very special man to win

That

SPECIAL

Woman!

She's friend, wife, mother—she's you! And beside each Special Woman stands a wonderfully *special* man. It's a celebration of our heroines—and the men who become part of their lives.

Look for these exciting titles from Silhouette Special Edition:

January   BUILDING DREAMS by Ginna Gray

February   HASTY WEDDING by Debbie Macomber

March   THE AWAKENING by Patricia Coughlin

April   FALLING FOR RACHEL by Nora Roberts

Don't miss THAT SPECIAL WOMAN! each month—from some of your special authors! Only from Silhouette Special Edition! And for the most special woman of all—you, our loyal reader— we have a wonderful gift: a beautiful journal to record all of your special moments. Look for details in this month's THAT SPECIAL WOMAN! title, available at your favorite retail outlet.

TSW1R

COMING NEXT MONTH

#805 TRUE BLUE HEARTS—Curtiss Ann Matlock
Rough-and-tumble cowboy Rory Breen and mother of two
Zoe Yarberry knew that getting together was unwise. But
though their heads were telling them no, their hearts . . .

#806 HARDWORKING MAN—Gina Ferris
Family Found
The first time private investigator Cassie Browning met
Jared Walker, he was in jail. Cassie soon discovered that
clearing Jared's name and reuniting him with his family
were easier tasks than fighting her feelings for him!

#807 YOUR CHILD, MY CHILD—Jennifer Mikels
When confirmed bachelor Pete Hogan opened his door to
Anne LeClare and her child, he thought he was saving them
from a snowstorm. But the forecast quickly changed to sunny
skies when they offered him the chance for love.

#808 LIVE, LAUGH, LOVE—Ada Steward
Jesse Carder had traveled far to rekindle the flames of an old
love—until she met sexy Dillon Ruiz. Dillon brought Jesse's
thoughts back to the present, but was their future possible?

#809 MAN OF THE FAMILY—Andrea Edwards
Tough cop Mike Minelli had seen Angie Hartman on the screen as
a former horror movie queen! Now he sensed vulnerable Angie
was hiding more than bad acting in her past!

#810 FALLING FOR RACHEL—Nora Roberts
That Special Woman!
Career-minded Rachel Stanislaski had little time for matters of the
heart. But when handsome Zackary Muldoon entered her life,
Rachel's pulse went into overtime!